BOUND TO END BADLY

R. L. TIOCHTA

For my best friend Neil, who is sadly no longer with us. Many years ago we had a crazy idea to write a book.

1

PETE'S STORY - 19 CRIMES

Mouth dry, heart pounding away with brutal intensity, I sit fidgeting as my thumb involuntarily tries to twirl my missing wedding ring for perhaps the fifth time in the last few minutes. A sick feeling forms deep in my stomach as I notice the faint imprint has almost entirely disappeared. Taking a sip out of my nearly empty pint glass, I glance over at the door again—and they say dating is fun.

I forgot how nerve-racking these occasions can be. This time is even more terrifying as my best friend Dave has set me up on a blind date. He is the one person you shouldn't trust with such a delicate task. His unerring belief in his own expertise with women is mainly based on his easy charm and ability to have them regularly falling into his bed. An image of lemmings going off a cliff edge plays in my head, those cute, pixelated ones off the computer game, not the real-life furry versions.

Thinking about it, I don't recall any of Dave's relationships ever lasting more than three weeks, but here I am anyway, waiting patiently in the Red Dragon. A deserted pub that has clearly seen better days, possibly in the early '80s judging by the nicotine-stained décor. The time is 7.25 p.m. on a Wednesday evening. I hope Dave hasn't set me up with someone utterly unsuitable or just plain mad - either of which is always possible.

The regional news is pouring out in thin crackling mono of the only working speaker of an ancient portable television, which is mounted extra high to ward off thieves.

All the local TV channels are talking about Derby's first official serial killer. Some twisted individual who likes to cut the head off women and deposit them in carrier bags at the roadside as an unpleasant surprise to those in the local biking or dogging community. At least I have nothing to worry about, but this is bound to affect the local dating scene.

I sigh. Derby is a decaying, forgotten city, slowly sliding into impoverished oblivion, but this newfound notoriety is something we could well do without. Why couldn't that world-famous mugger 'Robin Hood' have been born a mere fifteen miles to the west? Think of all the kudos and American tourist dollars we missed out on. To be fair, those same tourists would only have gotten abused, robbed, or molested when they made the mistake of taking a right turn out of the bus station and wandering through the misleadingly named River Gardens, which is much more of an unofficial shelter for the homeless and criminally insane.

Another glance at my wristwatch confirms my date is officially late. The thought she might not show up hadn't occurred to me until just now. What if she popped her head around the door and decided I wasn't her cup of tea and hurried off in disgust? Maybe she's even worried I might be the local serial killer.

I recall getting ready earlier in a new pair of jeans, straight leg, not skinny. I never understood how you are supposed to fit your mobile phone and balls into them at the same time; it's quite impossible. Next, a pure white T-shirt with a small V-neck; again, brand new as they are a real nightmare to keep clean. A quick check reassures me I haven't got any stains on it in the last few seconds. My choice of footwear is a pair of brown suede Chelsea style boots, and finally, my favourite mustard coloured bomber jacket completes the ensemble. My outfit says smart casual, thrown together in two minutes as I'm that kind of cool, laid-back intellectual guy who doesn't need to try too hard. It took me over three hours to get the outfit just right, and now I may have been mistaken for a mass murderer.

Pushing my self-deprecating thoughts behind a door in my head and locking them securely away, I decide the best course of action is a stiff drink or two as the pint of lager I have been nursing is dead.

"Been stood up?" the barmaid asks as I stroll over.

She's more pleasing on the eye than the craggy faced landlord who served me when I first got here. Pausing, I give myself a quick once over - checking for any giveaway signs I am on a date. Apart from the fact I've washed, shaved, spent ages getting dressed and gelling my hair into an acceptable shape, nothing too obvious.

"You've been looking at everybody coming through the door and checking your watch repeatedly. Such a dead give-away. Oh, and you seem nervous too. Luckily, I've got a cure for that."

She pushes a glass of some golden liquid over to me, a double or triple by the size of it.

"My treat," she says and smiles.

This simple act lights up her entire face, and I do the one thing we really shouldn't do and from a full two seconds of meeting someone, make a snap judgement based on their appearance alone. My eyes take in all the ingredients that make up my perfect woman:

---

1. Height – at around 5ft tall and the fact I'm 6ft, way too short. This will lead to weird stares if we hold hands in the street and a bad back when I lean over, and we chat or kiss - fail.

2. Age - I take her to be between 19-25 - She's probably too immature for me - fail.

3. Appearance – Slim verging on skinny with a mop of bright dyed red hair and matching lipstick. Semi goth looking in a pair of Hello Kitty converse high top trainers, fishnet tights and a barely there leather mini-skirt topped off with a tight white T-shirt featuring the mildly inappropriate, 'Fuck the Clock' slogan on the front—for a pub that allows kids in until 7.30 p.m.

She has a slutty rock chick vibe my parents would hate, but as they both died when I was young, this isn't going to be much of a problem - Pass

4. Body Art & Accessories - No sign of a wedding or engagement ring - pass.

An inverted crucifix on a silver chain – possible devil worship? (not a deal-breaker)

Large neck tattoo in a weird alien symbol - fail. I wanted a tattoo ever since I turned 17 but still can't make my mind up – those things are for the rest of your life. She's way too impetuous for me.

Universal Rating System of Attractiveness 6 maybe 6.5 out of 10

*My eyes take in all this information, sends it to my brain and
a split second later, I have an answer:
Possible life partner = ~~PASS~~ / FAIL
Just like that, the barmaid is written out of my future.*

I take a sip. It burns my throat, so I swallow it all in one swift gulp. The pleasant warmth of strong alcohol fills my belly.

"I'm Maze, by the way," she says, happily pouring me a refill and one for herself.

"Pete. Pete Walker, and yes, my date is late. The only trouble is I don't know what she looks like; she might have been and gone already."

"Ooh, a blind date, bad idea. You know it's bound to end badly, especially as I bet she resembles the lovechild of Mrs Brown and Boris Johnson." She giggles, and alcohol spurts out her mouth and over the bar, joining the other myriad of strange stains down there. "Get a few of these down you. At least she will look better."

I smile back at Maze. She is young and pretty, and even though my unconscious mind has ruled her out as a possible partner, I'm still basically a caveman. We haven't developed that much in the last million years, so yes, I still want to sleep with her.

My gaze wanders over to the strange symbol tattooed on the side of her neck. I hope it's a transfer, but I get the idea she's the type of girl who goes all in.

"What do you think?" she asks, seeing me looking. "It's a copy of the O.P.A. tattoo from the Expanse, isn't it cool?"

I haven't got a clue what the O.P.A. is or the Expanse, but not wanting to appear out of touch, I don't bring it up.

"I'm kind of psychic as well, and I can tell what you're thinking."

I raise an eyebrow at this.

"You think it's cool and sexy now, but what about when I'm ancient? Like mid-thirties, and everything goes droopy."

I had actually been thinking I'd see her on an episode of next year's Tattoo Fixers, but I go with it. "That's amazing; you read my mind."

"Well, the first thing is I don't think I will make it to forty, so who cares and second, laser removal keeps getting cheaper and easier, so there. Oh, and the third thing, never ever say anything sarky to your date if you ever want to get laid." I can tell she was teasing me now.

"Another drink?" she says, a cheeky grin firmly in place.

I already have a warm alcoholic flush. "Go for it. What do I owe you for these?"

"Nothing. The asshole landlord tried to feel me up earlier, so I'm helping myself. Going to quit soon anyway." She downs two more shots in quick succession. "It's okay; I can handle myself. Look, I have an idea. If your date is a minger, I will come over and tell you there's a phone call. You know, on the landline. Old people still use them so you can pretend your mum died or something. As a last resort, there is a tiny window in the ladies. Say you're going to the toilet and then climb out; you should just about fit if you breathe in."

"Isn't that mean?"

"Well, a bit. No wait, I thought of another one." Maze is obviously enjoying thinking up ways of ending my impending bad date. "I come over and announce you're a sex addict and you gave me a quickie in the toilets, or maybe fingered me behind the bar, wait, wait, this is the best bit, and then I say I'm only fifteen and ask you to help with my homework. What do you think?" She's laughing uncontrollably. How much booze has this girl consumed?

"Maybe not. Word getting around that I'm some sort of sex offender isn't quite what I was thinking of. Anyway, the date might go well."

She doesn't look convinced. "Well, the offers there. I'll keep nipping over, topping up your drinks. Give me a signal, I know, pretend to cough, and then say minger under your breath. I'll jump straight in and save you."

"Thanks. While we're on the subject, any dating advice you want to share. I'm suddenly terrified."

Two more shots get necked in quick succession. "Well, I only go out with men a lot taller than me ever since I walked in and caught my ex trying on my clothes."

Drink spurts out of my mouth, some running down my chin as I half choke. "Were you going out with a midget?" I only mention this due to Maze's tiny size.

"Hey, that's racist, you're supposed to say little people these days, and no, I wasn't dating a little person, though Jeff was," she wiggles her pinkie finger at me, "exceedingly small in some departments if you get what I mean. He ruined my best leather mini-skirt, stretched the hell out of it. Now I only date tall men who have no chance of fitting in my stuff.

"Got any advice I can actually use?" I say as one of the older regulars taps his glass impatiently on the bar, indicating he wants a refill.

"Hold your horses," Maze says, annoyed. "No manners, these oldies. Back in a minute." She winks and goes off to serve. "So, what will it be? Let me guess, a pint of Pedigree."

The old fella nods.

"You know, I can make over a dozen different cocktails. How about trying a Manhattan Iced Tea?"

"I only drink PG Tips. Why would I want one down the

boozer?" He shakes his head mystified. "I will try something different though, get me a pint of Ay Up."

"It's an extra 40p."

"Blooming 'eck, I'm not a millionaire. I'll stick to the usual."

"Looks like my mixology course was a complete waste of time." Maze sighs and starts pouring out a Pedigree. It splutters and froths into the glass. "Great, another barrel change. I'll be back in a second." She raises her eyes heavenward before opening a side door and disappearing into the cellar.

I smile. Raising my glass to my lips to take a sip, I notice my hand visibly shaking. To steady my nerves, I take a deep breath and think back several days to my conversation with Dave, which led to my current stressful situation. He offered to buy me a drink in an expensive city-centre bar, so I should have known something was off. The scene plays out in my head.

Dave puts his pint down on the table and stares at me with a solemn expression. "Look, I didn't want to bring this up, but you are turning into a miserable sod. People are starting to avoid you; nobody likes a sad sack. You're still young and in great shape. Much better than me," Dave sucks in his developing paunch, "and you still have all your own teeth and hair. Quite an achievement at our age."

"Hey, we only just turned thirty-one. I have my fingers crossed they will last a lifetime."

Thanks to Dave's old man passing down the baldness gene, he was follicly challenged by the time we left school, though this never troubled him much.

He continues, "Look at me. I'm an average-looking guy,

and I still get loads of action, with your looks..." he leaves a small pause, "when you fall off a horse, you need to get straight back in the saddle, and by saddle - I really mean the poonani express."

I hold my hand up at this point. "Mate, just stop. I'll go on a date if it shuts you up. I just never expected to be back on the market at my age. I thought I'd done with all that. How do people do it now, Tinder, Plenty of Fish? It all seems so clinical, seedy even."

Dave nods and takes up his wise man pose, hands together in a triangular prayer shape. "There's nothing wrong with seedy. But yeah, dating sites can be a minefield, no way you're ready for that. I signed up to a new one last week, and my date had this amazing profile picture, a stunning face with a fashion model's body. I should have known something was off, and when I get there, she was nudging seventy if a day. I thought she was trying to be arty with her black-and-white photo; turns out they took it during the Blitz."

"And did you do the dirty?" I interrupt, somehow keeping a smirk off my face.

"Ha, ha. Hilarious. You should be a comedian. Don't worry; I'm not going to rush you. We will go at a sedate pace till you are up and running. Rosie, the bird I'm seeing, she's got an attractive single friend."

My hand shoots up like I'm still at school and asking the teacher a question. "What's wrong with her?" I scrutinise Dave's face closely for any signs of deception. He doesn't have a convincing poker face, though he can lie to women with unbelievable ease.

"Nothing at all. She's tall, slim, attractive, and no kids either. Perfect."

I couldn't see any obvious signs of untruth, but you could hide a lot in what went unsaid.

"Okay. Why is she still single, and how come you haven't tried it on with her?"

Now Dave has been my best friend since school, but when it comes to women, he has fewer morals than a Tory MP up for re-election.

"Well, of course, I tried it on. Her name's Jennifer. I saw her at that flash new bar on the high street, the one that insists on sticking an umbrella in the top of every drink. Hookers or Lookers, something like that. I simply walked over and introduced myself."

I have always been envious of Dave's easy way with women; he possesses the ultimate confidence and will swagger over and use the most terrible chat up lines in history. Most of the time, this leads to a date.

"I used my best line on her, and she blanked me, but her friend Rosie pissed herself laughing, and we instantly clicked."

"Go on. What chat up line did you use?"

"Mate, listen and commit this to memory." He takes up his favoured chat up stance, stood sideways, feet slightly apart, stomach pulled in. "I've lost my favourite teddy bear. Can I sleep with you instead? See, what woman could resist?"

"Seriously, that works?"

"That my son is a Grade A panty dropper. Now, Jenny is sort of an intellectual. She reads books and stuff. We would never get on, but you would with all that gay stuff you like."

"Gay stuff?"

"That up its own ass television channel, you like to watch."

"What, Sky Arts?"

"Yeah, and you go to art galleries and museums as well. You two will get on like…" he pauses to think, "like Shrek and Donkey."

I raise an eyebrow. "I was hoping more for Romeo and Juliet, and you know you can't use the phrase 'gay stuff' anymore, don't you?"

"I guess I'm not allowed to tell you to stop being a bender either?"

"No mate, not for the last ten years at least."

He shakes his head. "You know your problem? You're a dreamer and a politically correct dweeb all at the same time. By the way, Romeo and Juliet is the most depressing love story ever; they both die in the end."

"You read the play; I'm impressed."

"Of course, I haven't. We watched the rubbish film at school, in English class."

I shrug; I'd forgotten.

"I feel sorry for you, mate. All those years at that stuffy I.T. firm have brainwashed you. That sexy Chinese receptionist over there had the hots for you, and I can't believe you never nailed her. Against company policy, I bet?"

"What Nicky? She's from Kettering. I think her mum is half Korean though. What, wait, she had a thing for me?"

Dave laughs, followed by a facepalm gesture. "And that proves you need my help. She was always smiling at you, laughing at your crap jokes, inviting you to every after-work party and the most obvious one of all, she straight out told you she didn't have a boyfriend."

I frown at this information. "Did she? I thought she was just being friendly."

"Don't worry. I'm going to teach you everything I know. Under my expert guidance, you're going to achieve many great things, and by many great things, I mean—"

I hold my hand up and interrupt. "Love, friendship, finding my twin flame?"

"Not quite where I was going, but yeah, those too if you want." Dave winks at me. "This is going to be amazing."

The noise of Maze slamming two more shots down on the counter brings me out of my reverie. We clink glasses, downing the putrid green liquid in one as the pub door creaks open. Turning, we watch as a figure emerges, no, two figures, one after another. The first woman, vaguely female, resembles an alcoholic homeless person, all red, bloated face and ragged coat held together with a piece of string. The second woman couldn't be more different, a flawless beauty, like one of those models who pretends to be somebody's fit mum in a washing powder commercial. She is wearing a simple but elegant outfit of a tight pencil skirt, high heels, and a plain white blouse with the top three buttons undone to show a tempting amount of flesh. A fur jacket (hopefully fake), full makeup, dark glossy shoulder-length hair, like she stepped out of a Pantene shampoo ad, perfection personified. I really must stop comparing women to television ads. Next, I'd be imagining them with a freshly baked loaf of Hovis bread. TV really disturbs your unconscious mind.

"Wow, she's a ten," Maze whispers in my ear.

"I bet my date is the bag lady."

"Don't be such a pessimist; the hottie is here for you. She's gorgeous, I would."

I do a double-take to see if she's serious. I can't quite tell.

"What, she's stunning?"

Both women search the near-empty pub until they get to me. I gulp in panic; Dave better not have set me up on a double-blind date as some sort of joke. I give the attractive one my best smile and a friendly wave. If she isn't my date, then I've made a right twat of myself and will be making use of the bathroom window shortly. She smiles back and starts to walk over. I sigh in relief. The older lady veers off as she gets near and goes to join an older man in a cloth cap who's supping half a bitter.

"See. You're going to have to up your game though, she's out of your league."

"Thanks for the support."

"You know what I mean? She's definitely a ten, and you're a nice-looking bloke, but you're punching above your weight there. You will have to try real hard. Go down on her a lot; that's my advice, like all the time. Us women can forgive a lot if we get to come every day."

My cheeks redden. Simply my natural reaction to a practical stranger talking about oral sex. I grew up in a household where S. E. X. was never discussed, even though I had a sister who must have come from somewhere. We were raised by our puritanical aunt, who refused even the smallest mention on this taboo subject. She also showed us zero affection. I only recall one awkward hug from her in my entire time living at her house. To be fair, though, she hadn't expected a ready-made family of two foisted on her with the untimely death of my parents. They are but a distant memory now. Any attempt to get my Aunt to talk about them is met with a wall of silence. I only vaguely remember pleasant parent-shaped silhouettes when I reminisce.

My date is now only a few steps away, and I freeze with dread as Maze forms her fingers into a V-shape and starts moving them towards her mouth. Quicker than I thought possible, my hand shoots out and stops her.

"I get what you mean. No need for a demonstration."

She grins. "Just trying to be helpful." She stands there looking all innocent, a mischievous twinkle at the corner of her unusually coloured eyes. Her right eye is a pleasant washed out blue colour which continues over to her left iris, where it abruptly changes to amber as if the artist has run out of paint. My needy Sphynx cat has sort of the same thing with one blue and one green eye. He can be a bundle of trouble too.

Gorgeous women can be quite intimidating, and I am momentarily frozen to the spot as my date stands before me. She speaks first.

"Hi, Peter, I'm Jennifer." She offers me her hand, and I shake it as if we are in a business meeting and not here to decide if we would like to rip off each other's clothes and perhaps make a baby. My mind automatically does its snap judgement thing, and it's passes all the way.

"Can I get you a drink?" I ask.

"A glass of red wine, please."

I order the same, and Maze offers to bring them over and gives me a not-so-subtle wink. We head to a nearby table. Jennifer drops her handbag on the top and sits opposite me, crossing her legs and leaving me with a view her shapely, waxed, and toned limb, ending in a sexy black stiletto heel. She casually adjusts the shoe off and on again, making sure I notice the undamaged red sole. I pretend this isn't a practised move on her part and try not to look, or at least glance subtly; I fail miserably on both counts. With no immediate drink in front of us, we both stare awkwardly at each other, trying to think of something to break the silence.

Jennifer goes first. "Sorry, I'm so late. The taxi didn't turn up, and I had to ring another one." Her silky voice has dropped an octave and taken on a sexy raspy tone; it makes even this innocent sentence sound somewhat thrilling. If she does say anything remotely sexual, I may need a cold shower.

"That's okay. I was wondering if I'd been stood up."

She smiles. "Well, I was having second thoughts. I rarely go on blind dates."

Maze now interrupts us with a cobweb-covered bottle of red that must have spent years in the cellar. "Nicest one we have by the looks of it, though I know sod all about wine. You don't want the rubbish we keep behind the bar. Why don't they have screw tops, bloody thing?" she says, securing it between her mini-skirted thighs - while inexpertly trying to remove the cork.

I nearly offer to help but don't want to appear sexist. In the world that we live in today, I am unsure if I should hold a door open for a woman anymore. Luckily, I never have to use the train. Deciding if you should offer your seat to an old person or pregnant lady would fry my brain with worry. The cork pops out without fuss, and Maze fills our two large glasses up to the brim in a true home measure. I take a quick sip to stop it from overflowing.

"Maze, is it safe to leave my car in the car park overnight?" I ask, now realising finishing this one glass will push me well over the limit.

"Depends on how flash your motor is. What you driving?"

I don't want Jennifer to hear, and I'm also somewhat embarrassed, so I wave Maze closer and whisper. She immediately turns and bellows, "Porsche, definitely mid-life crisis material there, but nothing to be ashamed of. My ex Jeff had a push-bike - a kid's one at that, and a small dick. What the hell was I thinking? I'll ask the regulars not to vandalise or steal it. But only leave it for one night." She wanders back to the bar to serve another little old fella who just walked in.

I shuffle uncomfortably in my chair, but Jennifer tries to reassure me.

"I already knew about the car. It's nice you don't want to

brag. Dave told me when he mentioned this blind date, and I quote, '*he's got a Porsche, and he reads books and stuff*'."

"Wow, what an incredibly sad description of me, but come to think of it, I'd quite like it written on my headstone when I die. So, what made you come on the date?"

"Well, after Dave gave me his sales pitch about you, I said no. I thought you would be a self-loving narcissist or something, no offence meant. He then surprised me by saying what a really nice guy you are - one of most genuine people he knows."

"Seriously?" A wave of emotion overcomes me, and I push back a tear threatening to form. This doesn't sound like Dave, at least not the one I grew up with. He is usually a self-ish, self-centred womanising prick, strangely also my best and most reliable friend.

"He thinks a lot of you, I can tell." She takes a sip of wine. "This is amazing. I haven't tried this one before. Did the barmaid say how expensive it is?"

"No, but I don't think she's going to charge me." Jennifer looks puzzled, so I fill her in on mine and Maze's recent conversation. We carry on chatting as the pub fills with around six more people over the next fifty minutes. Jennifer is easy to talk to and those odd moments of silence couples dread seem somehow natural as our conversation ebbs and flows.

"So, Dave was rather vague about what you do for a living. I take it your business is going rather well for you to drive a Porsche?"

"I do okay. Though the Cayman wasn't that expensive because it's registered as a Cat S crash repair. A real steal at the price I got it for. I just don't like telling people what I drive; they automatically assume I'm a…" I search for the correct word, "tosser, but it's an amazing car." A silly grin forms on my face at the thought of racing it around. "Now I've turned thirty, the insurance isn't even that steep." I don't know why, but I appear to have knocked a year off my actual age.

Jennifer smiles and asks me the same question in a different way, "Well, they do have a certain connotation, so what exactly do you do for a living? Dave mentioned toys? He said you left your full-time job at Rutgers I.T. Services but earn more working a handful of hours a week."

She's trying to check my suitability as a provider which means she likes me. The trouble is, I don't fancy talking about my job tonight.

"It's import-export stuff. Boring, you wouldn't want to know the details." Her face tells me differently.

"So, got any coke on you?" Maze half slurs as she stumbles over, our bottle of wine in one hand and what appears to be a triple brandy in the other. She finishes it in a single gulp before sliding onto my lap and latching her arms around me. Her pert bum is pressed against my groin area, giving me a pleasant feeling that I desperately try not to think about.

Jennifer's eyes widen, and her stare gets intense. Being a cat lover, I'm used to my Sphynx's moods, and this isn't a good sign—it's when the claws come out.

I try to defuse the situation by pretending nothing out of the ordinary is happening. "Don't you have coke behind the bar?" I say pleasantly.

"That's not the type of coke I meant. Got any Charlie?"

Now, I have never actually heard cocaine referred to as Charlie in real life - only in Guy Ritchie gangster movies, so I take it Maze is a fan.

"Why do you think I have cocaine on me?" I ask, puzzled.

"Cus, I overheard you saying you were into import-export. That's code for drug smuggler. No judgement. We all need to make a living. I just thought you might have a line on you. I could do with a boost."

Maze's eyes half-close, and I rescue our bottle of wine just in time as it falls from her open fingers. I pour the rest into Jennifer's glass, mainly to free my hand up so I can stop Maze from falling off my lap and landing facedown on the stained floor.

While shaking my head in denial, I mouth to Jennifer, "I'm not a coke dealer." My date has certainly taken a surreal turn when forced to deny being a major international criminal. I glance down at Maze again, who's head is against my chest.

"I don't think taking any illegal substances is a good idea, the state you're in. Or any time." I add quickly, noting Jennifer's disapproving stare.

Maze perks up. "Judgeee much?" she mumbles while grasping my cheek and squeezing it extra hard. "Look at this sweet, innocent face. You know he's snorted coke off at least one dead hooker?"

Jennifer's expression suggests she's no longer so sure; I find my head shaking in denial again.

"At least a live hooker then?" Maze slurs.

"I have never even spoken to a prostitute in my—" I stop suddenly because I have, and I am now remembering it.

"Dark past, told you," Maze says, her eyes closing again.

"Well?" Jennifer's tone suggests I'm a creep, and she should have listened to her instincts and not turned up for this date.

I can't believe I'm being unfairly vilified and try to tell my side of it. "I was in Norway or Sweden, possibly Finland. It was one of those countries, anyway. So, I was at the hotel bar, minding my own business, when I get asked by this woman if she can join me and practise her English. She's kind of attractive (I fail to mention she was a sizzling hot Scandinavian blonde with these amazing bright blue eyes that burned into your very soul). We get a drink and sit there talking pleasantly. I had no idea she was a prostitute until she said later that for 500 Euros, I could take her back to my room and do anything I wanted to her. (I also fail to mention I was sorely tempted.) Of course, I said no."

"Bet she meant bum stuff," Maze shouts, having awakened briefly.

The smashing sound of a dropped pint glass by a little old bloke on a nearby table informs me most of the pub heard this last statement. Then, for her final pièce de résistance, Maze collapses on the table with a loud thud, unconscious, cheek down with dribble escaping her mouth. Now, just as things can't possibly get any worse, the landlord appears. He's an overweight fifty-year-old with a ruddy complexion and an incredibly annoyed expression on his face, which turns to horror as he spots the empty bottle on our table.

"What the…?" He picks it up and glances between mine and Jennifer's wine glasses. His eyes finally come to rest on his unconscious barmaid. "That cost me five thousand pounds. It was going up in value every single year. You just drank my entire retirement fund." His face goes bright red, and his cheeks puff out. I'm just relieved I didn't leave my credit card behind the bar.

"It's very nice."

Jennifer gives me a light kick under the table to tell me that's probably not the best thing to say right now. While the wine is a step up from my usual bottle of 19 Crimes, which I normally get in Asda for around seven quid, it certainly isn't worth five grand. I decide its best not to voice this opinion.

"Would you like a try?" I hold my glass out; a minute amount sploshing about in the bottom. Jennifer kicks me harder this time. A prominent purple bulging vein appears on the landlord's forehead and thuds rhythmically in and out with increasing urgency. I shrink back as far as my chair will allow, unsure if he's about to attack. He casually takes the glass off me in one hand and the bottle in the other. Looking at both, he determines whether it will do him any good to pour it back in. Deciding against this action, he holds the glass up to the light, admiring the deep red colour and then inhales the aroma. Satisfied, he drinks it all in one go.

"That was excellent," he says, like a true connoisseur. "Right, now exactly how are you going to settle your five-grand bill?"

"Seriously, are you on crack? There's no way I'm paying. Take it out of her wages." I motion to Maze.

In a perfectly calm and controlled manner, he makes an announcement, "In that case, I'm going to get my baseball bat and beat you to a pulp." All said while staring directly at me. I don't know what I've done to make him so upset. We all drank it.

As he walks away, I give Jennifer a startled look. "I think we better call it a night. Give me a hand getting her up?"

We pull the semi-conscious, presumably now ex-barmaid, to her feet.

"I don't feel well. Why is the room spinning? Oh God, I'm going to—" Maze grabs the thing nearest to her, which happens to be Jennifer's designer handbag and does the best exorcist impression I have ever seen. She fills it to the brim with jets of multi-coloured spew, which quickly overflows out the top and down the sides. We all stare at it in utter shock for a second.

"I'm so sorry," Maze says. Turning towards Jennifer, she lets out another exorcist level stream of vomit, covering her from head to foot. Faux fur jacket completely ruined and now a strange puce colour. Now I am not proud of what I do next, but seeing the beautiful Jennifer stood there covered in sick strikes me as kind of funny. My dark sense of humour takes over. A small smirk appears on my face, which she sees. Her emotions go from shock to anger to full-on rage, all in a split second as I duck to avoid the empty bottle she inexpertly throws at my head. Turning, now in floods of tears, she runs out of the pub, leaving me alone with the swaying barmaid. We all know karma is a bitch, and I get mine as a stream of putrid-smelling sick erupts from her innocent-looking face and hits me directly in mine. How much food has this girl eaten? I step back, blinded, and crash into the table behind me. It was everywhere, in my hair, ear, nose and even in my mouth. I grab a pint of bitter off the table and splash it over my face.

"Sorry mate," I say to the little old man whose pint I have stolen. Normally I would offer to buy him a fresh one, but the crashing noise of the landlord coming back up the basement stairs brings me to a moment of pure clarity; *I do not want to be murdered tonight.* I pick Maze up and throw her across my shoulder in a fireman's lift position and make for the door. For a little woman, she weighs more than I thought. While I am in reasonable shape, I'm not the sort to go lifting weights at the gym every week, so carrying around the equivalent of a sack of spuds is no mean feat.

"Handbag." Maze points towards the cash register as we pass. Turning with a bag of spuds on your shoulder is no easy feat either as I grab her small white and pink bag. The feline face of Hello Kitty stares back at me with disdain or more likely some poor Chinese kid's sewing was off after a fifteen-hour sweatshop shift.

We barely make it to the door as the landlord appears, a well-worn baseball bat in hand and a manic expression on his face. Still, I find myself disappointed he hasn't got the where-withal to utter the immortal line *'Here's Johnny!'*, he won't get as good a time as this ever again.

Next, I'm out of the pub and sprinting down the street. After what seems like forever but is probably less than a minute, I collapse out of breath. Adrenaline can only take you so far, even with a complete nutter behind you. A quick check around the corner confirms he's nowhere to be seen. Now, if I can just get rid of the drunken barmaid and end this night of madness, I'll sneak back and get my car in the morning.

I put her down and gently slap her cheek until she comes around. "Where do you live?" This I repeat twenty-six times in a row before I get an answer I can understand. Google maps is now my friend, and seconds later after sticking the address in my mobile, a little arrow and voice gives direc-tions. It strikes me as odd that not one person tries to question or stop me when I am wandering around with an unconscious woman over my shoulder, British politeness, or apathy. Either way, I am disappointed in my fellow man. However, I get asked for spare change at least three times, which I refuse with a growing snarl of contempt.

After a five-minute walk, I arrive at our destination—a three-story block of flats with crumbling render, patches of the original yellow colour showing through underneath. A shabby communal door leads me into an even more neglected interior. The key I retrieve from Maze's handbag has 3A on the fob. Just my luck, she lives on the top floor. As expected, the lift is out of order, and I'm on the verge of a coronary as I make it up several flights of stairs, now breathing like a pensioner with a sixty a day smoking habit. I knock on her front door, an ugly off white gloss monstrosity with old rusty numerals hanging on with one screw. I bang my fist against it in an exasperated cry for help. Why can't someone be in there to take her off my hands?

Leaning her against the wall, my adventure continues as I unlock the door and enter a flat that makes most student accommodation seem luxurious and tidy in comparison. A variety of discarded bras, underwear and other women's clothing covers most of the available floor space, from small lacy things to more Bridget Jones wear and what appears to be a discarded sex toy. I get a pair of knickers stuck on my shoe and avert my gaze as they are on the crusty side. I briefly wonder if Jeff has tried this pair on. Now while balancing Maze in one arm, I pull them loose and throw them as far away as possible. Thankfully, I don't fall over, as I would probably catch Typhoid or worse from the eighties threadbare carpet.

Freedom is now within my reach. The place is small, just two bedrooms, an all-in-one kitchen/living room with a settee covered in an ugly teacup motif throw. There is a dark and dingy bathroom with no external window and the compulsory leaking tap, which most plumbers I know would happily charge two-hundred pounds to change the ten pence washer. Rip off Britain; you have to love it.

Making my way into the bedroom, I pull back the duvet and gently lay the unconscious barmaid down. Leaving her clothing intact and making no effort to remove her trainers, I cover her up. She's on her side in what I believe they call the recovery position, just in case she's sick. Done, I breathe a sigh of relief. Jennifer will never talk to me again, but at least I wasn't murdered; the worst thing is, I know Dave will blame me for tonight's mess. A choking noise stops me in my tracks as I'm about to close the bedroom door and make my escape. *What have I done to deserve this?* I ask myself as I rush back in to find Maze now on her back, struggling to breathe.

I'm not one for putting my fingers in another person's mouth, especially if I'm not sleeping with them. It's that British reserve thing, but I do my gruesome duty and fish chunks of vomit out of her mouth, and on clearing her airwaves, she breathes freely. She must be a gym bunny or have a fantastic metabolism to stay so slim with the amount of food she spewed over all and sundry tonight. Rolling her back on her side again, I realise I'm now screwed. I can't just go home and crack open an *'I didn't get murdered tonight, celebratory beer'*. I'm going to have to stay and make sure she doesn't die in her sleep.

I sigh and take a seat on a massive pile of dirty laundry in the corner of the room overlooking the bed, hoping nothing is living in there. The fact there doesn't appear to be any chairs anywhere bothers me way too much for my own liking. Perhaps I should pay it forward and send her a couple through Amazon. I know those fuckers don't pay any tax and are killing off an entire nation of shopkeepers, but they are incredibly handy, and who doesn't love free next day delivery?

I relax for a second, the adrenaline finally leaving my body. So tired now. Jerking awake, I force my eyes shut against the first rays of sunlight streaming in through the window. I only closed them a second ago. Guess I dozed off. The sound of a rampaging wilder beast hits me, and my head snaps back and forth in panic. Searching for a place to dive out the way when I remember where the hell I am. The horrendous noise originates from the single bed; I smile as I realise it's only Maze snoring. No wonder she lives alone. Now a sense of peace settles over me, and I decide to do a good deed before I sneak out. Taking my life in hand, I enter the grimy bathroom and search through the cabinet. The cheap plastic handle snaps off, and I place it on the sink as quietly as possible. I feel embarrassed and guilty going through a strange woman's bathroom, especially when I find some antidepressants next to the packet of painkillers I'd been looking for. Placing the painkillers in easy reach of the bed with some water in the least dirty receptacle I can find, which is a chipped mug with a smiley face emoji on the side, I leave a note.

Dear Maze, You were a bit worse for wear last night, so I brought you home and put you to bed. You are welcome. P.S. You let us drink the landlord's £5000 bottle of wine, and he chased us with a baseball bat. I wouldn't go back in there again if I were you. Hope you don't have too bad a hangover. Cheers, Pete.

I purposely omit my phone number from the message—we won't meet again. Now, I re-read the note several times, deciding to rewrite it to perfection, but I'm too tired, and it has all the basics, so I fold it and slide it under the mug of water. I sneak out quietly.

I zip my thin bomber jacket up against the winter chill that greets me outside the building. The street is quiet, apart from a few birds chirping. My watch reads 6.24 a.m. The city can be a beautiful place at this time with no traffic, no drunks, drug addicts or those ubiquitous charity chuggers on every street corner. I yawn and close my eyes for a couple of seconds to enjoy the perfect silence, then step off the pave-

2

MAZE'S STORY - DRY OCTOBER

B illowing fog swirls seductively around me, the silky texture caressing my bare flesh. Goosebumps form on my arms as it invites me onwards. I step slowly forward, my vision down to a few metres in any direction. My pulse races as my bare feet slap against the cold marble floor, small blood-stained footprints left in my wake. Excitement electrifies my entire body as haunted organ music echoes through the mist. He's coming.

Lightning smashes through the clouded sky and strikes the floor in a spectacular display of nature, and for a second, I see a figure silhouetted against the background. Tall, powerful, deadly. The light fades, and he's gone. My breath catches in my throat; thunder spills through the air like the last sound of a dying animal. The mist thickens, and I sense his presence. Hot breath licks my naked shoulder, and I spin around ready to face the master of the undead - about to be taken, ravished, and pleasured beyond all human knowledge, but instead of my vampiric tormentor, stands a bald forty-year-old man in threadbare dungarees leering at me.

"Are you Dracula?"

"No, Duck. The name's Terence. I'm with the council. You're going to catch pneumonia running around naked like that."

"Um, I was sort of waiting for Dracula to… you know?"

"What, In Derby? What's he going to be doing here?"

"Well, me. Hopefully."

"Don't think so, Duck. He might visit London every few decades, but I doubt he's ever been north of the Watford Gap. The traffic alone would be horrendous. Anything I can help you with?" He gives me a creepy stare, up and down.

"Err, no, thank you."

"You sure? Because I have these." Clasped firmly in each hand is a red brick, the standard house variety.

Nervously, I take a step backwards. "What are you going to do with those?"

As I finish speaking, he leaps forward and smashes them against either side of my head. Pain roars through my temples and into my brain.

My eyelids flutter open, and I sit upright, finding myself at home in my single bed. I glance around, which proves a mistake. Nausea adds to the pounding in my head; this is worse than when I got the ferry crossing to Calais in a gale force storm. I abruptly lean over the side and vomit. God, my throat hurts. The brief pain relief ends with the sight of my favourite pair of fluffy slippers covered in an unpleasant coating.

"Jesus, not again." I spend so much on replacement footwear—the market stall people I buy from probably think I have a house full of permanently ill relatives in and out of hospital.

Wait, *why am I fully clothed?* I do a quick check to see if I've been molested, but no, everything seems fine down below. Weirdly, my trainers are on. I usually take them off even when utterly wasted. I lie back down as the queasiness returns, and the retch at the base of my throat threatens to erupt in a volcano of overflowing vomit. Rushing over to the toilet, I hug the bowl like an old friend as more sick drips from my mouth.

"I swear I'm never drinking again." The words magically quell my headache, though promises made to the toilet hold no sway when said hungover. My mind is a blur. It takes a full minute to remember what day it is. Now, what the hell happened last night? I give up trying to remember and rest my head on the soothing ice-cold porcelain rim, closing my eyes for a second. Joining the banging in my head is another thudding noise, this time at my front door.

"Go away," I mutter as I hug my old friend some more.

"Sis, it's me."

"Go away." I remain perfectly still while listening to the sound of approaching footsteps.

"You should lock your door living in this dodgy area. Some chav with the strong whiff of cannabis let me in downstairs, and I think somebody got stabbed outside. There's blood everywhere. Why don't you ask mum and dad to help out and move somewhere more upmarket?"

Not that old story. I would usually argue that I am an independent young woman, resolutely standing on her own two feet, but as I lift my head, nausea returns, and I christen the toilet with more foul stomach acid. At least I seem to be out of food.

"Oh, Jesus, Sis." A familiar hand pulls my hair out of the way. "Dry October not going too well?"

"Dry..." Then I remember. Why do we agree to these stupid things? "I managed a night off."

"In two weeks. Come on, what happened last night? Give your big sister all the details." She runs the tap, filling a glass, while I sit there trying to remember. I gulp down the water like it's the best Champagne ever.

"I went to work."

"And?"

"It's semi vague after that."

"You have bits of sick everywhere and your makeup. Well, you resemble a pissed-up panda."

"Well, you look…" I try to think of something negative to say, but my older sister Angelina looks perfect as always. She got her genes from my dad's side of the family, so she's tall and muscular with strong features, whereas I got my mum's genes and am short and skinny. I'm used to her being in a business suit, but she still looks fantastic in the Tommy Hilfiger tracksuit she's currently wearing, "great," I say.

"Aww." She nearly puts her arms around me but decides against it.

"Why are you in fitness gear? Decided to slum it with us poor people?"

"Dry October and getting fit. You said you wanted to get in shape and start jogging." She waits for this to sink in.

"Oh yeah. I'm pretty sure I was kidding." I try to hug the bowl some more, but my sister pulls me to my feet.

"Come on, let's get these stinky clothes off, and you in the shower. You smell like the old homeless alcoholic man who lives by the river. You know, the one you asked out on a date."

"Ha-ha, very funny. How was I to know he wasn't a Hipster? It's difficult to tell them apart."

Angelina laughs. "Well, I suppose that's true enough."

I strip, and she supports me as I climb in the shower. Standing back, she squeezes an entire bottle of shampoo over me in huge dollops like I'm some filthy prisoner being hosed down. I watch the chunks of puke rinse out of my hair and try to recall more of last night. I turned up for my shift, nothing unusual so far, now I remember. The old perv landlord patted my bum, and I started drinking heavily? No, that doesn't sound right, but it's a blank.

"Have you got a robe anywhere?"

"Back of the door."

Angelina wraps me in my treasured extra warm *Hello Kitty* dressing gown and half carries me back to bed. I sit upright, supported by the pillows, and pull the hood up, the red bow against the top of my head. I feel safe and cocooned in warmth.

"You look about ten. How are you supposed to attract a man dressed like that?"

"Hey, I like it, and if men don't, so what. I'm sure some will love it."

"Yes, perverts."

"Talking of perverts, that date I went on a few weeks ago."

"Yes." I have my sister's rapt attention.

"Well, he asked me to dress up in a school uniform."

"The sick bastard, the dirty twisted… wait," she reads my expression, "you dressed up, didn't you? You dirty bitch. I can read you like a book, now tell me everything, how was it?"

"Sis."

"What? My sex life is practically zero since I got married. Mike is always in Brussels on some business meeting or another. My only pleasure is living vicariously through you and watching Chris Hemsworth movies where he takes his shirt off a lot. So how was it? Tell me every explicit detail."

"Well, I put on this school uniform: knee-length white socks, a short blue skirt and a white blouse. I feel kind of silly, but he gets excited, and I mean really excited. We kiss a bit. He keeps telling me I've been a naughty girl, and he's going to give me detention and lines. He tells me to write down one hundred times—*Mr Biggy Big Balls is my favourite teacher*—and he hands me a pen and paper."

"Umm." My sister is disturbed, disgusted, and intrigued all at the same time. "And?"

"And I didn't even make it to the second B when he makes this strange whimpering noise, and I guess he just explodes in his trousers. He thanks me all polite like and asks if I want to meet up again. Night over."

"Oh, my God, so sad, what a sicko. What a dirty perv... wait, you went on another date with him, didn't you? Sis, I can't believe you would go out again after that."

"I have a boring life, and I thought it might go better next time. We went to this expensive restaurant and—"

"And?"

"Well." Even I'm embarrassed by the next part of the story. "We order a starter, open a bottle of wine, it's going well, all normal."

My sister is willing my story on with an impatient wafting of her hand. "And then."

"I order the steak, medium-rare."

"That wasn't what I meant."

"I know, I'm getting to it. So, I order the steak and well..." I stare at the floor, embarrassed. "He asked me to do the one hundred lines for him, which I wrote before the meal. It took me ages, even hurt my wrist. Who writes anymore?

Anyway, I get them out and slide them over as we are waiting for the food to arrive."

"And?" Angelina stares at me, mouth half-open. 'Then what?" She tries to suppress the excitement in her voice.

"He gets a funny expression on his face and kinda goes a funny colour. Then he jumps up and throws some money on the table, telling me he doesn't feel well and runs out of the restaurant like his trousers are on fire. I think I saw a wet patch on the front."

"Nooo…"

"Err, yes. At least he paid for the meal. But no, you don't need to say anything. I won't be seeing him again, ever. It's just so hard to meet anybody nice in this city. They are either married, gay, married and secretly gay or just plain odd. You are so lucky to be with someone like Mike."

My sister wraps her arms around me. "You'll meet somebody special one day, promise."

"Special needs knowing my luck. I'm not so sure I will ever find anyone."

"Hey, who left you this note by the bed?"

"What?"

"A note." Angelina leans over and grabs it, reads it out aloud.

Flashes of the previous night start to return.

"Who's Pete? Looks like he brought you home last night."

"Somebody I met in the pub." More memories return as I hang my head in shame. "I may have vomited on his date, and she was hot too; a ten." The image sears itself painfully onto my retinas. I blink away the shame.

"May have?"

"Well, did. I covered her in vomit, head to toe. She looked like a Twister ice lolly after I finished, all green and cream."

My sister smirks.

"It's not funny."

"Was she beautiful?" I nod. "Well, on the bright side, I guarantee she loves herself. I never met anyone that good looking who wasn't a narcissist. Try not to worry about it."

"Pete seemed nice from what I can remember and what a gentleman bringing me home and not molesting me. I wonder if he might want to meet up? No wait, I threw up on him too." I tell my sister everything I can now recall from the previous night and look at her expectantly.

"So, let me get this right, you got drunk, vomited on his date and then him and got chased out of there with a baseball bat."

"Well, that about sums it up."

She shakes her head. "Sorry, there is no coming back from that one." She hugs me tight. "Drink some more water and sleep it off. I'll come back tomorrow, and we can try this getting in shape thing properly." She lays me down. Kissing my forehead, she says, "Love you."

I swear I hear laughter outside the door after she leaves. Probably just my imagination.

3

PETE'S STORY - 02 IS RUBBISH

Something gently hits my face. The unpleasant damp sensation makes me open my eyes and sit up. Millions upon millions of snowflakes are falling all around me. I see them all so clearly. Every one a different shape and pattern, glowing with an unexplained translucent energy. As they float around me in a maelstrom of multi-coloured violence, I reach out to touch one, wondering briefly if this is what an acid-induced trip feels like. Perhaps those hippies in the seventies were living in the true age of enlightenment, after all? And I dismissed it all because I dislike paisley prints and flared trousers.

Music fills the air, the beautiful violin piece from the film Platoon. Knowing I won't rest till I remember what it's called, I pull out my mobile phone. It shows a perfect full bar signal, and I still have the internet. This is when I know I'm dead; O2 is rubbish normally .

Adagio for strings offers Google. I press *play sample* to be rewarded with a far inferior techno remix, which I promptly switch off. Standing for the full nine-minute rendition as the magical show swirls around me, tears drop from my eyes as the music reaches a final crescendo. Every snowflake bursts into flame to disappear in a single perfect moment, and I am left standing all alone with a deep, profound sadness hanging over me. I slowly become aware of my surroundings, slap-bang in the middle of a long tunnel that stretches as far as I can see in either direction, with no discernible end in sight.

I take a moment to stretch my limbs, checking each still works. After all, I was just hit by a car. The last time I felt this healthy was in my early twenties. Things went swiftly downhill when I reached the lofty age of twenty-five: aches, pains, tiredness, the usual stuff.

Staring down the tunnel to the right, I see pure white lights along the entire length. Looking left, I notice the crummy half-broken lighting you find in a typical UK underpass, a third smashed and the rest yellowed and barely functioning. The shadows radiate a dark and ominous presence, and I'm afraid something squalid might be living in them like a second-rate Gollum. Pete Doherty from the Libertines comes to mind, and I make the hasty decision to go right into the light. I may have made the wrong choice as I am still walking two hours later, my legs aching, but it takes another three hours until the tunnel abruptly ends.

Before me are the Pearly Gates, that mystical entrance to heaven itself. The colossal iron railings run into infinity on either side. Magnificent pillows of marble reach skywards, their tops lost in the swirling mist. I touch one. My finger goes through the polystyrene side; that's peculiar. At least the air quality up here is fresh and crisp; it's almost as if I am in the Alps. I gulp down deep breaths, and my well-being rises. Back on Earth, I know that the government would tax this if they could. Ignoring the fake columns, I make my way forward. This must be heaven as there is no queuing, unlike my life in England, where even posting a letter requires fifteen minutes of boredom. A figure in a cloth cap and stained coverall wanders into view. Clipboard in hand, he looks me up and down as if I'm a turd he's just stepped in.

"What's with the polystyrene columns?" I have more pressing questions, but it's bugging me.

"Budget cuts," the figure replies, and I recognise him from television, he looks just like the comedian Eric Sykes. On closer inspection, he's all in shades of grey, not a modicum of colour to him at all, just like watching him on my Aunt's old portable television. She had a colour one but turned all the knobs till it went black-and-white to get a cheap TV licence. I tried explaining once that wasn't how it worked, but she was adamant and claimed programmes looked better that way, plus she said, "Holly Willoughby looks much less of a tart." My Aunt was a complex character, to be sure. Growing up, I sometimes sneaked over and turned the colour back on, usually at Christmas. My favourite movie - *It's a wonderful life* - looked so much better, but boy, did I get a slap when my Aunt glimpsed of James Stewart's new skin tone.

"The devil's work," she informed me. After slapping me, that is. I protested it was the Americans; they had colourised it. The results sure did look pretty to my developing eyes. Even now she receives a free TV licence—I'm confident that EastEnders will be in monochrome when I do my twice-yearly mandatory visit. On the other hand, I have developed an aversion to black and white programming and resolutely refuse to watch any. However, this has led me to miss such classics as Clerks and Schindler's List, though I think the Americans won't resist colourising the latter for long.

"Good deeds?" he now asks.

"What?"

"You need to recount your good deeds to gain entry to heaven," says Eric.

"I thought you just looked my name up in your book, and I get in." I point over his shoulder towards the entrance.

He scrutinises me closely, trying to work out if I'm simple. "Budget cuts," he repeats and turns his clipboard around so I can see a blank piece of paper. "Do you know how long it would take to search for your name alone?"

I didn't. "Couldn't you computerise it; make it quicker?"

"No. I bloomin' well couldn't. What do I look like? A bleeding computer expert, now I ain't got all day."

I stand there stumped, thinking furiously, but my mind is blank.

Eric offers some examples. "Did you join Doctors Without Borders and help the poor and sick?"

I shake my head.

"Cure any illnesses at all?"

Shake of the head again.

The list carries on.

"Help an old person cross the road?"

More head shaking.

"The last one. Give any money to the homeless?"

"Hey, I was too busy trying to earn a living. Paying for a roof over my head and putting food on the table. All while giving the government a massive cut of my money." I ball my fists in frustration.

"You're not getting in, no chance." Eric shakes his head.

"The beggars would only spend the money on drink and drugs. I can do that myself."

He stares at me blankly, without sympathy.

"Please, somebody is waiting for me," I beg somewhat pathetically.

"Sorry, rules is rules." And with that, he screws up the blank piece of paper and throws it in my face.

The damp sensation of snowflakes hitting me in the face is back. I open my eyes, realising I'm back in the tunnel where I began, but now the right-hand path is pitch black - all light extinguished along with any hope of going to Heaven. I start the long trudge left, which takes another five hours. Luckily, there isn't anything lurking in the shadows. It's actually safer than an average Saturday night out in Derby. No pissheads trying to glass me, and not a single Mamba addict is in sight. Mamba being the drug of choice in my home city. That's if you want to go into a zombie-like state, then shit your pants. It is surprisingly popular.

As I reach the end, a familiar sight greets me, but instead of the white columns stand red ones. A man I recognise blocks my way.

"Are you Hugh Grant, the actor?"

"No, absolutely not. Do you think I had to sell my soul to the Devil just to get film roles and spend every second Wednesday down here helping out until I die?"

"Well, it would explain a lot."

"Well, I'm not," he says, frostily.

"Okay, understood. What do I call you?"

"Hugh… Grant, but it's just a coincidence. Promise."

I nod. "Okay." I guess he's in denial.

He holds up an Apple iPad and taps the screen. "Now please recount your evil deeds and prepare to be judged."

I think for a while. "Well, when I was a teenager, I didn't return a library book." Hugh is unimpressed or maybe not as his features don't change a great deal either way; never have.

I carry on. "I got a speeding ticket once, and one morning after a night out, I drove to work, possibly over the drink-drive limit."

"Seriously, that's pathetic. You saw what I got up to on the news. And that's only the public stuff. You need to do better."

"Well, I cheated on my exams, not all of them, but I wrote a few answers on the back of my hand." I'm struggling now.

"Sorry, you get to wander limbo for all eternity." Hugh locks the iPad screen and throws it down, where it smashes by his feet. "It's okay. We get a generous Apple discount," he explains.

I hold my hands up, pleading. "Wait, there must be something you can do."

"Well, this isn't technically in the handbook, but—" His eyes glow red, and he grabs my collar and pulls me close. An intense pain sears my brain, and I sense he's looking deep into my very soul. After several seconds he lets go, and his eyes return to their natural colour. The vast iron gates let out a pained squeal as they slowly open inwards.

I clench to avoid soiling myself as an inhuman voice roars, "You are welcome to enter; we see your dark desires. This is your true home."

I don't know what Mr Grant has seen down there, but surely thinking of Lucrezia Millarini, the newsreader, while I made love to my wife once or twice shouldn't warrant such a warm welcome. Hugh escorts me through and down a long corridor with doors on either side.

"Torture rooms," he says casually, the sound of pitiful screams leaking out. We stand between matching red doors on either side. "We're not all bad here; you get to choose your punishment."

He pushes the door to the left open. Inside is a man in a

shiny black latex gimp suit, a single table with one solitary apple core dead centre, and nothing else.

"Bit weird, he a friend of yours?"

Hugh shrugs. "No, these scenarios are all taken from your mind." He pushes the other door open, inside having a party are the entire cast of The Only Way is Essex or Towie as fans know it. Drinks are flowing, and the party is in full swing. I never watched an episode, but see them so often while looking for news stories in the Mail Online that they have all become ingrained in my mind.

I stare at Hugh. "I didn't think they were dead... Oh yeah, sold their souls, sorry me being stupid again. How else would they get on television?"

"Decide?" Hugh demands.

I point right at the Towie cast. This surprises Hugh, or maybe not? It's hard to tell. "Booze and women, how bad can it be?"

"Well, if you're sure." He pushes me through, and the door slams ominously behind. I realise my mistake less than a week later as Joey shows off his piss poor acting skills again. On this occasion he pretends he can't tell the time and asks me to show him how using my watch. We're not even being filmed, and it's the twentieth time today. They tricked me. This slow torture is worse than anything I could imagine. I break down, sobbing at his feet. The horrible Essex accent is grating on me as well. Seven days and I already want to die, and I have all eternity or until one of these egotistical pricks gets a gig opening a supermarket.

"Would you like a cup of tea?" a voice says in a soft Jamaican accent.

This is new, I think, and glance around in surprise.

"Cup of Tea?" the voice repeats, echoing out of Joey's open mouth, but the two don't quite sync up. A hand touches my shoulder, and I force my eyelids gradually open. At first, everything is blurry and out of focus until my vision clears, and I'm looking up at a cream coloured, almost smoke yellowed ceiling with a dark stain which, if you squint, sort of resembles Jesus. I'm instantly in pain, my legs, arms, back, but mainly my face.

"Cup of tea?" The little Jamaican woman is bored of asking. I nod, and a wave of nausea rolls over me, so I lie still till it passes. She places the hot beverage beside me, all the while avoiding looking me straight in the face. Relieved, she pushes her trolley along to the next patient. *What the hell is wrong with my face?* My joy at not being dead fades. Life is a lot harder for ugly people. I know sometimes I slid through life on a smile instead of working harder, pretty privilege, sort of like white privilege. Wait, I have them both. I haven't thought this one through.

Now the idea that I'm disabled floods through me like a curry the morning after. The icy touch of fear shoots down my spine, and I'm moving all my limbs like some demented octopus. They all work, and nothing appears broken, but I remember a car hitting me. I grin, happy not to be paralysed. Surveying the room, I notice three beds in this hospital side ward, and my fellow patients all seem to be either asleep or comatose. The oppressive heat being pumped into the room by the hospital's new age heating and cooling system could have something to do with this. Later, I find out that it cost a fortune and never worked correctly like so many things in Britain. My hand goes to touch my cheek, but I stop, hearing a familiar voice nearby.

"So, apart from being sexy, what do you do for a living?" I recognise the voice of my best friend, followed by some coy giggling. I would have got a slap for using that line, and Dave has pulled again. I strain to hear the rest of the conversation.

"Yes, I'm here to see my friend Pete. He's the one in there looking like Elephant Man's more deformed brother."

My hand tentatively touches my pain-filled face. Jesus, it's massive. Can I even walk with such a colossal head? Panic fills me as I carry on listening to Dave's booming voice. I can only hear parts of what's being said, and none of the reply. "—my life will be ruined if you don't go out with me—say yes—how about a double date?—get one of your attractive nursey friends to come along for Pete?—no, he's going to look normal in a few days—spoke to a Doctor, just a fractured eye socket—no broken bones—pillock stepped out in front of a car—here's a picture—Porsche—reads books—here's my number."

Dave now enters the room on full volume. "Oi, Oi, how's the Elephant Man doing?" He's wearing a tracksuit, which must be for fashion reasons as I've never known him to work out ever. Perhaps there was an attractive woman selling gym memberships again? This got him every time. He sits on the edge of the bed ignoring the sign which tells him not to.

"I tried to buy you a porno mag, but they are waiting for stock. Everybody just jerks off online these days, low demand, said the bloke in the sex shop. Got you these instead." He holds a half-eaten bunch of grapes towards me.

"They sell grapes in the sex shop?" Images of sordid Caligula like scenes with various fruit play out in my head. "Sorry, not a fan," I say. My mouth feels strange and misshaped, but the words come out fine. I'm not sure why I would want a pornographic magazine while in recovery, but Dave's heart is in the right place, I think.

"Of course not. That would be weird. There's a Tesco Express on the corner. Anyway, more for me." He stuffs a couple in his mouth. "What's up with these geriatrics? Is it a Great War reunion?" I close my eyes and wish I were anywhere else, especially as one patient now has all his family around him, and they all turn to give us frosty stares.

"You can leave tomorrow. They gave you a full M.R.I. scan, and you're fine. Well, apart from the Elephant Man thing, but you'll be alright soon enough. One-night observation and you get to go home. Amazingly lucky is all I can say, a fractured eye socket, swollen head, and a few cuts to your face. Nothing that won't heal. Wait, I almost forgot. Somebody is here to see you." Dave rushes off before I can tell him I'm in no mood for visitors. He comes back in with an older man and woman who I recognise but can't quite recall where from.

"This is Fred and Doris, a super couple. They ran you over. Lucky they were only doing twenty miles an hour; if it had been a boy racer doing fifty, then you would be a goner."

I smile politely. I would have heard a boy racer a mile away, silent electric cars saving the environment. What are people thinking? We spend the next few minutes chatting awkwardly. I have no idea what to say to people who have mowed you down, conceivably some comment on how polished their roof is. We eventually find a joint interest, cats. All feline owners can talk absolute shite about their pets for hours; it's a talent. I tell them all about my beautiful Sphynx cat with his piercing multicoloured eyes, one blue and the other green and how vocal he can be. I don't mention how he leaves oily stains on my pure white bedding or that he sometimes bats me in the face when he's annoyed or wants food. Satisfied I am going to live, they leave happy.

"Sorry about your car," I shout as they exit.

"Dave, did you take a picture of my face?" I ask as he's looking suspicious, phone in hand. "Seriously, mate!"

"You will see the funny side one day. Well, maybe not.

ment. I am as shocked as the nice old couple Fred and Doris when their Nissan Leaf crashes into me. My legs buckle and fly from under me as my face smashes their windscreen. I see them screaming through my blood and the broken glass. Next, I'm somersaulting over the roof.

Would you like to know what your final thoughts are in those last few moments before you die?

Now I was raised Church of England. They didn't really care if you believed in God because they just wanted to fill some more pews. Thankfully, my local priest only had a drinking problem and no inclination to molest me. However, this left me thinking, Heaven, Hell, or never-ending nothingness? That's a lot to process in the last few seconds of your life. I'm also curious about who will feed my cat 'Mr Tiddles' when my body stops spinning and hits the rock-hard asphalt road with a thud, and everything fades to black.

I've got some more news. You are going to be buzzing about this. I got us a date with two fit nurses a week Saturday."

I wasn't. "No, I'm done with women, going to become a monk."

"Well, in case nobody mentioned it, you already have. Anyway, you must come. Rosie dumped me."

"I'm sorry. Why?"

"Jennifer said that I set her up with a dodgy coke dealer who drugged the barmaid. It sounds like you had a buzzing night to me. I defended you mate, told her there must be some mistake." He gazes questioningly at me.

"It was a weird night; you had to be there. Tell you all about it when I feel better."

"It's okay, plenty more fish in the sea, and by fish, I do actually mean poontang."

I hold my hand up. "Not the time or place." I point to my fellow patients.

"Right. Yes, sorry everybody," he shouts across the room before turning back to me. "So, are you going to come then?" He looks at me and puts on a fake sad face, but it still gets to me every time, and I agree.

"Okay, brill. I'll book you a taxi to take you home tomorrow. Now rest and get better. I want you on your A-game for this date." He throws the empty grape stem on the floor and wanders out, cracking a few jokes with the nurse at reception.

I'm exhausted and lie back down. That unpleasant damp sensation is on my face again. I can now make out a leak in the ceiling. Costing us £125 Billion a year, the NHS could at least fix the drips. Bored, I take a sip of my drink. Whatever else it is, it certainly isn't tea; lukewarm cat urine comes to mind. I lie back, close my eyes again and try to drift off.

Dave interrupts my rest. "Good news, Elephant Man." His loud voice booms directly in my ear, and I nearly jump out of bed in shock. He's sneaked back in the room for some reason. "Sorry about that. Look, they need some beds, so I volunteered yours. You get to go home and let a real ill person have your pit of despair."

"I am desperately ill. I think I want to stay the night."

"Stop being a wuss. I promised I'd get you out as a favour to the head nurse; they are running at maximum capacity."

I try to protest, but it's futile. Dave runs off and reappears out of breath with a dilapidated wheelchair after ten minutes. "I'm knackered; they only have them by the exit, four floors down. How are cripples supposed to get one?"

"I can still walk. Why do I need a wheelchair?"

"Hospital rules, mate. It's in case you sue them."

"What do they think I am, American?"

Dave shrugs, helping me into the chair. He grabs my few possessions and drops them on my lap. "Let's get the hell out of here." We get to the end of the ward and run into a fellow wheelchair user, an emancipated fourteen-year-old, blocking the exit. "Come on, baldy, we haven't got all day."

I'm mortified. "Dave, he's probably got cancer," I whisper.

The kid turns and gawps. "Jesus Christ, what happened to your mush? Did you escape a freak show? You should wear a bag on yer head mate, scare the pensioners, init. Wait, I gotta get a selfie." He searches down the side of his chair for his mobile.

My sympathy takes a severe nosedive. "Push past."

Dave wheels me around and out into the long hospital corridor, followed by the annoying patient in hot pursuit. As he speeds up, so does our new friend, though as he's wheeling himself, he can't get a picture till we stop. You would think that with Dave pushing, we could easily outpace him. But our wheelchair is bulky, and outdated, whereas our friend has a sleek new model.

"Want to race, do you?" Dave says to my horror. I can see where this is going. He possesses a competitive streak beyond belief.

"Dave," I say, but it's too late. Like two competing Olympic athletes, they set off—two sets of wheelchairs neck to neck. Dave goes from a fast walk to full-on run as I'm pushed back in my chair, terrified. A nurse jumps out of the way.

"Sorry," I shout as we shoot past. Next, a member of the cleaning crew quickly pulls his floor buffer out of our way. Now I realise we're in trouble. Dave slows slightly as his shoes can't grip the floor, then let's go of the chair. I see him hit the floor over my shoulder and bounce twice. Identical to a competing British athlete then. The corridor is fast coming to an end with a set of closed lift doors facing me. I guess I win as our cancer-ridden friend forces his chair to a skidding halt. Trouble is, I don't think mine has any brakes, or I just can't find them. I discard the foolish notion of trying to stop the tyres with my bare hands as soon as it enters my mind. Just then, the lift doors open. Inside is a solitary cleaner with a fully loaded cart, which I smash into. Dirty water soaks me as a barrage of mops and various cloths fly everywhere in a tornado of filth.

As water sploshes over the floor, a camera flash and a shout of "Cheers ya' muppet" add to my indignity as cancer boy peers inside. I am drenched and humiliated. My day is now complete as a bucket that has been balancing precariously now tips over and lands on my head, leaving me looking like a second-rate Tin Man from the Wizard of Oz.

4

PETE'S STORY - NEIGHBOURHOOD WATCH

Going to live with my Aunt wasn't nearly as traumatic as I recall. She never mistreated us, but my sister and I were unwanted house guests and shown little affection. A simple inconvenience to be tolerated. Christmas could even be pleasant. We both received a tonne of presents. It was only later in life that I realised this was a careful plan, so we didn't bother her with our needy company. She would put us together in a large room as far away from her as possible, where we played with our new toys late into the night. The one strict household rule was not to touch any of her dusty ornaments that littered every available surface. If Peter Rabbit or any of his friends were a millimetre out of place, we were in serious trouble.

One Christmas, I made my sister a solemn vow. As soon as I could afford it, I would buy us a house where we would both live happily ever after. A magical castle by the sea, every room filled to the brim with toys, and we would hire servants to bring us chocolate ice cream and that wonderful orange pop that resulted in a diagnosis of ADHD. We would set aside an entire room full of animal shaped ornaments just to smash to smithereens whenever the mood took us. I just needed to save up my pocket money.

In the meantime, my sister Kate suggested we write to Michael Jackson and ask if we could live with him instead, so we did. A reply was not forthcoming, though with hindsight; this was probably a good thing. Nothing would ever break our sibling bond. Of course, she married into money at the first opportunity. Now she hardly speaks to me, her poverty-stricken relative a crippling embarrassment. Despite that, I always imagined that one day I would live in the most fantastic house when I escaped my Aunt's grasp.

Growing up, I became obsessed with property programmes, Grand Designs being my favourite. All those houses in every conceivable design, art deco, colonial, revamped with a twist, and those ridiculously expensive modernist builds resembling a glass shoebox. Being fully visible to the neighbours while taking a pee, exhibitionist or what? A converted water tower was the one that took my fancy. It was only after I got my first average paying job that harsh reality hit me in the wallet. When I eventually scraped a meagre five percent deposit together, I bought a dated and characterless early eighties three-bed detached house on a modern estate—severely in need of modernisation. Period features that had once meant a lot to me were instantly discarded. The only ones my new home possessed were the rotting wooden double-glazed windows. Still, it is a step up from the semi my parents originally lived and died in.

Now, as somebody knocks on the door, I wish I'd bought a timber shack somewhere deep out of the way in the forbidding countryside where the wolves prowl or maybe just Ashbourne. They have some excellent pubs there, though a few of the locals are known to date their first cousins. Taking my still deformed head over to the front door, I put my eye up to the peephole, and sigh. Standing outside in his brown wool knit cardigan is Kev. The self-elected president and only member of the local Neighbourhood Watch committee. Which is simply not needed in a cul-de-sac where the houses are practically built on top of each other. I don't answer, because:

1. My face is still abnormally sized, and while slowly returning to normal, I still resemble Stewie from Family Guy.

2. Kev is a… I think of the correct term, yes 'dickhead' fits the bill. He still lives with his mum at forty-five and has no life, plus he wears socks with sandals, which is unforgivable in a grown man.

"I know you're in there; I saw you get back earlier."

I heavy breathe through the door, just so he knows I can hear him and still have no intention of opening up. This does the trick, and he hops from foot to foot with ever building pen pusher rage.

"Now you're being childish. We could handle this like gentlemen, but you're forcing my hand." He pulls a piece of paper from his pocket and tries to push it through my letter-box, which I block with my hand. A tussle ensues with Kev using his full weight to force it open. I abruptly relent and am rewarded with a loud crash as he falls against the door with a thud, then jumps back up as if nothing happened. I pull the single sheet of paper through and read it.

OFFICIAL FIRST OFFICIAL WARNING

1. Lawn approximately 20mm overgrown.

2. Blue bin overflowing with wine bottles.
3. Windows are dirty and could do with a clean.
4. Weeds growing through block paving.
5. Your car could do with a wash.

PLEASE RECTIFY THESE PROBLEMS – A TIDY
NEIGHBOURHOOD IS A FRIENDLY AND PROBLEM
FREE ENVIROMENT

I love how he's pre-typed the letter and underlined the official warning bit as he's the only member of his made-up group. It must have taken him ages, a shame he can't spell *environment* or work out how to use a spell checker. I go with my first instinct and draw a large penis shape over the message, pause, add some jizz shooting out the end, then pull open the door and stick it back in his hands.

"Well, that's highly immature. We made allowances for you, becau—" He stops dead, staring at my misshapen features.

"Kev, you are not elected to any position of power. Don't call again, or I will tell your mum you tried to touch me up."

I slam the door in his face. My smug grin of victory lasts until I go into the kitchen to make a coffee and discover my fridge is devoid of milk; I'm completely out. Usually, this wouldn't be a problem as the shop is nearby, but I can't walk anywhere without scaring children. I sit down at my computer and try to book a last-minute Sainsbury's delivery, no slots—all taken. Exactly the same situation with Ocado. What is it with lazy people these days? I desperately need a cup of coffee. While I gave up sugar a while back when the government said it would 100% give me cancer, then changed their mind again, I just can't drink it black. Twenty minutes later, I'm getting the shakes thinking of going caffeine free. Looking for something to take my mind off this mini-disaster, I search through the contents of my fridge freezer. The bottle of vodka hidden out of sight under the ice cubes is calling out to me. *No,* I tell myself. Earlier in the year, I was in a dark place and drank excessively, but now I have it back under control. I only drink heavily when I go out—I go out a lot.

Now annoyed, I stomp off upstairs to get my most over-sized hoodie from the wardrobe. The one with 'Tunnel Snakes' emblazoned across the back, which Dave presumably bought me for the endless joke making opportunities. Making sure the hood hides as much of my face as possible, I rush out to the car and sneak inside unseen by any nosy neighbours. Now I start the engine and reverse quietly into the street, making sure to wheel-spin past Kev's house, hoping this gives him another number for his official warnings. Luckily, there is a space directly outside my local shop. Pulling up and switching the car off. I wait until the street is clear, then rush inside. Heading straight to the milk section, I grab the larger six pints of semi-skimmed instead of the four-pint carton as it has to last. A game of Pac-Man ensues as I try to make it to the till while carefully avoiding the other customers. Head down; I put the milk on the counter.

"One pound fifty," the gum-chewing assistant says.

I prise a two-pound coin out of my pocket and try to pass it over; she doesn't take it. The chewing has ceased. Looking up, we make eye contact. The young girl is staring at my swollen head. Horrified, she bursts into tears and runs off into the back room.

"I was in an accident," I say, the sound of a sliding bolt

and sobbing my only response. "I'll leave the money on the counter."

I slam the coin down and grab my milk before skulking out, head down in shame. I feel for you, John Merrick.

Back home, coffee in hand, I search for my cat, Mr Tiddles. He must be in a mood and hiding from me. I shout his name only to be ignored, which isn't that unusual; he can be quite cantankerous. Pouring out some biscuits in case he's hungry, I go and watch television. Quickly bored, my thumb presses the up button on my remote, channel surfing through endless mediocre shows. Charlie Dimmock has certainly let herself go; I notice after watching three Garden Rescue shows in a row. Time passes with a surreal slowness when watching mindless TV programming, the effects of being sober and knowing I am unable to leave the house, I suppose. When I switch back to Channel 4, and find it's showing that all-time classic, 'The Elephant Man', I take this as my cue and turn in for the night.

I wake, disorientated, my sweat-drenched body cocooned inside the sheets that stick to me with cold, damp unpleasantness. I stare over at the bedside clock. The glow of the red digital display informs me I've been asleep for less than twenty minutes. So much for my plan of getting an early night and waking refreshed. The 9.20 p.m. readout taunts me with my lack of success, and I decide to get up, now tired and irritable. After a refreshing hot shower, I dry myself and move over to the condensation covered mirror, which I wipe clear with my hand. I take a step backwards as the bathroom mirror shows me a different picture to my eyes as I swear I'd just covered myself with a towel around the waist. My all-black outfit and leather gloves, while marking me out as maybe the new age Milk Tray Man, have more sinister connotations, and I tell myself *not to go*. Something deep inside is urging me onwards, and I try fighting it. *Go back to bed,* I tell myself. I try to resist the urge—a dark desire for violence that I know is wrong. The Church of England and that bible thing. It tries to tell us right from wrong. Well, apart from the bits where people are stoned to death, and that happens a lot. There seems to be a lot of smiting in there too.

But this need in me is like a giant boa constrictor slowly crawling up my leg and coiling itself around my body to crush me slowly—my breathing struggles and stops. My eyes shut, and I welcome the darkness. I'm in the car now, driving. I don't even remember leaving the house, but I know exactly where I'm going and the time it takes to get there. My breathing is slow and laboured as my hands grip the wheel tighter than necessary; the demister control set to full. The dull drumbeat of rage pounding in my ears cancels out the screeching air rushing through half-open vents as the screen gradually clears. I stare with tunnel vision at the road straight ahead; *nothing else matters*. I would turn the car around if I could, but the darkness inside won't let me. I call it that, but it's more an insatiable hunger I can't control.

I find myself outside a house. A family of garden gnomes adorn the front in scenes of tasteless joy. I don't recall leaving the car, but as I trudge over the garden, I angrily stick Papa Smurf upside down in the wishing well. I make my way to the living room window and stare through the gap in the curtains—where they don't quite meet in the middle. Mocha brown colour drapes that could do with a clean, I even make out a few loose threads coming awry. My hatred rises. I don't know why I am so angry; I've seen worse curtains out there before. My gloved right-hand caresses the window softly, and as I gaze inside, the boa constrictor squeezes tighter. My vision blurs, fades, then returns, now tinged in a blood-red haze. My icy breath fogs the windowpane. I see them now, the family inside going about their everyday business. The television blaring away in the corner and children glued to mobile phone screens, addicted to Candy Crush or sexting pics of themselves, whatever the hell teenagers do these days.

The girl appears to be around fifteen, a mop of curly hair and freckles disguising the wickedness underneath. She makes a stupid pouting face at her phone and takes a picture. I get the urge to give her a good hard slap, but this is how I feel with most millennials, anyway. The boy appears younger, around twelve, chubby fingers push his glasses back up the bridge of his nose before returning to his phone, moving animatedly over the touchscreen again, face lighting up as he clears another fruit or jewel-based level. Mum now appears with mugs of tea, possibly coffee. I make out the steam rising from the surface as she passes a cup to dad. I decide they are tea drinkers. My temper is building, and my right hand quivers with rage. I struggle to breathe; forcing in one more scant breath is agonising. I hate this overweight, slightly balding middle-aged man more than I ever imagined humanly possible. I can't make out what's on the television from my position, but imagine it to be EastEnders and want to euthanise the entire family. I want dad to suffer. I say want, but I need this man to experience real torment.

Pain erupts in my head as I try to remember his identity. I blink, and now I'm in the back garden, unsure of how I got here. My hand pushes the patio door handle all the way down. How stupid are you to leave your door unlocked in this crime-ridden suburb? The door glides silently open on its well-lubricated runner. I quietly close it behind me as I step inside. Now I am alone in the darkened dining room, facing a mahogany looking table with six red and cream striped chairs. My fingers brush through a layer of dust; this confirms my original idea that it doesn't host many family meals in here. The sounds of the television filter through the closed internal door. Which I now glide towards, pulled by an unseen force. My ear rests against the thin layer of wood, my hand pauses above the handle. I still don't recall where the man is from. The memory of his face is infuriatingly just beyond my recollection.

The handle suddenly moves, and the door swings open. I slink behind it, hidden as a bright light illuminates where I was previously standing. The boy enters the room. I hold my breath. If he sees me, I may do something terrible, but he turns to the left.

"Mum, where did you put my Gameboy?" he shouts.

I guess his phone is out of charge. God help him if he had to have a conversation with someone for a change.

"It's in the top drawer, on the left."

The kid opens the right-hand side. I despair at the state of this country's education system. Not finding it in there, he now opens the correct drawer. Moments later, the small screen illuminates. His anxiety at having to converse with an actual person fades. I'm enraged that his Pokémon edition yellow and blue Gameboy Color has been allowed to get in such a poor condition. Scratches snake across the plastic screen, and dirt stains the seams. My brain is also annoyed that the Americans can't spell the word colour correctly. Now the boy turns towards the living room; if he looks up, he will catch me trying to hide my six-foot black-clad frame behind the door. Part of me wants him to see me. He doesn't and wanders past me, oblivious. Not shutting the door entirely, he leaves a small gap which now becomes my view into this family's universe as my eye peers through the opening. I examine the man's face. I still can't work out where I know him from. My gloved left hand comes up, and for the first time, I realise what I'm gripping tightly. *Is this the time?* Hot breath streaming from my mouth, rage building deep inside, the giant boa constrictor of hate hugs me tight, and everything goes dark.

———

I wake, again drenched in sweat and stare over at the bedside clock, 12.40 p.m. Pulling the blanket over my head, I close my eyes and try to go back to sleep. I wish these weird dreams would stop.

5

MAZE'S STORY - FORTRESS OF SOLITUDE

I worry I'm suffering from early onset Alzheimer's and that by twenty-seven, I will be a wheelchair-bound dribbling wreck—abandoned in the corner of some grotty care home. I'm barely one street away from my flat when I realise I have forgotten my handbag. I would understand if it were a subtle easy to forget, small black clutch. Hello Kitty's feline face and ears should not be so easily forgotten, especially as I have on my matching watch, socks, and I pause to check, yes, pants.

My breathing is on the heavy side as I mount the top of three flights of stairs. I really should do more cardio. I swear I locked my front door? If my life were an American sitcom like Friends, which it isn't, then inside my apartment would be simple but lovable Joey with a turkey stuck on his head or perhaps Rachel with those perky nipples pointing at me like a Dalek's ray gun. Monica would sashay out of the bedroom in that now politically incorrect fat suit, giving Chandler a knowing glance as he sneaks another Vicodin to feed his growing addiction—all covered with a fake smile. But my life isn't a sitcom, not even close. I tiptoe over to the open door and listen. Someone is inside, ferreting through my drawers. Just as I'm about to rush to my neighbour Frank's, I catch a scent from inside. My teeth clench tight in anger as I recognise the cheap rubbish cologne my ex-boyfriend always drenches himself in.

I deliberately slam the door wide open, making sure it crashes into the wall with a loud bang. My ex Jeff is in my bedroom, rifling through my wardrobe. He is still wearing those ridiculous combat trousers with the extra-long tassels he bought for himself in the women's clearance sale at New Look.

"Find anything good?" I say, voice raised.

"Oh. Hi babes."

He doesn't even have the decency to look embarrassed. "What the hell are you doing?"

"Looking for my… old T-shirt."

"And how did you get in? I took my door key back."

"I err…" he stares at his feet, "found an extra one."

"Give." I hold my hand out and wait.

"I was going to leave it, babes." He unclips it from his keyring and places it in my hand. "Why would I want an extra key?"

"Why indeed? Maybe so you can sneak back and help yourself to my money anytime you're broke. What is it this time? Another business opportunity of a lifetime that's doomed to failure. You're not getting another penny out of me. Not now, not ever. You pathetic loser."

"You can be a real ball-buster." He steps forward, invading my personal space, spittle exploding from his lips, his true self surfacing. "You ruined my life," he shoves me backwards, and I nearly fall, "all I needed was some money, a little cash advance to invest, and I would be raking it in, but no," he grips my shoulders and presses his face against mine, "you were too high and mighty to ask your family for a loan. Do you know the worse thing? I only went out with you because of your rich parents. Look at yourself." He grabs my hair, drags me to the bathroom and forces my face violently against the cold mirrored glass. "Ugly and pathetic. No man is ever going to want that."

"Jeff, please let me go. You're scaring me." I smell the alcohol now, mixed with day-old sweat, his breath harsh against my cheek.

"You never gave me a chance," Jeff screams, smashing my head against the cabinet with all the force he can muster. It cracks, and I find myself face down on the floor, dazed, with blood leaking into my eyes. "Look what you made me do, Maze. You make me so angry. Why do you do that?"

"There is money in my handbag. Take it and leave me alone," I scream in anger or pain; I can't decide which as tears stream down my face. I shrink back as he steps forward, pulling his arm back like he's going to punch me.

"You know what? You're not worth it, and you owe me that money just for putting up with you. You will never find anyone better than me." He storms out the bathroom. After stealing my purse, he slams the front door angrily behind him.

I sit there, shaking, hugging my knees against my chest as I rock back and forth, the cold bathroom floor chilling my limbs. For over an hour, I sit quietly. Just me and my bleak thoughts, those that whisper to me from the dark recesses of my mind telling me I deserve this, I'm not good enough, no one will ever love me. I climb to my feet; I know what I'm going to do. Grabbing my packet of antidepressants, I press out every individual day until I have a palmful. Now I add my collection of various painkillers, an overflowing handful, now. Right at the back of the cabinet are a few expired tablets; I add these too. Now, before I think about it, I force them all in my mouth and go to retrieve my bottle of vodka from the freezer. Twisting off the top, I pause. *What the hell are you thinking*? They explode outwards like a freshly smashed piñata of multi-coloured sweets as I spit them into the sink. I carefully search through the remains and pick out a triple dose of my fruit loop tablets as I like to refer to them. Knocking them back with a full to the brim glass of pure unadulterated self-loathing, I retire to bed and pull the covers over my head, embracing the comforting darkness. Somehow life is better in my fortress of solitude. I might stay here forever.

6

PETE'S STORY - INFERIORITY COMPLEX

D ave isn't known for his generosity, and his choice of food venue proves this.

"Why are we at this dump?"

A worn sign with several missing letters welcomes us to the 'King Arthur ub & Restaur nt' while the shrill squeal of unruly children tell me all I need to know before I get through the main doors.

"Well, it's great value, and I have these." He holds up two meal deal vouchers.

"Seriously?"

"We asked the girls out, so we have to pick up the cheque."

"You asked them out. You can pay for this rubbish food; I'd rather chow down on a juicy steak somewhere decent."

He shakes his head at me. "I go on a lot of dates, some great, most average, and a few are plain diabolical. On every single one, the woman expects me to pay. Which is fine if they put out but very disappointing if they don't, hence spend as little as possible."

I shrug and examine my surroundings. I can tell it's cheap

because it's packed out with families, all getting pissed while screaming brats run around creating mayhem and breaking things. Every male specimen in the place seems to possess a *Peaky Blinders* style haircut along with a tattoo, denoting their love for mum or dad in a poorly depicted heart shape.

The insipid piped in music provides zero atmosphere and little solace from the cacophony of raised voices. It's but one of many identical outlets in a countrywide chain, with every single place designed to be as appalling and soul-destroying as the next. I inhale, taking in the odour of stale sweat and urine-soaked kids' pants. It could also be the parents.

"Seriously," I say again.

"It will be fine, and you know what they say about nurses?"

"What, they are hardworking and underpaid?"

"Well, yes, but mostly easy. Hear me out. It's not their fault. They work long hours and deal with death and poo regularly and, yes, get paid sod all. So, when they go out, they love to party and will be grateful for some nosh, even in a shit hole like this. I have it all planned out. Did you bring the Porsche?"

"Yes, why?"

"Your date, Tammy, works mainly in A&E and is obsessed with fast sports cars. After the meal, suggest going for a ride, and by ride, I mean..." He leaves the rest unspoken as a group of kids are in earshot.

"I'm not having sex in my car."

"Why do you think it's got leather seats? Wipe clean." He nods knowingly. "If I had one, I wouldn't be paying for all these hotel rooms; I can tell you that."

"And you wonder why I won't let you borrow it. You could just take your dates back to your place."

Dave stares at me in utter horror, like I've suggested he

join the priesthood and take a vow of celibacy. "They would have my address. How would I dump them, and what if they're married? An angry husband turning up is something I don't need."

Our conversation is interrupted by the arrival of our dates. Kim, I'd met in the hospital, but of course, she looks better out of uniform. NHS outfits are nowhere near those of the 'Carry On' films. She is wearing brown leather knee-high boots, a short skirt with a side slit and a tight-fitting polo top, accentuating her trim figure. Beside her is Tammy, who I greet with a peck on the cheek. I don't need to bend down as she's tall and wearing skyscraper heels which brings us eye to eye. She's casually dressed in ripped jeans and a figure hugging sweater. She brushes her long curly ginger hair out of her eyes in a very practised sexualised gesture and smiles at me seductively, her tongue lightly glazing her bright red lipstick. I'm reminded of a Tiger eyeing up a gazelle in the wild from one of those BBC nature programmes. I imagine the voice of David Attenborough saying in his posh semi whisper, 'This is a rare sighting of the near-extinct surgically enhanced female of the species, rarely spotted without an accompanying Homo Erectus who partakes in too many steroids and suffers from shrunken genitalia.'

My mind tries to do its snap judgement thing and fails because my caveman self has taken over and is staring at her double D chest, magnificently presented by her tight black jumper.

As we escort the girls to our table, Dave whispers in my ear, "You're going to need a full valet on those car seats."

I try not to laugh; I guess his caveman mind has picked up on her personality too. We all scrunch together on a battle-scarred plastic table that's too small for four adults and could do with an energetic clean with a liberal amount of disinfectant. Our server approaches and hands out menus. I nearly just shout out burger as that is the best this chav centric pub sells, but I take it politely and peruse the options so I can say burger after careful consideration. At least it gives me a chance to take my mind off Tammy's chest. I really think less of myself; I believed I was a mature, centred individual. Guess not so much. Dave makes easy conversation, and soon the girls are laughing at his inappropriate comments while they decide what to eat. Our server waits patiently for our orders. As well as paying minimum wage, these places like to humiliate the staff with the ugliest uniform possible.

Examining our waitress, I note the chunky flat black shoes, generally favoured by women who prefer the company of other women or who want to save the whale, not that these are mutually exclusive. Next, a pair of thick woolly tights that must be itchy as hell. These are covered by a poorly fitting grey skirt that hangs awkwardly at a weird length, not quite knee and not quite ankle. Next is a white starched nylon blouse covered by an ill-fitting jumper, embossed with company logo. It is probably to prevent it from being stolen but much more likely, so the staff can't make a break for freedom, all topped off with a please kill me expression and a brown mid-length bob. A name tag that reads Helen completes the outfit. Surely, dressed like this, you should be allowed to go incognito? I notice a sticking plaster on her forehead and another one covering most of her neck, and I wonder, is she trying to hide a love bite? *Have you been a naughty girl, Helen?* When she speaks, I then recognise the voice. It's Maze; my waitress is the goth looking barmaid I'd helped home several weeks previous, now devoid of any personality. Her speech pattern is different too, slow, monotone and obscenity free.

"A Burger and a side of chips, please," I say.

Writing down my order, she stares right through me as if I'm trying to sell her a copy of the Big Issue. Not a flicker of recognition. Everybody orders the burger as I knew they would. Maze shuffles off, and I get that tingle at the back of my neck telling me that something is wrong.

"I hear that you've got a Porsche." Tammy's leg grazes against mine, her foot rubbing suggestively against my shin.

I try not to gawp at her cleavage and keep eye contact, "Yeh, a Cayman, 24 valve, 3.4 litres, 295bhp." Tammy's foot edges nearer to my groin with every statistic uttered. Unfortunately, I've run out, and I can't think of the 0-60 time for the life of me.

"Perhaps you can take me for a spin later?" she says as her foot makes it all the way to my crotch. I glance over at Dave, who pretends he has a chamois leather and makes a cleaning gesture.

"Sure, I'll take you for a drive later. Now if you will excuse me, I'll be back in a second." Normally I'd say I was going to the toilet, but I'm not sure if Tammy might take it as an invite. I rush off down a long corridor where I saw Maze disappear and bump into her as she comes out of the kitchen.

"Hi, do you remember me? Pete, Pete Walker."

Her gaze gradually lifts from the floor, and I examine her face. Maze's pupils are a lot more dilated than they should be. Being British is difficult at the best of times; we don't want to pry into other people's lives and avoid a scene if possible. But now, looking into her dulled eyes, I know something is wrong. I gently take her by the shoulders.

"Maze, are you okay?" I search for any sign of her old self.

"I can't feel anything." Her eyes well up.

Stepping entirely outside the box of my own reserve, I give her a hug. I mean, I try to hug her, but sometime in the last twelve months, I appear to have become *Rain Man*. This simple act makes me uncomfortable and on edge. It takes all my resolve to wrap my arms around her slight frame, leaving me bent weirdly out of shape with my lower half not in contact at all. This is soon remedied when her two hands grasp my bum and pull me in tight. I stare down at her, and next, she pushes her tongue into my mouth. It's not unpleasant, and it only takes a second to respond. I press her against the wall opposite; we are full-on making out in the corridor. My hands are all over her appalling uniform, the static electricity building as we rub our bodies frantically together. My hand brushes over her jumper and ends up on the back of her head, where her hair starts to rise. Trying to pat it down, the whole thing comes off in my hand, and I stand there momentarily shocked.

"It's a wig, they don't approve of my red hair," she tells me, then pulls me back in for a kiss. Just as things are getting steamier, our passionate clinch is ruined by a loud voice.

"What do you think you are doing? This is a respectable family establishment." The woman's voice is a shrill shriek, and we disentangle to find Maze's boss looking daggers at us. She appears to be Miss Marple's even more tweed loving sister, completely dressed head to toe in the stuff.

"You, young lady, are fired." She points to Maze, who bursts into tears and runs off through the kitchen. I attempt to follow, but tweed lady intercepts me. Stepping directly in my path.

"You should be ashamed of yourself, corrupting a young woman like that. We don't want your kind in here. Please leave now, or I will be forced to call the police."

I'm unsure that consensually making out with your waitress constitutes a crime, but not wanting to create a scene, I turn to leave. But then decide that even though I am sort of in the wrong to give her a piece of my mind.

"You should be the one who's ashamed. Making Maze wear a wig and a fake name tag, and all that nylon." An involuntary shudder runs down my spine. I think about pressing home my rant with a strong pointing gesture, but she's quite scary looking, so I turn and leave quickly.

Getting back to the table, I whisper in Dave's ear, "Can I have a quiet word, mate."

I walk him a few brief steps away from the girls and inform him of the circumstances of my recent banning, and I see the flare of admiration in his eyes. He's so proud of me. I can tell he thinks that leaving your date to snog your server in the hallway is pure lad. He takes it all in as we return to the table.

"Girls, you will never believe what just happened." He winks at me. "Pete saw a waitress drop food on the floor and then put it back on the plate, disgusting. We're not going to eat here. God knows what they're doing in the kitchen. Get your things, and we'll go somewhere more upmarket. Can anybody recommend a good steak place? Because Pete has generously offered to pay for everyone." He winks at me again, and I smile back. Dave's super power of lying to women with little effort is another of his attributes that I envy. We agree to meet at a fancy restaurant nearby. He takes Kim in his car while Tammy comes with me.

She sits beside me as I start the engine, and give the accelerator a quick press. The roar from the exhaust seems to excite her as she caresses the leather seats with her palm.

"I love the sensation against my bare skin," she purrs, her hand now settling on my thigh and inching higher with each word uttered, "Why don't we miss the meal and go back to your place." Her hand now rests on my crotch, and I'm instantly aroused.

Twenty-five minutes later, and we're both nude in bed, spent and lying there awkwardly, mainly because the drive back was twenty minutes, with another four to get to the bedroom and undress. Not my finest hour or sixty seconds, if you want to be more precise. In my defence, I am out of practice. Tammy shifts uneasily, and I sense it won't be long before she makes her excuses to leave disappointed. Pain sears through my head as my wife's image comes to mind, which I block instantly. Now Maze appears, the sexy goth version, not the lobotomised one. My attempt at helping has resulted in her getting the sack for the second time. Now, as I gaze over at the resting Tammy, my trio of guilt is complete. I already said that being British is complicated, with all our inbuilt inferiority complex. Why wasn't I born American? They can wipe out entire nations while pussy-grabbing without a care in the world. I decide, while I can't do anything about Maze, I can't let Tammy leave unsatisfied.

I kiss her just as she's about to mention leaving. "God, you're so beautiful," I say, then pause. Talking dirty is hard to do when completely sober, and there is that British reserve thing I keep mentioning. I whisper some dialogue stolen from a French art-house movie, hoping it's just the right side of sexy versus misogynistic filth required. It works as Tammy pulls me around and our mouths mash together. We… my romantic side suggests the phrase make love, but it is much more primal. It's an animalistic catharsis of skin on skin, a frenetic grinding of bare flesh, until we eventually collapse, our sweat-drenched bodies exhausted.

Later, I hug Tammy goodbye, and we swap numbers. But we both know there is nothing here, she's a nice girl, but we have nothing in common. I decide to get some sleep and return to bed. My back is killing me; I massage the base of my spine, where most of the pain radiates outwards. Some of those positions we tried are too much for a thirties body to endure. Still, I return to bed happy that I have given Tammy an orgasm, possibly more than one, but she may have been faking. It's hard to tell. Crawling under the duvet, I text Dave an apology for not turning up, and I promise to pay for the next two meals out. Switching my phone to silent and placing it within reach, I slip into a fitful sleep—those dark dreams still haunting my subconscious.

7

MAZE'S STORY - ROOKIE MISTAKE

Pulling out my ancient laptop, I waste valuable minutes staring at the intricately applied stickers and running my index finger over the silky texture until I can procrastinate no more. Time to check my bank balance. Raising the lid, I hum a tune as Windows takes an eternity to boot and display the welcome screen. I manage to log into my NatWest account on that nerve-racking third and final attempt. How do people remember such long passwords with a sodding upper-case letter, number, and weird squiggle?

HelloKitty123! finally accepted; my stomach cramps as I sit here wishing I'd inadvertently blocked my account. How can I be £1500 overdrawn? My finances are well and truly busted. I sort of knew I was insolvent; bills continue to get paid while I have no income, but ignoring my present situation seemed the best plan. Staring at those bleak figures reassures me I have made the correct decision. I only have an hour to wait. Then I will be interviewing two potential flat-mates for my box room or, as advertised: an individual living space in a fashionably shared bijou apartment. Obviously, I'm not going to mention the broken lift, resident heroin users, increasing rat infestation, or the fact the hot water ceases to work after 9 p.m.

Pacing up and down the whole six steps it takes to cross the apartment, I hum to myself, nervously. Maybe I should have my sister here with me, just in case I inadvertently invited two complete lunatics into my property. My vision blurs as my breathing intensifies. No time for a panic attack right now. I stop at the fridge freezer and retrieve my bottle of vodka, cunningly hidden under the frozen peas. Taking a long glug and an anti-depressant, I press my back against the cool interior. Closing my eyes, I breathe in deeply. Yes, that's better, everything will be just fine. After last week's self-medication debacle, I dropped back to my recommended daily dose.

The buzzer sounds. Right, this is it, best behaviour. One last check around. All good. My floor looks unnaturally clean, as all my clothing is stuffed in my tiny wardrobe, doors straining to keep them prisoner. Nothing is going to go wrong. My face forms a friendly smile, and I practically skip over, press the buzzer release and fling open my front door.

An enormous dead rat greets me, and my meticulously constructed visage of carefree happiness crumbles as I scream and give it a mighty kick. It flies a mere metre away and lies there, giving me a baleful stare, dead eyes full of accusations like where was my cheese? I have a family of ten to feed. The grinding sound of the ascending lift stops me in my tracks. How is it possibly fixed? I've never seen it working in all my time living here. The single strike of a bell announces the end of any potential flat share. There's only one thing I can do. I make the hasty decision to run forward, grab the dead rodent by the tail and hide it behind my back. The lift doors judder painfully open, and I give a friendly wave with my free hand. My first potential victim, I mean flatmate, has arrived.

The first interviewee of the day is wearing a slim fitting dark blue tailored trouser suit, high heels, hair up in a business-like bun, her face thin and pinched as if experiencing a bad smell. She strides over in precisely measured steps and sticks her hand out.

"Cassandra Winter, here to view the apartment." Her voice betraying the tiniest Germanic lilt.

I shake with my free hand. "I'm Maze. Please let me show you around." I almost don't recognise my own voice, automatically having switched to my posh tone, hard to do while grasping the rough tail of a dead rodent behind your back.

"Follow me." Carefully I shuffle backwards into the flat, rat body, hitting my backside with every step. *God, I hope it's not decomposing.* My smile falters as my trainer catches on the carpet, and I nearly end up sitting on my hidden friend.

"This is the open plan living room and kitchen."

Cassandra walks around examining the room as I swivel to face her as she circles me.

"Balls," I mutter as I see the tip of my broken vibrator peeping out from under the settee. How did that escape my clean up? Cassandra's shoe is moments from discovering it.

"And your room is over there." I point.

As she turns, my foot clips it and knocks it out of sight. Until this very moment, I never understood the appeal of professional football, well apart from the tight shorts. In my opinion, they are all overpaid child men, kicking an air-filled piece of plastic between themselves when they got time in between the raping, that is. But the exhilaration I now experience must be like scoring a goal in the World Cup, as I force myself not to celebrate by pulling my top over my head and running around the room like a complete idiot.

My fixed grin is becoming more manic by the second.

"And the bathroom, let me just check it's clean before you go in." Backing into the small space, I pull the light cord and push the door shut. All the air rushes from my body in one deep exhale as I slump, but only for a second. Feverishly, I search for somewhere to dispose of Mr Ratty McDead face. I try stuffing him in the small bin by the toilet, his ugly mush sticks out, and the lid resolutely refuses to close. "Oh, come on."

Cassandra knocks on the door, two powerful raps of her knuckles. "Everything alright in there?"

"All good, no problems at all. Just be a second." Choosing my only remaining option, I drop the rodent in the loo. Forcing my manic smile back into position, I slam the lid down hard and sit on it. "Come on in."

Cassandra enters and stares at me sitting there.

"Plenty of room. Isn't it great?" My smile wavers.

She briefly examines the worn tiles and broken cabinet. "I have seen enough. Your ad is disingenuous at best. This place is… unclean, grubby, and ridiculously small."

Cheeky cow, grubby indeed. If I weren't so desperate for somebody to pay half the rent, I'd throw her out.

"I could clean up a bit," I suggest hopefully, but her expression tells me all I need to know. "Thanks for coming round," I say as she marches off. Should I sit here and cry or drink more vodka? A tear streaks down my face, ruining my makeup. I guess I will do both.

"Hello, anybody there?"

Someone is knocking on the front door.

"Sorry to be early. Hiya?"

Brushing away my tears, I venture into the living room to meet India Wilkins, a twenty-two-year-old, who's new to the area, and that's all the information I possess. She appears more my type of person, dressed in a canary yellow wool jumper and torn jeans. The cut-out sections revealing a variety of artwork. I make out a pentagram amongst a storm scene. India carries in her hand an over-sized Victorian carpet bag, red and gold tapestry. Just the kind of thing Mary Poppins would love.

"What's up Chick, you having a bad day?" India folds me into her arms, hugging me tightly.

I intuitively know we're going to be best friends. "Thanks, I needed that." I sniff away the remnants of my tears. "I'm Maze. I'm not always like this."

"That's okay; I'm always bawling at the slightest thing. You'd think I was menopausal. I'm India, India Wilkins, and you guessed it, my hippy parents named me after the place where I was conceived. I'm only glad it wasn't Luton." She laughs, a genuine chuckle full of friendship.

"I'm going to level with you. This place is a bit of a dump, but it is incredibly cheap."

India grins. "But what's the men situation like, any fitties in the building?"

"Well, Simon from number 5 is hot. So pretty, but he has a boyfriend." He is always limbering up on the stairwell, hot muscular body covered in a fine sheen of sweat, like a male stripper on his day off. To make things even worse, his boyfriend is even hotter, a tall olive-skinned Italian looking thing of beauty. Seeing them together sent my fantasies into overdrive, hence my broken vibrator. The sad truth is that I am all but invisible to them and barely receive a nod of acknowledgement.

"Hey, eye candy at least, and I'm always up for a challenge, anybody else?"

"Not really, unless you include Frank, who lives opposite. He always wears a stained wife-beater vest, with his beer belly peeking out. I see it most days when he's fetching the milk in."

India laughs. "Well, I'm not that desperate yet, though I have been single a while."

"Hey, I could show you around the local pubs, you know, if you decide you want to move in." *Am I being too pushy?* I don't want to scare her away.

"Love the tattoo, by the way. That's intricate work," India says while takes a closer look. I tilt my head sideways, exposing the full design. I can imagine us now, two single women doing a pub crawl, getting hammered and scoping out the available men, we're about the same level on the attractiveness scale, so it won't be all one-sided when we're out.

"I can tell I'd fit in here already; I'm very spiritual and can sense these things. Before I move in anywhere, I like to do a reading." She pauses, waiting for my reaction.

"I get where you're coming from; I'm a bit psychic myself."

"Thanks, Chick. I had a feeling you would understand." India impulsively hugs me again, and I feel the real warmth of our newfound friendship surrounding me.

She lets go. "You should see some of the strange looks I get when I mention doing a reading. Now my mum used to have a genuine talent; the stuff she could do was verging on spooky. I only get flashes. Here goes."

Snapping open the leather catch on her bag, she rummages around. Sneaking a peek inside, I spot a crystal ball, tarot cards, gemstones, some bits I don't recognise and a bottle of Pinot, my heart races in joy, a fellow drinker. The rummaging stops.

"This is it." India pulls out two copper pieces of metal, bent at right angles. "Divining rods."

"Are you looking for water?" I ask, puzzled.

"Rookie mistake, finding water is only one of their uses, I use them to sense bad juju, simply a precaution, I'm not expecting to find any here. Um, I'll start at the front door." Rods held outward; she marches to the door and turns around.

"Okay, so far," she says, giving me a reassuring smile as she scans the room. As she reaches the settee, they twist and crossover, and I remember what I kicked under there earlier. She kneels to peek under. Now she turns and faces me, her expression neutral. I hold my breath, expecting the worst.

India grins. "I sense some pent-up energy in there." She winks, don't worry. I bought this monster vibrator just to get my last boyfriend to leave me. I even left it sticking out of his sandwich box. He had the smallest todger. Still, it took weeks for him to get the hint. In the end, I wet it under the tap then plugged it in the USB port of his laptop to charge, dripping over the keyboard. That did the trick."

I smile back. I know we will be swapping stories of Jeff's tiny cock within the hour.

"Mind if I check your bedroom?"

"Knock yourself out, sod all happening in there recently." And nothing to see as I've stuffed everything in my wardrobe.

India again ventures forward; rods held out like ant antennae. I breathe a sigh of relief as they stay unwaveringly straight.

"All fine here too."

My good humour takes a hit as the thin white doors holding all my dirty clothes prisoner make a loud creaking noise. India hears this too. As she turns to look, the small catch explodes from the pressure, and a confetti shower of dirty garments fills the air, pants, socks, bras, towels, jumpers, even my missing suede mini-skirt that I haven't seen for six months. A trainer narrowly misses hitting India as she quickly ducks. "Wow, now that's space-saving."

"Yes, I sort of cleaned up in a hurry, sorry." I shrug, embarrassed.

"Don't worry; I'm a messy cow. One last room to check." She marches into the lavatory. "All good," she says, just as both rods jerk right and left as if possessed. "Strange. I've never seen them move like that." She walks around the confined space, and as they pass over the toilet, they go crazy. India pauses and goes to open the lid.

"No, don't open that," I half scream.

"Why, what's up?"

"I... I did... a big poo." *Jesus Christ, what did I just say?* I wish the ground would swallow me up. An angry, scraping noise erupts from the toilet. India's expression goes from puzzled to concerned, then terrified as the lid rocks up and down.

"Are you a witch?" I scream while rushing forward and putting my full weight against the lid. India has somehow resurrected the dead rodent with her divining rods. The snarling noise is horrifying. "It's a rat," I admit, "I stuck it in there earlier, but I swear it was dead."

"White witch only babes, no necromancy powers here and certainly not with these." She holds the rods up.

"Sit on the lid; I know what to do." We exchange places, and I rush off, my hopes at a new friendship all but destroyed.

———

Ten minutes later, I'm sat cross-legged on the living room floor: a triple vodka and coke in hand. I simply can't believe how monumentally dreadfully that went. The bathroom door opens, and resplendent in his best pure white wife-beater vest emerges Frank, cage firmly held aloft and a massive smile on his face.

"Girls, I can't thank you enough for finding Henry. I've been worried about him; poor little sod has been missing for a whole week. Who's a good boy?" He pokes his finger through the cage bars. "Hey, if there's anything I can do for you, just ask." He leaves the apartment with a big beaming smile.

India now appears from the bathroom, laughing. "How could you mistake that man's cute gerbil for a vicious killing machine?"

"What do I look like, David Attenborough? It had claws and a long tail." I stare down at the floor, saddened. "I guess you'll be off then?"

"Well, I did bring this," she holds up the bottle of Pinot, "to share with my new flatmate."

"You still want the room?"

"Are you kidding? I haven't had so much fun in ages. You are one crazy girl; we are going to have a hell of a time."

I can't help but grin.

8

PETE'S STORY - OBSESSIONAL LOVE

"I so love Hugh Jackman in the Showman; he's just the best."

Now, this isn't what I expect to come out of the mouth of a nearly six and a half feet tall, shaven-headed black guy called Jace, who appears to have the muscle mass to bench press an entire gym. Sky movies is playing in my living room as we wait for 8 p.m. to come around. He is being paid the princely sum of £250 for an hour's work to be my muscle on tonight's job. Just in case things go wrong. As he breaks into a rendition of 'Never Enough' I have second thoughts. His deep soulful singing voice and appearance are in direct contrast to his overt ostentatious nature. I'm glad Dave isn't here; he would be wandering around saying, 'Ooh Matron' in a nasally Kenneth Williams impression and enquiring if Jace could get RuPaul's autograph. Drag Race surprisingly being Dave's favourite television show. I instantly like Jace, his cheery demeanour being in direct contrast to mine.

I leave him to pace up and down my kitchen, casting a sporadic glance at a plain brown cardboard box sat on the counter. What's inside will net me a £10,000 profit in the next hour. But they want to pay me in cash. While the buyer is an acquaintance of mine, he lives in a poor area of Normanton. That melting pot of immigration and failed integration in my home City of Derby, which the police judiciously avoid. Concentrating their best efforts on major crime like catching speeding motorists, and starring in channel 5's Traffic Cops.

My mobile phone rings, or more accurately meows as the ringtone kicks in. My sister is calling, and I mistakenly accept the call as my fat thumb hits green instead of red to reject.

"Hello, darling sister, what's up?" I change into my false happy to chat voice.

"Finally, how good of you to answer my call? I've been phoning all week."

She has, and I've avoided at least ten so far. "Sorry, been busy. Must have missed them."

"And the voice mails?" She sounds annoyed.

"Kate, I'm sorry, business is manic at the moment."

I choose to lie as I have been avoiding my sister and her ridiculous renewing of her wedding vows ceremony, which they think is going to be the event of the decade. Her snob of a husband Roger hasn't even been banging the staff, so what's the point? His secretary is scorching hot though, so maybe he has and they're keeping it a secret. It's a lot more likely that they just want to flaunt their middle-class wealth to impress the neighbours. I do not wish to participate.

"So, are you going to make it?"

"Of course, Kate, I've been looking forward to this all year. I wouldn't miss it for anything."

"And you're bringing a date?"

Shit, I forgot they were expecting me to bring somebody to their tedious affair. "Yep, totally bringing a date."

"We worry about you so much, you know after... It will be

good to see you getting back out there and enjoying yourself. Perhaps you can pick up your bloody—"

I interrupt before she can finish. I've heard enough. "Yes, little sister, it will be brilliant. See you Saturday, got to go, some of us work for a living." I end the call and stand there looking perplexed.

"What's troubling you? "Jace asks. "You look like Philip Schofield when he found out Gordon the Gopher was selling the News of the World an exclusive expose." How he moved so silently into the kitchen for such a huge bloke is a mystery.

I smile. "Sorry. That's my sister making sure I'm not going to miss her renewal of the wedding vows ceremony this Saturday. I'm expected to take a date, and I can't think of anyone to invite."

"Well, I'm always free if you need a plus one."

"Are you asking me out, Jace?"

"Simply being friendly, honey. One shouldn't suffer these things alone, and by the way, you're not my type."

I really want to ask what's wrong with me? But decide I don't want to know. The thought of taking Jace as my date strikes me as a potentially brilliant idea. The pained expression on everybody's middle-class faces would be something wondrous to see, under their polite demeanour would be an explosion of prejudice that would make a Klan rally appear tame. The fact my sister's husband is so uptight, if not downright homophobic, makes it even more tempting. At least I would never receive an invite to another family occasion. I nearly take him up on his offer right there. "Thanks, Jace, that's very generous, but..."

"Yes?" He raises his eyebrows extra high in a way that makes me want to laugh.

"They wouldn't be very nice to you." I shrug.

"Well, baby. I can take care of myself, but mixing with

the unenlightened can be tiresome. You shouldn't either; those folks will drag you down."

"Thanks for the offer. But family, what can you do?" I glance at my watch—time to go.

"Showtime," I say.

I think Jace is rubbing off on me as I've never used the expression in my life, but now we high five each other and head down to the car. He squashes his muscular frame into the snug racing seats and starts to flick between the radio stations. Jace treats me to a soulful performance of 'Summer Nights' and a few other classics as we drive across the city. Thankfully, he doesn't expect me to join in; my voice is only acceptable for Eurovision's UK entry. I try to find a parking space as near as possible, but my buyer lives in a terraced house, and the closest I can get is two streets away.

"Okay, I'm not expecting any trouble, but keep an eye out and act mean."

Jace winks at me. "No problem." A dour expression comes over his features as he stands upright to his full, intimidating height. I resist the urge to say *show time* again, and we make an uneventful journey to our destination, the box heavy in my arms. I'm nervous now; I glance at Jace for reassurance. We don't see another soul in the brief journey, and moments later I knock on a nondescript front door. Checking my watch, I see I'm less than a minute late. The door cracks opens a few inches, the chain engaged, and a small round bloated face stares out.

"Hi, Tony."

"Do you have it all?"

Tony is obviously nervous, and I glance sideways for any sign of trouble. "Everything is in the box." I lift the lid a fraction to give him a view of the merchandise.

His eyes go wide with excitement. The door slams shut,

followed by the jingle of the chain, then opens fully. "Quick, come in."

I almost ask why he doesn't live in a nicer area, but I don't want to appear rude. I enter directly into Tony's front room. A tiny television hangs on the wall, and apart from a blocked-up fireplace, there is only a small settee and chair surrounding an old teak table. Hideous seventies brown flock wallpaper adorns the walls, and I'm only surprised it doesn't feature any flying duck ornaments. The bare floorboards squeak with each step as I carefully place my box down on the table and take a seat. The door is locked behind us.

"Do you have the money?" I ask.

Tony glances at Jace, wipes sweat off his brow, then nods. He doesn't look well. The pallor of his skin suggests he may be undead—that and the unpleasant odour.

"Jace, why don't you stand by the door."

I now turn to Tony, who appears calmer. "Ready?"

He takes a seat opposite, and I place my hands on the box, gently teasing it open like a burlesque dancer showing a hint of naked flesh. He sucks in a lung full of air and holds it as I take out the most valuable item and pass it over.

In Tony's chubby trembling hand is a brand new and factory sealed copy of Clay Fighter Sculptor's Cut. This Nintendo 64 game is extremely rare - under fifteen thousand copies exist. The fact Blockbuster of America routinely destroyed the boxes and instructions when they went for rental didn't help.

He stares at me in awe. "You did it." His lips quiver and I hope he doesn't cry or even worse, try to hug me.

I nod and smile. "I did. I pulled off a miracle and got you the holy grail of Nintendo 64 game collecting. A full new and sealed set of the Blockbuster USA exclusives." Next, I hand over Stunt Racer; he holds it in reverence. He inspects each game in turn for any sign of damage. Razor Freestyle Scooter follows, then Beast Wars, next Indiana Jones, and lastly NFL Blitz Special Edition. Tony stares at the Nintendo 64 games with pure obsessional love. I mention the extra playable characters, including the unlockable Earthworm Jim in Sculptor's Cut, but I know he's never going to play any of these. They will be placed lovingly on a shelf and admired from afar.

"Did you get the rest?"

I grin and pull out the Nintendo 64DD games Japan Tour Golf, followed by Doshin the Giant 2, both incredibly rare. I'm not entirely sure but there now appears to be a small bulge in Tony's trousers. I pretend not to notice.

I also get out a copy of Mia Hamm Soccer. "On the house, as I know you wanted a sealed one."

He takes it, but nobody gets excited by Mia Hamm Soccer, even for free. He's now stroking the boxes cradled in his arms like a newborn. I realise this is what Gollum would look like if he happened to be an overweight forty-something video game nerd.

"Did you get—?" He leaves the question hanging.

"What this?" I pull out the final item, the Nintendo 64 game Tarzan. This special edition features the new and sealed game with two small plastic figures in an oversize box. Even though this is an American version, the entire stock ended up in Germany, where I picked this one up.

He takes it from me. "They're so beautiful; I now have the full U.S. set." He brushes away a tear.

"Do you still want every big box variant Rampage with the monster keyring? You have the one with the Lizzie plush, right?"

"Yes, I still want the others."

"Okay, it might take me a while."

I know he has a full Pal set as I got him a Snowboard

Kids 2 and HSV Adventure Racing (it's Beetle Racing remodelled with Holden muscle cars for the Australian market). However, he still hasn't completed the Japanese set, so there is always room for more profit.

"Happy?"

He grabs my hand. "Thank you so much."

I'm just grateful he doesn't hug me. "Money?" I say, a warm smile appearing on my face as I contemplate all that filthy lucre.

"Yes, of course." He pulls up the cushion next to where he's sitting and hands me bundles of twenties, which I now count. "It's all there," he says, eyeing Jace's menacing figure.

"Just for future reference, I take bank transfer." I lift one bundle and smell the beautiful wedge of cash, but get nothing from it. Stupid plastic money ruining my fun. You can't beat the aroma of paper mushed in thousands of people's grubby hands that's been used to snort cocaine and passed to strippers in seedy nightclubs. Plastic money is just too hygienic. Still, you can't stop progress. Things went so smoothly, I'm already thinking of spending my profit, and Dave tells people I sell toys. If only he could see me now.

The sound of heavy boots on the pavement outside causes me to stop counting and glance up. That sixth sense that something is wrong tickles the back of my neck, and everything goes into slow motion. The front door implodes, sending splinters of broken wood across the room as a battering ram takes out the lock and something metal clatters across the floor, exploding in a deafening bang. I'm blinded by the flare of intense light. Through my muddled senses, I hear screams of 'Police' echo through the air. Figures in black now rush through the doorway like ninjas out of a badly dubbed Chinese movie. I turn to see Jace lit up by at least four different tasers. He hits the floor, shaking violently like a junkie going cold turkey.

I raise my hands, "I surrende—" when an extendable police baton hits me squarely in the face, and my world goes dark.

9

MAZE'S STORY - IT'S YOUR LUCKY NIGHT

Biting my lower lip, I nudge India with my elbow. Not as it's needed as we are both already staring at the same thing. Walking down the corridor with an enormous box held over his head like it's a toy is an absolute specimen of manhood: tall, broad muscly shoulders, a pure white T-shirt filled with rippling promise. I wipe a spec of dribble off my mouth as he gets nearer. Arm muscles Pop-Eye the sailor man would be envious of hold India's new flat-screen television in a firm, unwavering grip. India now nudges me back as he gets closer, and we both stare at his package, proudly displayed in his spray-on black jeans. Though I bet it takes him half an hour to get them either on or off. His blonde hair isn't in the most fashionable cut, it's more bowl around the head done by your mum, but it does give him that He-Man vibe. I'd certainly ride him like battle cat.

"Where would you ladies like it?"

"Definitely the bedroom," I blurt out.

India bursts out laughing. "I think we're good with it in the living room. Can you put it on the floor over there?" She points through the doorway.

He carefully drops it down and pushes it against the wall.

"It's very nice of you to hump it up three flights of stairs." I don't know why, but I emphasise the word hump. *Get a grip,* I tell myself.

"All part of the job." He smiles, and I notice his eyebrows are more finely sculpted than mine. This sends off warning signals as his T-shirt hasn't a single crease. Gazing downwards past the obvious, his trainers are pure white, without a single stain, and in a delivery job too. This can only mean either of two things. I glance over at India and motion with my eyes; she gets it too.

"How do you get your top so crease-free?" India asks.

"Oh, my mam does all that."

Bingo, he lives with his mother; all my excitement instantly drains away. "Thanks again." I usher him out the door as quickly as possible. "Such a waste of potential."

Indian nods in agreement. "Have you got any scissors?"

Ten minutes later, and I still haven't found a pair anywhere. All the sharp cutlery is also missing; I swear a resident poltergeist is hiding things. Five more minutes of sawing away with the only thing I can find, the butter knife, and I give up. The indestructible strap around the box has defeated us.

"I know we are independent, free-thinking women, but should I?" I motion over to Frank's flat.

"Yes, why not?"

Five minutes later, Frank comes over. In one hand his toolbox and in the other a cage. "Henry is dying to see you." He hands me his pet gerbil.

"Who's a good boy then," I say. The little sod recognises me and hisses.

"See, he likes you."

I smile politely and pass him over to India, who is trying not to piss herself laughing.

Frank breaks open his toolbox and gets out one of those extendable knife thingies to cut the plastic seal and open the box. He has removed the wrapping, screwed on the feet, and even set the thing up in no time at all.

"Feel free to nip over anytime to visit Henry." Frank leaves happy, having proved his masculinity.

"We will." India closes the door and points to me. "You should be ashamed, poor Henry. You've scarred that cute gerbil for life. He's going to need therapy."

I display my middle finger in an immature gesture of disrespect. India laughs hysterically. My attention moves to the new television, 65inch of ultra HD goodness. "My God, that's a cinema in this tiny flat." My hand caresses the sleek black edge. "How can you afford it?"

"I got it from Very, interest-free credit for twelve months."

"Hey, put something good on." We snuggle up together on the settee as India flicks through the channels. How many episodes of *Come Dine With Me* and *A Place In the Sun* did Channel 4 make? Unfortunately, I seem to have seen every single one. Rubbish quiz show after quiz show follows. Bradley Walsh desperately needs some new material.

"We should probably go halves on Netflix," I suggest.

India nods in agreement; she stops flicking channels as East Midlands Today comes on. Bubbly blonde presenter Anne Davies appears on the screen in a slinky red dress with black boots.

"She always dresses so nicely; I hope I look that good when I'm eighty."

"Yes, she's fantastic," India agrees.

"And now to our reporter on the scene," Ann says from the TV.

The screen now shows a middle-aged man in a raincoat holding a microphone. Behind him is a taped off area complete with a white tent and police officers in forensic suits.

———

We believe the horrific scene unfolding behind me, in front of the Greyhound Stadium, to be the fourth victim of the serial killer now labelled, 'The Bagman'. Discovered in the early hours of this morning, the victim is as yet unidentified with the only description, being female between the ages of 18 and 28. Only the head has been recovered; the torso is still missing.

Police believe that, once again, this is only the dumping site, and the murder took place elsewhere.

Derbyshire Constabulary are appealing for witnesses or any information. They have also issued a warning to all women in the relevant age group of 15-35 to be extra careful and go out in pairs if possible. Now back to Ann in the studio.

———

India switches the TV off. "You know you might have had a lucky escape with the delivery man."

"How come?"

"Well, serial killers always live with their mum, then they murder them and start wearing their clothes."

"I suppose I never thought about it much. I feel much

safer since you moved in. It's depressing news though. How about a drink? Wait, I forgot we're all out. Pub?"

"Sure, you did promise to show me around."

It takes approximately forty-five minutes to get ready. I'm secretly envious of India's effortless style; her outfit is a pair of light grey cotton trousers and a cream polo neck jumper. Still, what truly makes it is the yellow high heels and matching chunky wool knit three quarter length coat. I would resemble Big Bird, but India looks fabulous, hence my jealousy. I try to compete in black ankle boots with a wedge heel, black tights, leather mini-skirt, favourite T-shirt and a cute denim jacket with rips and smiley badges.

"You look amazing." India compliments my outfit, but deep down, I know she's just saying that. Still, we're only going down the local pub on a weekday, so we're both over-dressed.

We survive the uneventful three-minute walk to get there, unmolested.

"It doesn't look much," I warn India, seeing her looking doubtfully at the peeling exterior, broken lights, and pool of vomit outside the entrance, "but there are normally a few single men in here."

Things get worse inside, only two men on their own and both on the wrong side of fifty. The barman approaches, and I'm about to suggest we try somewhere else when the door behind us is flung open, and we get accosted by a whirlwind of chavvy charm in a pint-sized package.

"Wow, beautiful ladies, let me buy you both a drink. I'm Disco Dan. I'm known as the man who can, and it's your lucky night."

He fast draws both hands as if they're six-shooters and points one at each of us, making a *pow pow* noise before blowing imaginary smoke from the barrel, his finger. He now turns his ridiculously pre-aged John Deere baseball cap sideways, cheekily winks at India and spins around a full 360 degrees on the spot. He waves his embarrassed friend over to join him. He's cute, tall, and handsome, like a young, scruffily dressed Brad Pitt.

I exchange a questioning glance with India; she raises her eyebrows in a *what's the worst that can happen?* expression, as Dan is barely taller than either of us and just as skinny, he's judged mostly harmless.

"Go on then; I'll have a pint of Kronenbourg, India?"

"A vodka and coke, please."

Our newfound acquaintance gets asked for ID as he orders our drinks. He hands over a card to the barman, who barely examines it before passing it back.

"India, right?" He passes over the vodka and coke.

"And what do I call you, gorgeous?" He hands me the pint.

"Maze."

He almost goes for another spin but decides against it as he's holding his own pint of Carling. I don't know what to make of him. He is young, probably just turned eighteen, his deep baritone voice at odds with his youthful features. His dress sense is awful, tracksuit bottoms with a hoodie and black patent leather shoes. Still, he did call me gorgeous and under that baseball cap sits a handsome face. He just needs a makeover.

"So why do they call you Disco Dan?" India asks.

"Hold this." He hands me his pint. His feet turn into a tap-dancing blur as he outdoes Billy Elliot. It is impressive, and I've always had a thing for Jamie Bell, the older one obviously, not the movie version. He finishes and again does a full 360 twirl. India puts her drink down and claps.

"Impressive." I hand back his lager. "Are you a professional dancer then?"

"I will be when I leave… I mean, I'm looking for work, but dancing gigs are a bit thin on the ground right now."

I nod in sympathy. "I know, the job markets' tough at the moment."

"What's your friend's name?" India asks, checking out Dan's pretty friend who hasn't spoken a word yet.

"That's Zed; he's cool."

He mumbles, "Hello." Turns red and stares down at his feet.

"He gets more fun after a few drinks," Dan says, handing him a pint. India subtly positions herself closer and engages him in conversation. He replies shyly, hardly looking up.

Dan leans in and cheekily puts his hand on my hip. "So, are you going to give me your number? Perhaps we can go to the movies?" His voice falters on the word 'movies', going from a deep baritone to a high-pitched squeak. He steps backwards, taking a drink and trying to clear his throat.

He smiles nervously. "Went down the wrong hole." His deep voice is back.

Just then, his mobile phone rings—that annoying *'doo doo doo doo doo doo'* from the *Baby Shark* song. Zed immediately starts dancing away with matching arm movements like some manic toddler.

"Stop it," Dan hisses, ignoring the ringing.

"Do you want to get that?" I ask.

"It's nothing, wrong number." His voice once again slides into a high-pitched tone.

India senses something isn't quite right. "Are you okay, is

your voice alright? Because it's almost as if... Wait, just how old are the pair of you?"

"Nineteen. I have proof." Dan removes his ID card from his pocket and holds it out like some sort of talisman.

Zed coughs and goes a deep shade of red.

India takes a closer look. "Fake, I bought one of these off the internet when I was fifteen, so I could go clubbing."

We both stare at Dan.

"What? I'm nineteen. Promise."

The pub door crashes open, and in storms a beast of a woman, twenty-five stone plus with arms like hunks of beef.

"Oh, shit." Disco Dan examines his shoes with microscopic intensity.

The woman stomps over. "You two slappers get away from my beautiful son. You." She jabs a finger towards my face. "I know your type, desperately trying to hang on to your fading youth. Well, you can't have him. He's only fourteen years old. If you go near him again, I will call the police. Now Asquith, come on, we are going home right now. You have your homework to do." She turns to Zed. "And you, Rupert, you have school in the morning too, get home this instant."

"Mum, you're embarrassing us."

Asquith hesitates, so she grabs his ear and twists it painfully, dragging him outside despite his protests. Rupert follows meekly behind, giving us a goodbye wave.

I just stand there stunned and upset. Is my youth fading?

"Should I give Rupert my number and tell him to give me a call in five years?" India laughs.

"Am I looking old?—Is my youth faded?" I ask, devastated.

Her laughter fades. "Ah, babes, don't listen to a thing that nasty woman said. She's just jealous." India wraps me in her arms, a warm hug of friendship as one of the lone drinkers at the bar leers at us and winks.

"Oh, for God's sake, we are just two friends having a hug, nothing sexual here. Find some friends to drink with, you saddo. Come on; I've had enough of this place. Let's grab some wine and watch First Dates."

We buy a bottle of Cava from the local shop on the way back home, the only choice available unless you want the alcoholics favourite, a four-pack of 9% Tennent's Super. As we trudge up the stairs to our flat (the lift broke down within hours of being fixed), I hear a commotion. Knocking loudly on our front door are two police officers. They turn as we approach.

"I don't know what that woman told you, but I never touched her son." I protest.

10

PETE'S STORY - NOTHING TO DECLARE

I wake cold and disorientated with a sharp pain pounding away in my head like a toy drum; some annoying brat won't stop bashing. I'm lying on a concrete cot in a small cell with a rusty metal door as my only company.

Somebody has drawn a penis on the wall in what might be his own excrement. It's all rather artistically done. They have some minor talent, if only they tried actual paint and perhaps a canvas. The only other thing in the room is a small metal toilet, minus any seat cover. Now that's going to be cold on your backside, and what about germs? I grimace in disgust and hope I won't be here long enough to use it.

Never being in a police cell before, I find it a disquieting experience. My body aches all over, especially my face. I tentatively check the damage to my nose. It's tender to the touch, but thankfully not broken. My fingers come away covered in dried blood, which continues down my shirt in long black patches. Great, that's never going to come out in the wash. My shoelaces are also missing, which is annoying as I have no intention of topping myself.

Hours pass with only the occasional clang of the metal

hatch for company as somebody checks up on me. When the door does finally open, I'm in a foul, morose mood. The pain in my skull just won't let up, and I feel sorrier for myself than normal. I'm escorted to a bland interview room. While I've been expecting Luther to come in at any minute and strangle a confession out of me, the real thing is less impressive as a couple of overweight middle-aged white men come in and sit opposite. I resist the urge to ask how they pass the police medical every year. They remind me of my rights or lack of them and start recording the interview.

Only the one on the left speaks. "Make it easy on your-self. We got you on tape receiving fifteen grand in cash, bang to rights. Now do yourself a favour and tell us where the drugs are?"

"What drugs?" I have no idea what he's talking about.

"The narcotics you smuggled," he slams his hand on the desk, "we have been watching you. Interpol checked your last few trips out of the country, none lasting more than a couple of days, and now we have you with a shed load of cash. Now, where are the drugs, son? We might be able to give you a deal if you name your suppliers."

"I sell video games, and pay tax. This is ridiculous." I make sure not to use the phrase *import-export* since Maze told me it was code for a drug smuggler.

The Detective now places a tray of mangled cardboard and broken plastic on the table. "Do you honestly expect us to believe that somebody paid fifteen thousand pounds for these?"

I stare at the tray in horror. They have torn apart every box and cartridge.

"Did you say you had me on tape accepting the money?"

The Detective grins back at me. "Oh yes, all on tape."

"Great, can I get a copy. I'm going to need proof that

Tony received his games and paid before you mangled and destroyed them."

The wrecked box of rare games makes a sad spectacle. Somebody will be out of pocket, and I want to make sure it's not me.

"Do yourself a favour and tell us where the narcotics are?"

I point to what's left of Sculptor's Cut. "A poor condition cartridge gets a hundred quid, two-fifty for a reasonable one. Boxed, they fetch up to a grand in good condition. A sealed copy is worth a small fortune. Every single game in that box is irreplaceable." I let this sink in as he examines the wreckage.

"I'm sure Tony will kick up a fuss about the destruction of his property. And I will sue for wrongful arrest, just look at my battered face." I point at the dried blood, but while Tony is sure to do something, I am bluffing. I didn't pay import duty on any of the games, just brought them through the green - nothing to declare lane, so I won't be making a fuss.

The two detectives retire to the back of the room where they have a heated debate. The interview is abruptly suspended as I get returned to my cell. Less than an hour later, an officer opens the door and informs me I am free to leave. No apology is given, and when I collect my personal effects, I am told that I must apply in writing to claim my money back.

"That will probably take six months to a year to go through," the Sergeant on the desk tells me with a smirk. I ask for the relevant paperwork to annoy him and step out into the freezing British weather a free man. Also, an impoverished one, as all my money is tied up in this failed deal.

"I knew you were a drug dealer."

I turn as I recognise the voice. "Hi, Maze." She's dressed

similar to when we first met, apart from now her hair is a different colour. I'm glad that she appears to be her old self again.

"They let me go, a simple misunderstanding."

She doesn't look convinced. "What the hell did they do to you?" Her hand touches my face. I pull back, not wanting her to get blood over them.

"They didn't want to chat much, just hit me in the head with a truncheon. It's okay; I'll live. You do believe I'm not a drug dealer?" I notice something about Maze. "You're a bit dishevelled yourself like you spent an uncomfortable night on a concrete slab. Have you been in the cells?"

Maze glances down at her feet before responding. "Well, yes, but it's your fault."

"How is it my fault?"

"Because you drank a rather expensive bottle of wine. And the landlord made a complaint."

"How come they kept you in overnight? Seems excessive?"

"Well, I may have told the policeman to eat a bag of dicks."

I laugh, imaging a feisty Maze giving the officer hell.

"This isn't funny; the landlord is going to press charges. I'm off home to fashion my toothbrush into a shiv. I'm too pretty for life inside. Having to lick prison noonie for a packet of fags isn't going to be much fun."

"I didn't know you smoked."

"I don't, but you get the idea."

"Have you been watching Wentworth again?"

"Yep, that and original Prisoner Cell Block H re-runs, even OZ. I'm worried."

"Hey, maybe you might get a rake thin extra tall Russian

fashion model called Olga as a cellmate, or do you think that's too much to hope for?"

Maze clicks her fingers an inch from my nose. "Focus, this is serious."

"Sorry, I know. I'd help, but I'm completely broke."

"How can you be broke? You have a Porsche?"

"It's on finance."

"All fur coat and no knickers, as my mum likes to say."

"Snap. That's just what my Aunt used to say too." We both laugh and join pinkie fingers. Now we stand there awkwardly, trying not to mention our kiss at the restaurant, and I try to stop admiring her legs, which her tiny mini-skirt shows off to good effect. I also hope she doesn't think I got turned on by her hideous nylon waitress outfit; she may now think I'm a weirdo.

My British guilt decides to make an appearance. "Maze, I can't promise, but I'll try to sort something out with the landlord."

"You will?"

"I'll do what I can."

"Brilliant. I knew my luck was changing; I even managed to get a new job that starts this Saturday."

"That's great; I hope everything goes well for you." Fate intervenes to keep us apart as I had been on the verge of asking her to accompany me to my sister's renewal ceremony this weekend. It seems a silly idea now; we aren't compatible. She's screwed up, and so am I. What am I thinking? A shooting pain starts off in my left temple and sears through to my right. My vision fades like I'm entering a tunnel as I grab my head in agony.

"Are you okay?"

"Sure, just a headache," I say, but it's a lot worse than that as before me Maze splits into two, now three separate people. I sway unsteadily as my legs almost buckle beneath me; it's hard to stand straight while the world fractures around you. A small pair of arms steady me as much as possible for a five feet tall woman as I stagger. The pain flares one last time, then disappears as the world reforms back into one. I stare down at Maze. She's whole again. I should get checked out at the hospital, but I know I'd run into Tammy in A&E, which would be awkward.

"I'm fine; you can let me go."

Maze steps back. "You should get your head looked at; you're deathly pale. I hear head injuries can be serious. Promise me you will get it looked at." She's genuinely worried.

"Yes, Mum," I say because I know it will annoy her. It does, and I grin.

We stand there awkwardly again, not because we have nothing to say but because we are afraid of what we might say. There is a connection between us, or possibly the start of something that I now purposely stamp on with my next sentence.

"I have to go now; you take care. Have an amazing life." With that, I turn and walk away, forcing myself not to look back.

11

PETE'S STORY - DUNGEONS & DRAGONS

M arie Kondo has made me late for my sister's ceremony. I shouldn't blame her, but I can't take my eyes off this tiny Japanese woman fixing everybody's life problems by decluttering their homes. I'm stumped at the first hurdle and just can't throw out my favourite Goonies T-shirt that I haven't worn since I was seventeen. I force myself to switch off Netflix; I imagine if you lived with Ms Kondo, she would soon become tiresome as you discover everything you don't wear for a month is now being modelled by a homeless person.

Perhaps it's the complete apathy I feel towards Kate's renewal vows that led me to organise my closet into different sections and dispose of some of my worn out stuff. I find an old pair of Reebok trainers that my cat has chewed to near-total destruction; I guess these don't spark joy anymore and sling them on the get rid pile. Strangely, he isn't here. Mr Tiddles usually can't resist the chance of breaking into my wardrobe and scouting around.

Now, realising my sister isn't going to accept my Marie Kondo excuse and will probably kill me, I retrieve my suit from the closet and discover to my horror that a family of hungry moths have lunched on it for the last several months. Several large holes soon become apparent. Not having time for anything else, I grab my barely worn tuxedo out of a thick indestructible plastic cover and dress in a rush. Jumping in a taxi, I pick up my plus one for the evening, and we arrive at the exclusive country house venue a bare fifteen minutes late.

"Wow, fancy," Jace notes as we stroll up the long gravel pathway.

This gothic mansion, complete with castle buttresses' and ugly gargoyles, must have cost several thousand just to hire for the night. We join the queue of people entering the building, parading past Kate and her husband Roger, who are acting like stuck up minor royalty.

"Impressive, I guess. I apologise in advance for well—everything that is going to happen." We reach the entrance.

"Hi, little sister." I kiss Kate's cheek and try not to smirk at her horrified expression. "This is my plus one." Her husband looks equally as appalled.

I hold in a laugh. "Jace is my..." I leave the sentence hanging, "good friend," I say in the most ambiguous way possible.

"Pleasure to meet you, honey." Jace sticks out his hand.

I think Roger may suffer a coronary at any moment as he locks a smile firmly in place and forces himself to shake the offered appendage.

Jace is wearing a subtle brown striped double-breasted suit which must be tailor made to fit his muscular frame. But we are still attracting a lot of attention as he towers over everybody else here. My sister takes time out to usher both of us to a back-corner table as far out of sight as possible. It's right next to the toilets, judging by the smell. The seating plan is hastily re-ordered as she rushes to change place cards.

"Told you."

It doesn't take long for Kate to come back and corner me. "A word?"

"Yes. What can I do for you?" I keep my expression as upbeat as possible.

Jace smiles at me; he's been fully warned on how the day is probably going to play out.

"What the hell are you playing at?" she asks in a harsh whisper.

I feign ignorance. "What?"

Her face contorts with rage, but she keeps her voice down, "Are you trying to ruin our day?" She casts a displeased glare at Jace. "If you two dare hold hands, I'm never going to speak to you again."

I'm almost tempted to take her up on the offer, but fearing a flood of tears, I decide not to wind her up anymore. "Love you too." I give her a peck on the cheek before I return to my seat.

"And why are you dressed like bloody James Bond? It's a suit and tie event," she shouts at my retreating back.

"Why are you dressed like Bond?" Jace asks as I sit back down, so I tell him about my moth problem.

The large round tables slowly fill up around us. It's now I realise we are seated in the kid's section, being the only two people older than twelve. Well, at least this means all the wine is ours as they stocked it with six bottles, three red and three white. Grabbing a different grape variety in each hand, I pour out four glasses.

"Just white for me, honey." I pass him two over. "It's probably not going to be that bad," Jase muses.

"Yes, it really will." As I take a healthy slurp, I notice one of the waitresses at the event has bright green hair, and upon closer inspection, I recognise Maze. This only happens to be her new job. What are the chances? I slump down low in my chair, and for the next hour, avoid her. Luckily, she's not allocated our group, and I nip off to the toilet whenever she comes close. I am in there so often people must think I'm suffering a urinary infection or snorting obscene amounts of cocaine.

Eventually, Jace confronts me. "What is it with you and that waitress?"

"Waitress?" I feign innocence.

He raises his eyebrows so high I now laugh. "She keeps looking over, and you keep scuttling off whenever she's within twenty feet, so what's going on?"

I give him a brief rundown of what happened and how we met. "We are just not compatible; she's way too short for me."

"Oh honey, everybody is the right size when it comes to the bedroom."

Well, that's not what Maze thought about her ex Jeff.

"She looks fun. I'll be back later." And before I can stop him, he marches over and engages her in conversation.

I take the opportunity to wander around and soon find I'm now suffering from the middle-class version of leprosy as I'm cold-shouldered by the rest of Kate and Roger's desperately posh friends. Still, it's okay as I can't stand any of them.

"Hi, it's Pete, isn't it?" a female voice says.

I turn to discover who dares to speak to me. It's Roger's secretary, and if they invited her, it means they didn't have an affair after all. I do my snap judgment thing:

---

1. Height – 5ft 10 in heels, so about 5ft 7 - pass

__2.__ Age – I remember somebody saying she is 30 - so age-appropriate - pass

__3.__ Appearance – she's wearing high heels making her legs appear slim and defined, skirt an inch above the knee with an opaque white blouse with enough buttons undone that I can make out a lacy black bra underneath.

She's also immaculately made up with blond hair in a short pixie cut, which really suits her—all women believe they can pull off this style, but 90% end up looking like a backwards Albanian goat-herder.

The hours she spends in the gym might mean she would want me in better shape and possibly even try Kale - (not a deal-breaker)

__4.__ Body Art & Accessories – No wedding ring – pass

Little jewellery and no visible tattoos but there is a rumour she has an intimate one; I would like to find out.

Universal Attractiveness Rating Score – numbers out of ten suddenly become meaningless as some women are more than their total, so my rating sticks as a hot pass.
My mind takes this all in and spits out the following answer – Possible life partner – Yes, please.

———

"Hi, I'm Pete, you're Roger's…" I nearly say secretary but remember she's his personal assistant. I don't know the difference but suspect that just like a Canadian who you mistake for an American, the offence taken will be the same, "P.A." I finish.

"Penny," she says and holds out her hand, which I kiss gently, mostly because I'm already half-cut and think I'm flirting.

"May I ask you a personal question?"

I almost blurt out, *'it's huge,'* which seems hilarious in my drunken state, but control myself and reply yes with a nod.

"You're not a couple, are you?" She motions over at Jace.

"Nope, just friends, I only brought him along to alleviate the tedium and maybe annoy my sister. The people here are so unenlightened." I steal Jace's phrase.

"I didn't think you were, so does this mean you're single?"

"Yes."

"Well, in that case, I was wondering if you would like to go out for a drink sometime?"

Wait, what just occurred? My brain takes several moments to process the fact that a beautiful woman just asked me on a date, and I almost freak out and say no automatically as this is so unusual it's never happened before.

"Yes," I say eventually, still unable to string a coherent sentence together. A warm smile greets my answer as my pause made it look like I was going to say no, and we would have had to act like adults and hide in opposite ends of the venue while avoiding eye contact all night long. We swop phone numbers while agreeing on a day.

"Isn't this a wonderful ceremony," Penny says, and I agree politely, keeping my *you should only renew if caught cheating* opinions to myself.

"What's Roger like to work for?" I'm hoping for some salacious gossip.

She replies with all mean nothing phrases that don't tell me anything when I boil them down. We don't know each other well, but if Penny is happy working for Roger and thinks this is great, maybe we aren't suitable.

I put Penny on the spot. "I think Roger's a bit of a dick." I immediately regret speaking my mind, but the booze has lowered my inhibitions. Now I wait in anticipation for the reply.

"He can be difficult to work for sometimes." She chooses her words carefully, a playful smile on her face.

I grin at her, so we do both agree. I decide to go all-in and lean over and whisper in her ear, "Has Roger been having an affair? Why else renew your wedding vows?"

"That's what I thought; I mean, if you're happily married, what's the point? I've been getting funny looks ever since the announcement, like I'm the other woman. I have much better taste."

"Perhaps not; you did just ask me out." I regret my joke as soon as I utter it, but Penny laughs.

"You're funny. I feel like I can talk to you straight out. Sometimes when you meet somebody, there's this fake façade, and you never see the real person underneath."

My head is buzzing, and I get shooting pains—soon to be a raging headache.

"I'm only talking so freely because Roger stuck me on the kid's table, so we are hammering all the free booze. Normally when I'm around a beautiful woman, I clam up." I realise what I've said out loud and cringe inside.

Penny seems to like my last comment as her fingertips playfully stroke my tuxedo lapel. "You look extremely dashing."

We stare into each other's eyes, and for a second, I think we might kiss. My sister shatters the moment by stomping over and announces the ceremony will begin in five minutes, and we should retake our seats. I give Penny a goodbye peck on each cheek as I'm drunk and feeling all European. Jace is waiting at the kid's table as I stagger back and crash down next to him with a stupid grin on my face.

"She's fun," he says.

"Who?" I'm still thinking of Penny.

"Maze. She thinks you're annoyed because you have been avoiding her all night long."

"What did you say?"

"The truth, when somebody goes to that much trouble to hide, then it's not because they don't like you."

"Jace." I shake my head. "Why did you say that?"

He fixes me with one of his commanding stares. "When the ceremony's over, I want you to go and talk to her." I can tell there is no use arguing this one, so I agree.

Over on a small stage in front of the assembled crowd, the ceremony is about to begin. The view is half-obscured from our side-lined table, but I make out Kate and Roger mounting the stage. I examine my watch. It reads 4.30 p.m. - Clapping erupts, and I glance around to see Jace has a tear in his eye. "That was so beautiful."

"What?" I recheck my watch; it now reads 5.02 p.m. I am missing thirty-two minutes of my life. My brain feels like it wants to explode out of my skull and run around swearing at any vegans it finds.

"Are you okay?" Jace asks.

I nod and pour myself a generous glass of wine, which I down in one—like a mum who's just put her child to bed at half-past five. Dutch courage in place, I go over and chat to Maze. Her uniform today isn't half as ugly as her old one, it's a white blouse and dark-coloured skirt, and she gets to keep her new hair colour and real name.

"Hi." I try to sound casual.

"So, have you stopped being a dick and avoiding me?"

"Sorry, I didn't see you till Jace pointed you out." I go with the lie, even though it's clear she doesn't believe me.

"You two make such a cute couple."

"I know Jace told you we're only friends."

"Damn, I have so many jokes. Next, I was going to ask if you were the tunnel or the train, and… well, it's no fun now. Why are you wearing a dinner jacket? Nobody else is."

"The moths got to my only suit; I noticed like ten minutes before I was due here. This was all I had. Kate, my sister, would have killed me If I turned up in jeans. So, what do you think of her husband?"

"Well, I envy how you managed to go to sleep with your eyes open for all the vows, boring or what? You need to show me how to do that. Is that some sort of yoga technique? Oh, your brother-in-law is a perv, by the way. I caught him staring at my tits earlier."

"You sure he wasn't checking if you were a boy?"

"Oh brilliant, misogyny, you know that gets all us women so wet, don't you? Anyway, how dare you! These babies are impressive in the right push-up bra. You didn't seem to mind before."

I blush a full deep red. I knew what she was referring to, and I try to change the subject. "I bet arriving with Jace got us gossiped about?"

Maze's tone turns serious. "I guess you pair are the talking point of the night. I overheard one couple asking if the kids were safe with you. Unbelievable. Look, I overheard something else, and I wanted to say I'm so sor—" Maze carries on speaking. I watch her lips move, but the pain in my head flares up, and I can't hear what she is saying. The intense agony is so bad I might pass out. I can see her worriedly looking at me, but I can't tell her about my headache, or she will nag me about the hospital again. The torment slowly subsides, and I'm able to nod. She carries on talking, and now I hear her clearly again.

"You okay? You've gone a shade whiter than Casper the Friendly Ghost."

"Too much to drink, one can't be sober at these things. I've done my duty now, so hopefully, I can sneak out as soon as the first person leaves."

"Lucky you, I better get back to work. I can't afford to lose another job."

"That does keep happening when we meet."

"It does, doesn't it? Oh, can you pick me up at one on Wednesday? That would be fantastic."

I'm puzzled, but before I can ask what she means, she's disappeared and is back collecting glasses. I walk back to Jace at the kid's table.

"Did everything go alright?" Jace's huge grin tells me something more is going on.

"Maze asked me to pick her up on Wednesday, and I don't know why." Jace's grin widens.

"What did you do?"

"Well, honey, it's for your own good," he pauses, "I sort of said you would go and meet her parents while pretending to be her new boyfriend."

"Why on earth would you do that?"

"Look at her, such a sweet girl." I briefly wonder if he's been talking to somebody else by mistake. "We got chatting, and she said she was dreading her family meal and how they give her grief about not having met a nice man so..."

"So, you volunteered me to be her pretend boyfriend." I finish for him.

Jace smiles sweetly. "You got me tasered four times, do this for me, and I'll consider us even. The pair of you might even get on."

"Well, I don't have a choice now, do I?" I notice our table is now two-thirds empty, "Some parents are worried we are going to molest their children," I mention to Jace in an explanation for our lack of companions.

Ice-cold rage appears in his eyes that I haven't seen before, and I'm worried he's going to Hulk out and smash the table to pieces. Just then, the music changes. *'Gloria Gaynor's - I Will Survive'* starts blaring out over the dance floor. Jace's whole demeanour changes back into his usual happy self.

"Love this one. Hey, let's go for a boogie?"

I glance over at the few old couples on the dance floor and the people sat at the tables who would be watching.

"That's a hard no." While I like to think I'm free-thinking and open-minded, I can be socially awkward and care more about what people think of me than I know I should. Dancing with Jace would be out of my comfort zone. So far outside, I'd need my passport to get there. Plus, I know my sister would take it as a slight against her perfect middle-class life.

"Sorry, I can't be the human hand grenade that destroys my sister's happiness, even though these people are all dicks."

Jace shakes his head, disappointed. "Well, if you change your mind, I will be the one with all the moves." He disappears onto the freshly crowded dance-floor, which comprises a lot of angry divorced women. He's right; he has got the moves as he dances effortlessly out there.

I feel a small hand pull my sleeve. Looking around, a ten-year-old kid with chocolate smudges all over his face speaks to me.

"What revision do you play?"

"Sorry?"

"What revision do you play?"

"Revision?" I repeat back, mystified.

The kid stares at me as if I'm simple. "Dungeons and Dragons, what rule set are you using?"

"Do I look like I play Dungeons and Dragons?"

The kid nods, "I play fourth revision; it's way cooler. Would you like a game some time?"

I feel the need to go to the bathroom and check to see if someone has scribbled nerd on my forehead while I zoned out a while back.

"Sorry, kid, I don't do S&M. I mean D&D," I think my mind had briefly gone back to thinking about Penny.

"Squirtle is my favourite Pokémon. Who's yours?"

"Charizard." Shit, I just made the mistake of proving I'm a fellow nerd.

"Why?" he asks.

I nearly say because a mint condition first edition shiny can be worth a small fortune, but I feel the kid will be disappointed in me. Then again, I possess zero knowledge about Pokémon apart from how much collectors are willing to pay.

"Because he's a dragon." Is the best answer I can think of.

The kid shakes his head and moves to a seat on the other side of the table. "Lame," he says under his breath.

"I heard that."

It's at this point one of the guest's mutters, "You should be ashamed of yourself," as he makes his way past the table and disappears into the toilets. I have had enough of this stick up the ass crowd, and I'm suddenly glad I drank enough wine to send Ben Affleck back to rehab as I work up enough courage to join Jace.

My sister's expression turns to horror as I make it to the heaving dance floor edge.

"Don't you dare," she mouths at me and gives me a glare of hatred. No Christmas present this year, I guess. Is she really expecting us to slow dance?

Jace is encircled by a wave of plump women happily dancing away to *'I Will Survive'* in what resembles an excitable witch's coven. I want to say I overcame my sister's bigotry, but what happens as I edge forward is a white-hot pain explodes in my head. I stagger and collapse; all I vaguely remember is the ambulance siren and flashing blue lights.

12

MAZE'S STORY - DON'T MENTION 5G

It only takes a few seconds to find my sister Angelina in the crowded restaurant. Her chic and insanely overpriced cream silk blouse draws my attention. She sits at one of the better tables that offers a window view of a beggar with a compulsory underfed dog on a piece of string—a fairly common scene in this decaying city. I wasn't expecting an invite out, but I always enjoy her company, plus she offered to pay—a win-win situation. I kiss her cheek and sit down opposite.

"Husband still absent?" I ask.

"Yes, he's still away on business."

"Are you sure he hasn't left, and he's just not mentioning it?" It's so long since I've seen him, I find it hard to remember his face.

"No, we're good, I spoke to him last night."

There's something about my sister's smug expression. "Oh my God, you had phone sex. Didn't you?"

"Perhaps you can shout a bit louder? I don't think the table by the toilets heard."

"Oh, sorry," I lower my voice. "How was it? No wait, I

don't want to hear the details—old people at it." I shake my head in disgust. "Was he all like," I do the appropriate crude hand gesture, "all blue in the face, extolling his undying love before making the keys all sticky." I smirk at my sister's glare of disapproval as her hand reaches out and pushes mine firmly to the table.

"This is an exclusive restaurant, less of the wanking gestures, please, old people here. They may suffer a heart attack."

I make a cross my heart gesture. "Sorry, best behaviour, especially as you're paying."

"And you're a cheeky cow; I'm only six years older than you."

The smirk drops off my face when I notice our table is set for three. "Why are there…? No, just no." I stand. "You have to be joking. You're setting me up with a crusty old git from the office. Do I look in need of some mercy shag?" I'm raging.

"Hey, calm down. Ian is a great bloke, and he's… here now, sit."

"No way, I'm off." I turn to see Ian striding over to join us. Six feet tall, well-muscled in a slim-fitting suit. Tie loose with his top button undone, showing a small piece of chest hair. The face of a model, chisel-jawed, blue-eyed, perfect floppy blond hair, obscenely good looking. A smile shows his perfect white teeth, and that beautifully kissable mouth sends me weak at the knees.

I sit. "Well, I guess I could stay for a bit. Wipe that grin off your face, Sis." She doesn't.

"Sorry to be late. Ian is now in the room. Wow, ladies, you are both too stunning for words." He removes his jacket, revealing a respectable bulge in his trousers, so respectable I immediately forgive him for referring to himself in the third person. He sits down with a flourish; he even smells sensational.

I go to say, *I'm no lady*, but a light kick under the table from my sister stops me.

"Shall we order some wine?" Ian clicks his fingers, and if by magic, a waitress appears. She's as impressed as I am —*keep your hands off him, you tart*. She giggles as he requests a 98' Bordeaux. He doesn't bother to ask our preference. This would normally rankle my feminist side, particularly as I wanted a pint of Stella. Still, I now go along with it, even managing my own coquettish laugh to outdo my competition. My sister's smile becomes a wide beam, my rising annoyance directly matching its increasing size. She glances at her watch and gives me a subtle wink; her phone now rings.

Angelina answers, "No, really?—You need me there right now?—I am just sitting down for dinner—Can't it wait?—You need me extremely urgently?—Okay, I can be there in ten minutes."

I almost shake my head in despair at her awful acting skills. Any worse, and she would get a job offer on Hollyoaks.

"Guys, I am so sorry; they need me in the office. Would you mind keeping my sister company, Ian?"

"My pleasure," he says, his stunning eyes enticing me in.

Hopefully, it will be my pleasure. Now sod off, Sis.

The urge to hump him is so unrelenting I wonder if he's a vampire exerting his power over me. No, just horny, I guess.

Angelina kisses me goodbye, then whispers in my ear, "The meal is on my business credit card. Good luck and don't screw this up."

She leaves, and I am alone with ever so pretty Ian, who I can hardly tear my gaze from.

"So, Maze, what do you do for a living?"

Wait, Ian asked me a question. This is unusual; I assumed he would just want to discuss himself, which I'd be alright with as he is so gorgeous.

"The hospitality industry," I reply vaguely, unemployed skivvy not sounding the best.

"Have you ever thought of modelling?"

I glance over my shoulder in case he's talking to someone else.

"You have this stunning presence. I'd love to paint you sometime." He smiles.

My God, is he asking me to get nude for him? Because he doesn't need a brush. My inner doubt whispers—*he's making fun of you*.

"I have been painting for the last few years, and I don't claim to be a professional, but I am improving." He pauses, seeing my reluctance. "I only paint portraits, nothing inappropriate if you're worried. The line of your face is simply perfect."

The smitten teenage waitress makes another appearance, fawning over Ian as he orders us both a steak—good job, I'm not a vegan this week. We chat some more, and I melt as he tells me how he visits his grandparents in a care home at least once a week. The steak arrives. It's beautifully tender with just the right amount of blood oozing out of it, perfect, even better as it's free, and we pause the conversation to eat. Before I realise it, nearly a full bottle of wine is gone, leaving me lightheaded. After some harmless flirting, I find I have placed my hand over Ian's.

"So, what do you think of the Royal Family?" he asks.

Apart from yearning for Meghan Markle's figure, not much else.

Ian sees my pause as more than it is. His hand squeezes mine. "I knew you were a fellow believer."

"Sorry?"

"The world is ruled by the powers and principalities of darkness in high places." He winks as though I understand him.

"Exactly," I say, having no idea what I'm agreeing with, but if it helps him remove his shirt, I'm fine with it.

"I just don't know how so many people don't see it; the Queen's reptilian features stand out so visibly. They must be blind."

"The Queen's…?"

"The Royal Family are so clearly shape-shifting lizards. They think they can just consume the brains of ten Canadian children on a picnic and get away with it, but not for much longer. We Maze, are a growing group. One day soon, we will achieve justice."

I smile politely; this has taken a strange turn. *Do Not Mention 5G. Do Not Mention 5G.* "What do you think of 5G?" leaps out of my mouth in an uncontrollable outburst much like one of Prince Philip's racist comments.

"Exactly," Ian whispers. "Mind control on a hitherto unmentionable scale. You get it, Maze; I'm so pleased your sister asked me to lunch today." He sits staring with those mesmerising blue eyes. I so want to kiss his pouty, luscious lips.

He breaks the spell. "I need to be back in the office soon, but would you like to come to my apartment later to talk some more?"

My head nods—*Yes Please*—before I can even speak. I only hope by talk, he means something a lot more horizontal.

"This is hopeless," I throw my hands up in despair. My entire wardrobe is splayed out before me. Every single item I own or borrowed from my sister and never returned. Even the red beret I'm determined to wear one day without resembling a mime artist.

"I liked the summer dress, the one with the flowers," India suggests helpfully.

"Didn't it make my hips look enormous?"

She shakes her head. "No babes, you looked really trim."

"I don't know. I can't look desperate or like I'm trying too hard. This is impossible." I sit down in frustration, causing a small avalanche of clothing to cover me.

"Got it," I exclaim, grab some items and rush to the toilet to change. "Ready," I shout through the door to India like some catwalk model about to walk the runway.

"Ta-Dah," I say when I jump out. "What do you think?"

"Err, lose the beret."

I discard the headwear. "Well?"

India examines my outfit of azure blue raincoat and matching suede high heels. "Stunning, babes, show me the rest."

"This is it. I've shaved my bits. What? Too much?"

"Hey, no slut-shaming here, but… what if he lives with his mum?"

"Shit, is that even possible?" Maybe he wants to introduce me as his prospective future wife. Wait, no, don't be so ridiculous.

"Christ, this is a nightmare." I return to the bedroom. Maybe sexy underwear, just in case? I search through my wardrobe till I find it, an unopened cellophane packet containing a suspender and basque set in a garish shade of red. The Primark price label means this is a present from Jeff. My first instinct is to burn it, but I get excited by the thought of another man sensuously removing it. Five minutes later, I stand before the mirror. But instead of the burlesque vamp I was hoping for—the image is more low-end sex worker who does anything for a tenner. Still?

My right hand forces the hem of my raincoat down, while my left grips it tightly together at the front. Who knew that running for the bus would be this problematic? I almost trip as my heel slips on a wet patch, so I am forced to slow to an unsteady walk. Brilliant, a pensioner is trying to pay his bus fare with an expired book of Green Shield stamps. I will make it, after all. After a long conversation where the driver falsely promises to take it up with his bosses as to why they don't take the aforementioned stamps anymore, I show my bus pass and take a seat. Excitement races through me that even the worsening weather can't dampen. Though the bus is deserted, I get the obligatory nut job sitting next to me while talking to his knitting. The reek of stale body odour fills the air. I should have splurged on a taxi. Luckily, the journey is only a short one as I get off in the city centre. Ian lives in one of those fancy new apartments with a balcony overlooking the river. Though how exciting it is to count the condoms and used nappies floating by remains to be seen.

I receive only two requests for 'any loose change' as I make the short journey. As I enter the building through a set of dark mirrored doors that open with an efficient swish, I spot the bored-looking security guard behind a small desk on the right.

"Top floor, Flat 28." He doesn't even glance up from his book.

"Thanks." A clairvoyant security guard, what next? Well,

at least he didn't offer to take my coat. I check my makeup in the lift's mirror as I ascend. My excitement rising by the second. As I stride the last few paces to Flat 28, the image of a freshly showered Ian still damp and covered in a towel so small and thin that I can work out his religion crosses my mind, causing my stomach to flutter. I take a deep breath and knock. Disappointment floods through me as the door jerks open and a heavily overweight man with a bulbous, red-veined nose and ridiculous bouffant mop of ginger hair stares out at me. His brown shirt, whose buttons are only just holding on under the barrage of his extended belly, has a badge that reads 'Security' over the breast pocket. A large red food stain half covers the S, and his shoulder epaulette is hanging loose.

"Password?" he demands.

"Sorry."

"Password?"

"I didn't know I needed one. I'm here to see Ian."

"Sorry, you can't come in without the password."

I stand there puzzled, looking behind the overweight security guard I can make out other people. He moves his bulky frame to block my view.

"Illuminati." The phrase just pops into my head.

He grabs my arm and roughly pulls me inside before slamming the door. "Never say that out loud; they have surveillance satellites and unmanned drones listening for any mention."

"Sorry I didn't know," I apologise profusely.

"That's alright, that's why you're here to learn. We give the newbies some slack." He holds his hand out. "Roger, oh shit, no real names, sorry."

I shake his hand. "I'm…" His ridiculous pinched warning

expression tells me to give a false name. "Susan, Susan Storm." He nods, satisfied.

Ian now makes an appearance. Looking elegant, even though dressed down, in a snug-fitting pair of jeans and a jumper. "Maze, so glad you could make it." Unfortunately, he only kisses my cheek instead of sticking his tongue in my mouth, but still, nice. "You've met Roger already, I see."

"No real names," he hisses.

Ian produces his perfect pure-white toothed model smile. "Roger can take things a little too seriously, a by-product of working security over at Rolls-Royce."

Roger goes pale, his actual identity being revealed so easily.

Ian laughs a beautiful warm chuckle. "We're all friends here," he says, gently punching him on the shoulder.

"Maze, I have to say hello to a few guests, but please stick around, and I'll give you my full attention later."

I really hope full attention means what I think it does.

Ian notices I'm still in my coat. "Where are my manners? Let me hang that up for you." He holds his hand out.

My mouth goes dry. I swear everybody in the room is looking over at me. My heart beats faster as I fumble with the two fastened buttons. What will Ian think of me? As I slide my coat off, I make a mental note to get India a bottle of Prosecco for talking me out of my original choice. Still, my outfit is on the racy side. My extra short black leather mini-skirt that barely covers my bum paired with my thin knitted crop top and no bra. I haven't eaten a thing all day, so my stomach is relatively flat. As Ian takes my coat, my nipples decide they are in Friends sitcom territory and do a Rachel. If only my hair would copy Jennifer Aniston's. He leaves me with Roger, who stands there staring at my cleavage, mesmerised. Shame it didn't have the same effect on Ian. I break his trance with a question.

"So, how often do you have these get-togethers?" The apartment is full of around fifteen people, chatting over drinks and nibbles.

He stares back up at my face. "About once a month. Sometimes we have a slide show or a talk. The last meeting was all about the Nest Carbon Monoxide Detector and how it's a remote surveillance device—the blue light even hypnotises you when you're asleep. Have you got one?"

I shake my head, and his entire body relaxes a level.

"Good. Now we all know about Amazon Echo speakers sending everything you say straight to GCHQ, but they are also a vicious tool for misinformation. Try asking Alexa if the Queen is a lizard. It bare face lies and denies it."

He is staring at my chest again.

"Roger, any chance you could get me a drink?"

"Sure, stay there."

He wanders off as I search for Ian to save me, but he's deep in conversation with a couple in the corner.

Roger returns with the drinks. "White wine, alright?" he mumbles. With a packet of Monster Munch held firmly between his teeth.

"Sure." I grab the plastic glass and take a sip, still searching for someone to rescue me.

"You wouldn't believe the people who come to these parties. Once I met Kylie Minogue." He holds his hand at chest height. "She's tiny, only comes up to here." A half-eaten Monster Munch falls into his drink as he speaks. I step backwards to avoid more spittle as he excitedly confides in me. "The most famous person I met at one of these was Princess Diana." He pauses to see my reaction.

Don't ask If she was a shape-shifting reptile. Don't ask if she was a shape-shifting reptile. My mouth remains firmly closed.

"She was one of the few Royals who wasn't a shape-shifting lizard."

"How did you know?" I ask.

He winks. "We were very intimate."

I choke, a fine mist of alcohol spraying everywhere. "Sorry, went down the wrong way."

He carries on regardless. His gaze once again dropping to my cleavage. "Where do you think Prince Harry got his ginger hair from?"

"I—" Thankfully, Ian comes to my rescue.

"Stop monopolising our guest, Roger. Maze, come with me, and I will introduce you to a few of our other members." His arm slides around my waist, causing a hot flush. I spend the next hour chatting away. Most people are charming and seemingly normal; I even enjoy the video on how to mask the camera on your mobile phone—so the government can't spy on you. As the evening comes to an end, my excitement rises with each guest that leaves. Roger is the last person to go, and Ian practically has to push him out the door, finally giving him a bottle of red wine and a sausage roll to have on the way home.

Finally, we are all alone.

"I hope that wasn't too much for you. They are a great bunch of people. However, some can be slightly over the top."

I don't know if it's the alcohol giving me a confidence boost or something else, but I feel invincible.

"Ian, I was wondering if you still wanted to paint me —naked?"

Without waiting for a reply, I grasp my crop top's thin material, removing it in one slow, hopefully sensual movement. I am left standing there in the full glare of the unforgiving light, stomach pulled in, twisted sideways with my chest pushed as far out as I can, displaying my assets in the best way possible.

Ian gulps, "Maze, I would—"

Roger comes crashing back through the front door. "I forgot my keys," he mumbles through his half-eaten snack and stops dead, staring. The bottle falls from his open fingers, exploding violently in a tsunami of Shiraz, reducing Ian to a Carrie lookalike. The remains of his sausage roll drop out of his open mouth and land in the expanding puddle.

"Don't leave me hanging. What happened then?" India asks, breathlessly bounces up and down on my settee. She's sitting cross-legged, dressed in her striped pyjama bottoms and an old Grateful Dead T-shirt.

I clink my wine glass against hers. "Do you really want to know?"

"I wouldn't have waited up half the night for you if I didn't." The first rays of daylight pierce the darkness outside, and I'm wrapped up all comfy in my Hello Kitty dressing gown. I smile, glad to have my friend to confide in.

"Well," I take a healthy slurp before I continue, "I try to put my top back on, but it catches on my nipple piercing, and wraps itself tight. I have to stand there with my arms folded with that disgusting perv staring at me. Ian resembles a horror film murder victim, and the room is a minefield of broken glass. Roger still hasn't moved. He's just staring; I swear he's never seen a naked woman in real life before. Ian takes control and ushers Roger back out with his car keys, and breaks out the vacuum. I love a man who knows how to hoover."

India nods her approval.

I pause to fill our glasses up to the brim. "Ian is being so nice. I'm all embarrassed, but then he says he'd still like to paint me. He even asks if it's alright to take his top off as it's covered in wine."

"You said yes, right?"

I grin. "I did, and he does. He's magnificent, makes me feel a bit insecure. So I untangle my top and drop it to the floor. The tension is killing me. He leads me through into another room; I think it's going to be the bedroom; it isn't."

"My God, was it his sex dungeon full of all Fifty Shades kinds of kinky shit?" India is excitedly bouncing up and down again.

"No, it was his art studio, and you will not believe this, he insists on painting me. I have to pose for sixty minutes until I'm cramped and nearly falling over." I drink some more wine. "It gets worse."

"How?" I have India's undivided attention.

"After what seems like an eternity, he announces that - *Ian has completed his masterpiece.*"

India raises an eyebrow at this.

"I know, talking about yourself in the third person, but he has his top off, and he's so beautiful. Anyway, I stumble over; my leg has gone to sleep as I've been in the same position way too long. I keep expecting him to kiss me, but he doesn't. I put my hand on his hip, nothing too obviously sexual, but we are inches away from each other. He's topless, I'm topless, it's inevitable until I get, *Maze, I have to tell you something.*"

"No… he's gay?"

"Far worse."

"He's been in a car crash and had his cock removed?"

"Worse, because it's there all right, working and quite substantial."

"What then?"

"He doesn't believe in sex before marriage, nothing, no kissing apart from a greeting peck on the cheek and no groping or even dry humping."

"Not even a finger?" India is incredulous.

"Not even the pinkie." I shake my head, sadly disappointed. "And his masterpiece could have been painted by a ten-year-old in five minutes. Have you noticed my eyes are different colours?" I point to the left one.

"I have babes, and they're stunning."

"Aww, thanks. Anyway, in the painting, they are both identical, green with a jet-black vertical pupil like a—"

"Reptile," India shouts.

"Exactly, the guy is obsessed."

"Come here." India wraps me in her arms. "I will personally check the aura of the next man you go out with, just to make sure they're normal."

"Thanks. Will a quick check tell you if they have a job?"

13

PETE'S STORY - DEPRESSING IN THE DAYTIME

Usually, the sight of somebody referring to his pint of Guinness as Jeremy while crying would trouble me. Unless it happens to be Saint Patrick's Day, then it's perfectly acceptable. Sitting on a shabby bench in the smoking area outside the Red Dragon pub is one such individual. His worn tracksuit bottoms and football top sporting numerous jagged rips suggest somebody best avoided. While the fact his nicotine-stained fingers are almost squeezing his glass with enough force to break it has me a little concerned. I give him an extra-wide berth and make zero eye contact as I take a deep breath and enter the dilapidated pub.

Shoving open the main door, I am once again assaulted by the stale smell of decay and urine. Hopefully, this will be the only thing attacking me today as I was only just released from the hospital and have no wish to return, especially as this time it could be with a lot of broken bones. Memories of running for my life flash before my eyes, but I made a promise to sort this out, and if there is one thing I have always believed in, it's always to keep your word, no matter what.

I told Dave this once, and he agreed with me at first, but

after thinking it over, "Promises to women don't count, though, do they?"

I said, "They do."

"You're so weird; I'll knock that out of you one day, mate." Dave's general outlook towards the female population was less than salutary. It was something we would never agree on.

I feel guilty about drinking the landlord's retirement fund. If I'd know it was so costly I would have savoured it more, and not had a pack of extra strong mints before I even got to the pub. Personally, I would have stored the bottle in a locked cage with Mission Impossible style laser alarm system or something even better, but I will try to fix the problem for Maze. Usually, I'm the sort of person who puts off unpleasant tasks with the motto *I'll do that tomorrow* or next week, but here I am. The place is even more depressing in the daytime, old worn mahogany tables and chairs finished in that seventies fabric that taverns seem to have the exclusive rights to. The same regular male customers are supping half a bitter. Probably so they don't have to go back to their wives. I hope some of them have been home since I was last here. The landlord sees me as I walk in, and his hand reaches under the bar.

"Wait, I come in peace." I raise my hands in a conciliatory gesture; his face remains neutral as he slowly brings his baseball bat out and places it on the counter which I guess is his offer of parley. There is a name etched on its worn handle I didn't notice the last time I was here, though to be fair, I was fleeing with an unconscious barmaid on my shoulders.

"*Killer Bastard*, what an interesting name." I'm now unsure if I'm going to escape in one piece. Maybe I should have taken Jace up on his offer to accompany me.

"This bat has served me well over the years," he says, rolling it gently back and forth under his palm.

"I'm sure." I gulp, a bead of sweat dripping off my head. "About the wine, Maze didn't realise that was your retirement bottle; she would pay you back if she could." His expression doesn't change. "I'm not in a great financial situation, either." Now it does change, and not for the better as his hand closes around the handle.

"My offer is this if you drop all charges." I place a wooden box in front of him, temptingly just in reach. I mean, who can resist the mystery of a closed container? Apart from Schrödinger's cat, who is probably angry at being stuffed inside so many by bored quantum physicists.

The landlord pulls it nearer, undoes the two metal clasps and opens the lid.

"This is my mint condition Omega Seamaster Planet Ocean divers watch, automatic, waterproof to six hundred metres. A true piece of art."

He carefully removes it. I made sure to leave the original receipt next to it. My wife bought it for me as a present a few years back. I think for a shade over £4000; financially, we were doing well, so she wanted to treat me. Now I can't even bear to look at it.

I fail to mention it's gone down in value since purchase. Now, worth a little under £2900, according to eBay. Still, it is a thing of beauty, stainless steel with a mostly black face, offset with an orange segment. This timepiece is my only possession of significant value I own outright. He examines the intricate automatic movement through the transparent back panel and tries it on; it doesn't quite fit as his wrists are thicker than my more girly sized ones.

"It comes with extra links and the original guarantee card in the box," I say, trying to upsell it. The landlord places it down and examines the receipt closely.

"Deal," he says and sticks out his hand for me to shake. I take it, pleased this is going to be easier than I thought.

"You know I didn't want to cause Maze any trouble; she's a sweet girl. I was sort of hoping she'd ask her parents for the money, but she can be stubborn. I'm sorry about the baseball bat thing as well." He returns it under the counter.

"I'm Shaun, by the way. Now let's have a drink and make this official, a drop of the good stuff."

He pours us both a whisky, adding a single ice cube. It may be quality, but it all tastes the same to me, burning your throat on the way down. I do have a pleasant alcoholic warmth in my stomach afterwards.

"Another one?" Shaun is in a chipper mood, and we retire to a nearby table. I guess he's not expecting a rush anytime soon. A quick glance around informs me Shaun won't be making his millions today or even the rent. Three pensioners are sipping their drinks, and one underage teenager is shaking the fruit machine vigorously as he loses his last pound coin.

"Break it, and I'll break you," Shaun growls, and the lad calms down, searching through his pockets, hoping to find some more silver to fund his addiction. We spend the next couple of hours bonding over a several more alcoholic beverages as Shaun tells me his life story.

"I wanted to make this place something special," he indicates the pub, "but the brewery is intent on screwing me, I can't make a decent living, while those bastards live in their Penthouses, raising the beer prices every month. Do they think I'm swamped with customers who want to spend six quid a pint? These old gits make a drink last four hours. I need more alcoholics or the Irish; now they like to down a few." I nod in agreement. "I thought about having a topless barmaid night, but it might kill off the few regulars I've got left."

Judging by the state of his customers, I tend to agree. The sight of a naked breast could put anyone of them into cardiac arrest and effect Shaun's future income. It also seems a strange idea; even strip clubs have fully clothed bar staff. I'd find it distracting ordering a drink, I wouldn't be able to make my mind up, and the bar would always be full, a bad idea all around. Dave has made me go to the odd seedy venue with him in the past and is disappointed with my behaviour every time. While he is quite at home giving a woman twenty pounds to gawp at her naked body, I wonder if she suffered a childhood trauma that led them to this and simply sit there feeling uncomfortable.

Shaun keeps topping my glass up, and I'm feeling happily intoxicated. I'm a good listener, and being a pub landlord, he's naturally a good talker, so time passes quickly.

"I have a new girl starting next week, a beautiful young thing. Hopefully, that will attract some younger punters. What else can I do?"

I make a mental note to tell Dave; he will be down instantly to try it on with a new barmaid. I find myself liking Shaun even though he threatened to kill me. Now glancing at my watch, I see it's time to go. We part on friendly terms, and he says I can bring Maze back in if I want—all is forgiven.

Outside, I pause at my car door. I'm well over the drink-drive limit and decide discretion is the better part of valour and get my phone out to ring a taxi—Ubers being non exis-tent in our third-world city. I type the first couple of digits, pausing as my vision wavers. The numbers on my mobile blur then expand, flying directly off the screen and towards my eyes, like daggers from a dodgy knife-throwing act. Now I get that familiar crushing sensation, and my breathing becomes ragged. I stagger backwards and put my hand on the car roof to steady myself as nausea sweeps over me, but the pain is overwhelming, and I shut my eyes tightly. I lose consciousness.

The blaring noise of the car horn brings me back to reality, my hand white from the pressure I'm exerting against the steering wheel. I try removing it, but an invisible force is holding it solidly glued there. Glancing out through the side window, I make out the street from my dreams. The day is long gone, and the half-moon shines down outside, giving the scene an ominous silver glow. Curtains are twitching, and I see the vague shape of faces peering out to see the moron honking his horn at this hour. Now the invisible force fails, and I pull my hand away from the wheel, the blaring dies. Rubbing some life back into my dead digits, I stare outside. A few doors are opening, and a few brave souls appear to see what the hell is going on. I get the feeling I've been making a nuisance of myself for several minutes. Slamming the car into drive, I speed off before anybody gets my number plate. Being arrested for drink driving won't make my day any better.

Later, back home, I gulp back a large vodka and coke, heavy on the vodka. What the hell is wrong with me? Thoughts automatically turn to cancer. Ever since I was ten years old, I believed the slightest ailment life-threatening. Now we can self-diagnose with Google; everything is terminal. A quick search tells me I have a brain tumour and maybe Gonorrhoea. After another half hour, I also have rabies and the first case of the black death since the fifteenth century. Growing tired, I throw my phone down in disgust. I'll be fine, a British stiff upper lip and all that. I know I should go to A&E, but as my headache recedes, I use a well-known cure-all, excessive alcohol consumption and fall asleep in the comfort of my armchair. As I close my eyes, the familiar weight of Mr Tiddles presses down on my lap. No more bad dreams invade my sleep tonight.

14

MAZE'S STORY - CHRISTMAS IN NOVEMBER

"Bastard, bastard, bastard," I swear repeatedly as I stub my toe and hop up and down in pain. Then my tights rip as I pull them on, and now I can't find my heels. My parents have banned me from wearing trainers to their house, saying it's unladylike. They insist I wear heels to family get-togethers. To top it all off, I'm being picked up in ten minutes by my pretend boyfriend for the day, and I just know Pete will be punctual to the second. Looking at the multiple piles of clothes that litter the floor, I suddenly realise he might want to come in. It takes approximately fifteen seconds to grab huge handfuls of dirty clothing and throw them in the bathtub. Now, thinking he might want to use the toilet, I pull the shower curtain across, hiding them from view.

India is no help as she went into a statue-like yoga meditation pose forty minutes ago and hasn't moved since. I'm tempted to poke her just to make sure she's not dead. My luck changes as I find a brand-new pair of tights in a drawer; with a cute diamond pattern. I now remember my heels are in a shoebox under the bed, hardly used because I prefer the company of my Converse high tops, of which I own seven pairs in a variety of colours. My hand nudges my broken knock off Rampant Rabbit vibrator that seems to haunt the flat. It broke at a crucial moment, and I threw it on the floor in frustration. I need to buy a new one, the dreams I've been having recently all seemed to feature Pete and his huge... my mind wanders. I think of our encounter in the restaurant; him pushing me against the wall, hands all over. The hard bulge in his trousers pressing urgently against me. I really hope it wasn't his oversized mobile phone in his pocket; I've been deceived before.

Now focus, damn you. Down to eight minutes. I knock the rabbit back out of sight and pull out my shoes, a perfect fit. Now for a skirt. Back in the bathroom, I rummage in the tub till I find the one I want, short and tight in shiny PVC. Pulling it on, I admire my legs in the mirror. They are my best feature, and I like to show them off.

Pete thinks he's being subtle, but I've caught him looking at my legs numerous times. Next, I put on the jumper my parents insist I wear, and now with less than five minutes to go, I slap on some makeup. I try to style my hair, and of course, I'm having one of those days. It currently resembles a dead ferret. I saw the blond tart with her pixie cut trying it on with Pete, and now as I stare in the mirror, I imagine how much simpler life would be. Yes, I could easily pull off that hairstyle. Now, I manically spread styling mousse through my unruly mop. I'm down to four minutes. I grab my antidepressants out of the cabinet, wander over to my small fridge freezer in the kitchen, and down them with a sizeable slug of vodka; it takes the bitter taste away. These are a new type, the other ones made me numb. The in box leaflet warns, and I quote *'may bring suicidal thoughts'* that and a possible hundred others. I check my pink plastic watch just as there is a knock on the door. He's two minutes early. I could do with another ten or twenty, but tough. As I go to answer it, my flat-mate India stirs back to life and beats me there in an impressive sprint that would put Usain Bolt to shame. She bursts out into the corridor, a crystal on a chain dangling from her hand.

"Hello," Pete says as she swings the charm left to right over various areas of his body.

"This is my flatmate, India."

"Pleased to meet you."

She gets to his crotch area as he stares over at me and raises his eyebrows.

I give him a broad grin and pull India away and back inside the apartment where she gives me a smile and a thumbs-up. She will have a lot more to say when I return, but I go with that for now. Outside, Pete is looking puzzled.

"She was checking your aura."

"I think my aura is on amber alert after that once over." He grins. "Hey, there's something different; you're a real-sized person today." His gaze slides down my mini-skirt and legs, and not even subtly this time, so I turn sideways and give him a view of the diamond pattern and my extremely tall high heels; two drinks in, and I will be tripping over. He's impressed. *Take that, you pixie-haired bitch.* Pete even gives me a wolf whistle.

"More misogyny. You can't whistle at women anymore."

"Hey, I'm not a builder with my bum hanging out, abusing women in the street. I have never wolf-whistled an unknown woman ever; it's just a way to show appreciation unless you are a builder with your bum hanging out. The modern age really has passed them by. Now while the bottom half of you looks amazing, why are you wearing a Christmas Jumper with an elf popping out the middle?"

I press the hidden button, and the elf's nose glows red.

Pete looks perplexed. "It's November."

"My parents like to celebrate Christmas early when they have the family around; they always put the tree up in late November," I explain.

"That's slightly weird." He stares at the glowing nose, mesmerised.

"Well, why are you wearing your tuxedo?" I ask, even though I told him my parents are holding a black-tie event for a laugh. He gives off a sexy spy vibe, tall, broad-shouldered, with his dark hair lightly gelled in place and clean-shaven. His light flint coloured eyes have a friendly but now slightly annoyed gleam to them. I try not to stare downwards to see if I can make out a bulge in his trousers.

"I didn't need to dress up, did I?"

A small smirk appears, which I hide quickly. "My parents will appreciate the effort made by my pretend boyfriend for the day."

"I hope so. I'm having second thoughts already; parents scare me."

"Well, I'm always happy to be your pretend girlfriend if you ever need it."

"My parents are both deceased."

"I'm sorr—" He stops me with a raised hand.

"No need for platitudes. We all die sometime," Pete says somewhat rudely, and I sense I've hit a nerve, so I don't press it. "Shall we go?"

"Wait, you haven't told me what the hospital said."

"Oh, it's nothing."

I place my hands on my hips. "You collapsed and got taken away in an ambulance. That isn't easily forgotten. I thought you were having a heart attack."

"Stress," he says, so I hit him in the shoulder which I immediately regret thinking he might keel over and die.

"Well, they did some scans, and I get the results in a few

days. It probably didn't help getting run over by a car outside."

"You got hit by a car?"

"Yes, didn't I mention it?"

His vague answers annoy me. "No, you didn't mention getting knocked down by a car. Tell me now, or we aren't going anywhere."

"You do remember I'm doing this as a favour for you?"

I hit him in the shoulder again; I can't help myself.

"Okay, stop attacking me. I'm an ill man," he says, and my face drops till I see him smirk, and I do everything in my power not to knee him in the nuts.

"It was when we first met, I brought you back here and put you to bed. Well, I stayed and watched you all night to make sure you didn't die in your sleep or anything. The next morning, I step into the road, not thinking, and this old couple half kills me in their Nissan Leaf. Ridiculous electric cars, I didn't hear it coming."

"You watched me all night?"

He coughs, embarrassed. "Yes, but not in a creepy way."

I can't help myself, and I fling my arms around him in a hug. He shuffles awkwardly and only half-heartedly returns the embrace; I hope I haven't been reading the situation all wrong. I let him go.

"And I was just going to thank you for not touching me up while I was unconscious. You looked after me all night long as well. You're my hero."

He stares at me, momentarily at a loss for words. "Maze, you know that's simply normal behaviour."

It must be brilliant being a man. I change the subject, only happy thoughts today. "So why did you collapse?"

"Could be anything. I've gotten hit in the head a lot recently." He raps his forehead with his knuckles. "Luckily, nothing in here to damage—possible concussion. Who knows? That's what scans are for. Lack of sleep and stress can also cause it. Which is why you should let me off the hook."

"Not a chance, and my parents are nice, so get ready to be a perfect pretend boyfriend for me."

"Um, let's go before I change my mind."

We go outside to his newly washed and waxed car, and I slide into the passenger seat, kick my shoes off and place my feet on the dash, much to Pete's disapproval. He doesn't say anything, but I can tell. This doesn't stop him from taking sneaky glances at my legs as we drive.

"So, where are we going?" Pete asks.

"Quarndon."

"Really?"

"Yes, why? Do you think my parents live in a caravan park?"

He smiles and clicks on the radio. We make the twenty-minute drive in relative silence, with only Prince singing Purple Rain and some of his other classic hits along the way. Watching the countryside speed past the windows has a pleasant, calming effect on me. There is some stunning scenery once we break out of our dreary, crumbling concrete city. I'm reminded of the original ending to Blade Runner where Deckard escapes with Rachael, and they drive off through the lush green landscape to freedom. Only last week, I had the most erotic dream where Roy Batty and Pris seduce me into a wild three-way, using all their android stamina to satisfy me. I haven't come so hard in ages; I really must replace my vibrator or get laid really soon.

I catch Pete staring at my legs again. "Oi, eyes on the road," He looks away sheepishly, and I smile, feeling happy. Too many days, I wake up feeling like crap, never good enough, a deep-rooted emptiness inside that won't go away, no matter what I do. Glancing over, I resist the urge to put my hand on Pete's thigh. *Remember he's your pretend boyfriend, not the real deal.* Now I can't move my gaze away from his upper thigh; it appears muscular under those thin silky trousers. My eyes creep higher.

"Are we there yet?" His question breaks my train of thought, and I glance away quickly.

"Here." I point as we are about to drive past.

Pete brakes sharply and makes a hard-left turn, and as we crest the drive, my parent's home comes into view. A vast one-story building, which they steadfastly refuse to call a bungalow. Off to the left is a separate annexe that houses the guest house and swimming pool, which I have many fond memories of learning to swim in.

My sister is already here in her husband's Silver Porsche 911, parked up left of my father's near-identical but different shade of Grey 911. Mum's bright red Range Rover Evoque stands out, off to the right.

"Park there." I indicate the space between the two sports cars. "It will be like a Porsche three-way." *I really must stop thinking about sex.*

"Apart from my car will be the only one legally old enough to take part," Pete says in a deadpan voice.

We stop, and I slip on my heels. "Ready?"

"Sure, looking forward to it." His tone suggests otherwise.

Getting out, I hobble over the rough gravel towards the house but come to a stop when I get to a soggy patch. I don't want to ruin my only pair of stilettos. "Can you give me a lift over?"

"Seriously, don't your parents have servants for this kind of thing?"

"No, now don't be a dick, my boyfriend would carry me across, plus I can't afford a new pair of shoes."

"Jesus, you're heavy," Pete groans as he picks me up in his arms. "Maybe you should think of going on a diet."

"Cheeky git, you can put me down now."

"No, your perfect boyfriend would carry your heavy ass right to the front door." He huffs with exertion. "Why didn't you mention your parents were millionaires?"

We are a few steps away now as I feel Pete's arms tremble slightly. I think of saying he should get down the gym more but change my mind; it's lovely of him to carry me this far.

"My parents aren't millionaires. They just have a successful business. Why would it have made a difference if I'd told you?"

"Well, I would have thought twice about giving Shaun my Omega watch."

"You did what?" I ask, puzzled.

"Shaun, I gave him my Omega watch so he would drop the charges against you. He can now tell the time six-hundred metres underwater whenever he wants. Didn't I mention it? My head, sorry, I'm having trouble remembering things."

"You did that for me?" The trouble with deadening your feelings with antidepressants is that when they make a re-appearance they come back big time . My emotions now surge through me, and I put my hands on either side of his face and press my lips gently against his. This quickly turns a lot more passionate as he drops me to the floor, and we stand there kissing wildly, his hands cupping my bum and pulling me in towards him. That isn't his mobile phone sticking in me now; I saw him put it away in his jacket pocket earlier.

A coughing noise brings us back to reality, and we both turn to find my parents staring sternly at us from the open doorway.

"Hello, dears," my mother says while my father's welcome is somewhat frostier as he simply offers his hand.

"Pete, this is my mum, Bethany and my dad, Michael. Mum, Dad, this is Pete."

An extra firm handshake follows, but Pete gets some brownie points as dad spots he drives a Porsche. As my previous boyfriend owned or maybe even stole a push-bike, they will view this as a definite upgrade. Both my parents are sporting a Christmas jumper, one with Santa's face and the other a Xmas tree. Both will light up on demand, I know from previous get-togethers. Last to leave the house and greet us is my sister, all tall and alluring in high heels, tight leather trousers, and a Star Wars At-At themed jumper.

"So, you're the mysterious, Pete." Angelina winks at me and hugs the life out of him. "Nice tux, did my sister tell you it was black-tie? Don't worry, she told her last boyfriend it was fancy dress, and he arrived on his push-bike dressed as a chicken." She carries on the embrace way too long.

I catch Pete staring at me. "What? It was funny."

As we make our way into the house, Pete stares in wonder or maybe shock at the total Christmas experience, every surface is covered with tinsel and baubles, and the centre-piece is a colossal Blue Spruce tree.

"Wow, simply wow." Pete stops and takes it all in. "I can't even put up a tree, the cat destroys it in seconds, and last time I put up tinsel, the little bugger tried to hang himself, so I have fewer decorations than Scrooge." His hand touches one of the ornate baubles hanging down. I take this all for granted, I've forgotten how amazing it is and the effort my parents make. I'm suddenly happier than I have been in months.

"So, Peter, what do you do for a living?" Mum asks.

"Mum, can we leave the interrogation till after dinner at least? That way, you can catch him unaware."

"Helen, I'm simply an interested mother who wants to know what's happening in her daughter's life."

Pete now turns to me and silently mouths, "Helen," while raising his eyebrows in a comical questioning way.

I link arms with him and pull him into the dining room and our awaiting Christmas meal with all the trimmings. Helen is such a dull, mundane name. I choose the name Maze when I left home. The trouble is my parents resolutely insist on calling me Helen and nothing else. I smile as I know I'm going to get at least some gentle ribbing.

My stomach rumbles now as I get a whiff of the turkey. It's a beast of a bird. I purposely arrived late, so we go straight into the meal and avoid major questions, like, how are you? I fill my wine glass up to the brim as dad reaches over and moves the bottle out of my reach like I'm some kind of drunk. Pete smirks and checks his watch. I grin back as he gets a tiny measure of wine. He is driving their precious daughter; after all, I guess we will both have to remain quite sober.

"Can I ask why you celebrate Christmas in November?" Pete asks politely, then emphasising my name. "Helen never told me." I kick him lightly under the table.

"Well, as the children left home, it was harder for us all to get together on Christmas Day, and our old bones don't take the winter so well anymore, so we spend December in Tulum, Mexico. Have you ever been?"

"Yes, well nearby Playa Car, I went on my hon—, on holiday about four years ago, beautiful place and glorious weather."

"We just love it, but we always make a Christmas celebration for the family, hence turkey dinner in November. Do you visit your parents over the holidays, Peter?"

I have already drained my glass, but the bottle stays resolutely out of my reach; we could both do with a top-up.

"Unfortunately, I don't," he says.

"You should make more of an effort; they won't be around forever."

"Mum, he's being polite. They both passed away." A shocked silence follows, and Pete gives me a nudge. I was only standing up for him.

"I'm so sorry," Mum sympathises.

Pete finishes his glass of wine in one. "No, it's fine."

"How did they die?" asks my emotionally tone-deaf older sister.

"In a house fire." Pete's eyes shut tight. His hand massages his left shoulder while the colour drains from his face. I want to slap Angelina in the face. I decide to take him outside and away from the inquisition.

"I think we better get some fresh air." I give everybody a reprimanding glare as I grab Pete by the elbow and snag the bottle of booze with my free hand. I walk him out the front door where we sit on the front step. A minute of cold air and several large gulps of wine help the colour return to his face.

"Sorry," he says, as if he should somehow apologise.

"No, I'm sorry, my sister has no filter."

"No, this is my fault. It shouldn't affect me like this," he takes another gulp, "it was so long ago, I hardly even remember them, that's the worst thing. I can't even picture their faces anymore. I try sometimes, and all I get is a blurry shape."

I place my hand on his thigh in a comforting gesture, and it's as solid and muscular to the touch as I imagined.

"Should we go back in? I don't want to ruin everybody's

November Christmas, now do I, Helen?" He grins, and I know he's okay.

We wander back in, and all conversation abruptly stops. As we take our seats, Pete apologises again. "Hi, sorry, simply a headache. A car knocked me down recently and the Doctor told me to take it easy." He now briefly relays the details of the accident, leaving out the fact he carried me home (I imagine Pete would use the word inebriated but ratted fitted my state much better).

Now we eat. Dad carves the turkey. Not being much of a religious family, we don't bother saying Grace; we just tuck in. Pete stares judgementally at my plate of food, which is piled ridiculously high.

"What? I'm hungry." His plate is about half the size of mine. Near silence descends for the ten minutes it takes to consume.

"That was beautiful. Thank you for such a delicious meal," Pete says. I'm sensing he meets with my parent's approval. My ex Jeff said, "Cheers for the nosh," after last year's meal, which doesn't sound as polite as Pete's perfect English. Now conversation starts up again.

"Peter, why don't you leave the car and have a few drinks with us? I'll pay for your taxi home." I'm hoping Pete agrees to my dad's offer, I could do with more alcohol, and my parents are restricting me to the paltry amount my designated driver can drink.

"If you don't mind me leaving the car overnight? That would be fantastic. I can't let you pay for the taxi, but thanks for the generous offer."

Thank God, I can start some serious drinking. The feel of a full glass of wine in hand gives me a warm, happy feeling. Dad will think a lot more of Pete for refusing the taxi money. Jeff would have asked for a doggy bag and some beers to go.

We now retire to the lounge and sit there on huge leather sofas, which must have cost many cows their lives. Once when I was younger, I was walking happily through a field, picking flowers, and minding my own business when this huge ruddy cow took an instant dislike to me and chased me for half a mile before I could escape, so I do appreciate their sacrifice. A colossal 85-inch television adorns the wall and shows an 8K video of a roaring fireplace; this and the under-floor heating makes the room very cosy. Angelina comes in and sits on the arm of the chair, immediately draping her leather-clad legs across Pete's lap in a way too familiar gesture. Her hand resting on his shoulder now crosses the sisterhood line.

"Where is your husband today?" I ask.

She smiles back at me. "Away on business again, what can you do?"

Get off my pretend boyfriend for a start.

"He's hot," she mouths at me.

My parents can't wait any longer and go back to the mild interrogation of Pete.

"So dear, where did you and Helen meet?"

He pauses for a moment. I hope he doesn't mention having to carry me home; he's too much of a gentleman. The trouble is we haven't done any rehearsals for actual lying.

"We met at the ballet."

I'm as surprised by this as everybody else, including my parents.

"I saw Helen during the interval; she was easily the most beautiful woman there, elegant, stunning, and utterly perfect. I had to go over and meet her, so I introduced myself, and we clicked." I sense the emotion in his voice, and my heart sinks as I realise he is thinking of somebody else altogether.

My mother is beaming over at us. "I didn't know you've grown to appreciate the arts. Which one did you see, dear?"

Uh-oh, why didn't he think of a better lie? I know nothing about the ballet, having never been to one and having no intention of either. I take a furtive glance at Pete, hoping nobody will notice. He's trying to tell me, it's two words, and the one I can make out is swan.

"Black Swan," I say.

My sister sniggers. Wait, wrong answer, my brain tells me. That's the movie where Mila Kunis gets to lez up Natalie Portman in a hot scene I still fantasise about when trying to get off. This film caused me to turn full-time lesbian for a period of approximately two weeks. After all my rubbish boyfriends, the answer must be another woman. Turns out not so much. While I enjoy being gone down on, it's weird when I try it. Soon, she was getting on my nerves, borrowing my makeup, and stealing my clothes. I broke it off when she shaved off the beautiful mane of hair that attracted me to her in the first place. The final straw being when she brought home the biggest strap-on ever that would have broken me in half. Movies are always better than reality. I went back to crappy men soon after.

"Swan Lake, I mean." Disaster averted, the evening continues as I subtly hoof my sister out of the way and snuggle up next to Pete.

"Do you play chess at all?" Dad challenges Pete to a game later in the evening, and he agrees. Jeff couldn't even play snap. So Dad's happy.

I hear Pete say, "I'm only an average player." As they go off to the corner.

Mum joins me and my sister on the sofa and puts her arm around me. I swear there is a tear in her eye.

"He's lovely. Where have you been hiding him? I think your father rather likes him too."

My sister Angelina just can't help voicing her unwanted opinion and interjects, "Mum, stop it, just because he's got an expensive car and can string a few words of more than two syllables together, he could be a nutter for all you know. He could even be the Bagman." This is the moniker the news had now given to Derby's new serial killer. The police also came up with the theory that he shops for victims where he gets his carrier bags. It brought some much-needed excitement to the city and made the weekly shop so much more interesting as the person next to you might be the last face you ever see.

"Don't be so ridiculous, Angelina. I can sense a good person. Anyway, Maze's last boyfriend was an absolute loser."

"Cheers," I say. Now I feel guilty for lying to her, but I don't have the nerve to admit I might want my pretend boyfriend to become something more.

As the evening wears on, I watch Pete let my father beat him at chess. He then jokes about his early career in I.T.

"Honestly, we went around fixing people's computers by turning them off and on again. I spent half my time fixing laser printers which weren't anything to do with my job, you pull out the toner and re-insert, and you guessed it, turn it off and on."

I sense my parent's interrogation is now in full flow, but he appears to be enjoying himself and doesn't need my help.

"And what made you change career?" mum asks innocently, but I can tell she wants to know why leave a job if you don't need to? I know my mother thinks he got the sack for stealing, screwing, or drinking.

"A car accident."

My parents are suitably shocked.

"Yes, I know, another one. I don't appear to have much luck. Anyway, I had to take a few months off to recover, and I found I didn't want to go back and do the nine-to-five thing anymore. So, I became self-employed, and now I buy rare computer games and toys. I spend a lot of time in the Scandinavian countries as they have so many PAL exclusives. Some of these get a shocking amount of money. Sometimes people want cash, but more often, they will only part with their games if I have another rare item for them. You meet all sorts. I met this one man who was a big game hunter. He had all these poor animals' heads mounted on the wall and loaded guns just lying about on every surface like discarded coffee cups. Quite mad, he was, but I couldn't help but like him. Like that insane uncle, they only wheel out at Christmas. Anyway, we just got on. He collected Tec Toy Brazilian Master System games, and some of those are super rare. I got him what he asked for, but then he wanted to swop a stuffed Eagle for them. I said I didn't need a dead animal, and he offered me a hunting rifle." Pete laughs, then pauses, lost in thought. "Strange, I can't remember what we ended up agreeing on as payment. Anyway, it's something I found I have a skill for, and it's so much more interesting than my old job."

I can tell he enjoys what he does, unlike me. I either get groped serving pissheads down the pub or ignored by ungrateful couples at restaurants who don't acknowledge I'm a real person. Valentine's day is an absolute pit of despair, especially as Jeff disappeared on a three-day bender last year.

I pry Pete away from my adoring parents, and we sit down in the corner, only to be interrupted again as my mum passes me a card.

"Happy Christmas, dear."

"Thanks."

"So, what's in the card?" Pete asks.

"My parents give out the Christmas gifts early, and it's up to us if we open them now or wait a month. I always mean to wait but never quite manage."

I sneakily open the envelope. Inside the beautiful hand-made card is some much needed cash, and then I see it and my mood changes, a pre-paid course of laser removal treatment, open-ended. I'm raging. I make the mistake of showing Pete, who clamps his mouth shut in a desperate attempt not to laugh. I'm going to have it out with my freakishly controlling parents, I make a move to stand up, but he surprises me by leaning over and gently kissing me; all my anger fades away as he pulls back.

"They mean well. I grew up with my Aunt, with just a red-hot poker for company, and all I got every Christmas was a half-eaten apple."

"Really?" I don't know why I said that because it's obvious he's joking to lighten my mood.

"No, I was a spoiled kid with lots of toys, but it never made up for this, genuine love and affection." He indicates the room around us. My lousy mood instantly passes as he carries on talking. "So, how is my perfect boyfriend act going?"

"This is all an act?"

"I'm going to want triple time for being so pleasant; it's hard work. Pete now reaches over and holds my hand, which surprises me as Jeff never did. "We need to look convincing; I'm only joking about triple pay. I'm enjoying myself. This might be the nicest day I've had for a long time."

"How fucked up does that make you?"

"Very." He stares directly into my eyes, and his hand moves to touch the side of my face. I feel a tingle of excitement and want him to kiss me again. He moves closer.

"Maze, you may be the most beautiful woman I have ever met." My mind tells me it's a line, but my body says—*take me, I'm yours.*

"Let's go back to your house?" I say, suddenly decided. He nods.

I shout to my parents, "Mum, Dad, can you ring us a taxi? We are going to go now."

We make our goodbyes, which I don't remember because we are both now sitting in the back of a yellow cab, not speaking, just holding hands, and mine sure is sweaty. I'm extra nervous as I realise I'm going to be naked in the next twenty minutes. Why did I eat such an enormous meal? Pete is going to see my belly sticking out and think I'm fat. Just how many positions is right for the first time without looking like a slut? I'm so stuffed I can probably only manage two anyway. All these thoughts swirl around my head as we sit in total silence for an excruciatingly long journey to his place.

It turns out Pete lives in a modern three bedroom detached with garage. All the houses on the street are so identical I wonder if he's ever tried to stagger into the wrong one when pissed. He pays the driver and lets him keep the change, and we go inside. All the time, he's holding my clammy hand. We go straight to the kitchen.

"Drink?" He offers. "I have beer, wine, vodka, Southern Comfort and a decade-old bottle of Cinzano in case you're really desperate.

"I'll have a vodka and coke." As soon as he turns around, I rub my sweaty hand on my Christmas jumper, followed by a quick sniff of the armpits to see how ripe I smell. Pete gets out two glasses, some ice, then a dash of coke followed by a generous shot of alcohol. I hammer back half in one gulp. We now go into the living room, which has an enormous corner suite more than big enough for... I finish the rest in one go.

"Maze, I wanted to warn you that I have some scars and my left arm's got some burn marks."

It strikes me he is as nervous as me about getting naked for the first time, and I feel a whole lot better.

"Touch me," I say in my sultry voice, or at least I hope so and don't just sound simple. Pete places his hand on my hip, and I can't help myself; I light up my Christmas Jumper. "I've come. Thanks, I'll be off now."

He laughs, breaking the tension, pulls me toward him, and then the moment is ruined as the doorbell chimes repeatedly.

"Ignore it," I say.

Impatient knocking follows.

"I'll just be a minute." He goes to answer it.

I do what every woman would do in my position and snoop around. First, I check his music collection. Jeff only had free Spotify and nothing else. Here are real compact discs. If he organises them on an A-Z basis, I will have to dump him. I'll probably still sleep with him, but he will need to be fantastic in the sack to change my mind. If I find any Jazz, I walk straight away. I slept with a Saxophonist once, big mistake. He referred to his music as *experimental, impro-vised, freestyle* and based his sexual technique on the same principles. After he tried to twist my nipples off, I suggested it was time for his solo and left.

The CD's aren't arranged alphabetically; his favourites are at the top of the pile. The worst thing I find is some Shania Twain, but Rage Against the Machine evens it out, so it's all good.

Next, I snoop in a high-quality antique bureau, the type with the pull-up lid Sherlock Holmes was fond of. I open it carefully, making as little noise as possible. Inside are some pens and bills, nothing too exciting. It has four pull out drawers inside. One is full of spare carrier bags. The next two are empty and in the fourth is…

"Shit." I push it back in, pause, then pull it out again. The only thing in there is a handgun, one we have all seen before if you happen to be a Clint Eastwood fan, a .44 Magnum.

The weapon seems to be emit a magnetic force that pulls me towards it, and I take the worn wooden grip in my hands and feel the weight; Smith & Wesson is emblazoned across the barrel. I think it's real, but I've never seen a genuine firearm before. I press the catch at the side, and the chamber slides out. A total of three bullets are inside. I check one by pulling it out and weighing it in my hand; now I'm almost sure it's real. Still, perhaps it's a replica, and Pete's a Dirty Harry fan. We haven't discussed movies as we keep sticking our tongues in each other's mouths. It's a good job guns are illegal in the UK. Can you imagine the carnage when your neighbour sticks his car in your parking space or someone cuts in front of you at the supermarket? England would quickly turn into a bloodbath, the amount of emotional repression we are all suffering from.

There is no way my small frame would be able to shoot this monster of a weapon; I wonder how Pete fares. I decide it's real, and I put it back gently, trying to remember the exact position. The drawer carefully shut; I pull out the one full of Asda and Sainsbury's brand carrier bags, the sort a certain maniac is using. And I know the first decent man I meet in a long time is a crazed serial killer. I knew my man radar was skewed, but this is ridiculous. I can still make out raised voices in the hall, so I'm alright for a while longer.

Sneaking into the kitchen, I open the massive double-door American fridge freezer with one quick motion, ready to scream at the sight of a severed head sitting there. What greets me are eight bottles of lager, a bottle of Champagne,

Vodka, milk, eggs, cheese and little else. Thankfully, no murder victims. It's a comforting sight as it resembles the interior of mine, except I can only afford Prosecco. Stealthily making my way to the living room door, I sneak a peek outside. Pete is arguing with two police officers at the front door; maybe he's been caught already? He holds his hands out in a handcuff me gesture. They don't, and he slams it shut. I step forward about to call out, and Pete turns to me.

"What was all that about?" I try to sound calm.

"Simple misunderstanding."

My heart hammers away in my chest; *surely, he can't kill me with the police outside?* Another side of me is saying I'm being ridiculous. My parents like him, so he must be okay, but the gun and carrier bags? Perhaps even Dirty Harry shopped at Asda. No, *trust your own poor judgement in men,* I tell myself.

"Look, I'm sorry, but this was a mistake. I'm going to go now. Thanks for the pretend boyfriend bit, but I don't think we should see each other again."

"What? Hey, that was nothing. You don't have to leave."

"I'm going to go now," I repeat, taking a step towards the door he's half blocking.

"We were getting on so well, I don't understand. Have I done something wrong?" He stands there, puzzled.

I take another half step, wondering if I can make a run for it. Pete locked the door when we came in, but the keys are still dangling in the lock. Perhaps I can get through before he can grab me.

"Let me call you a taxi at least. It's not safe out there. You do know there is a serial killer on the prowl?"

Maybe right in front of me. "It's alright; I'll phone a cab outside."

He pauses about to say more but stops, unlocks the front

door, and holds it open for me. He indicates the gap with his free hand. "Okay. Well, take care of yourself."

Edging carefully past, I find myself outside in the chilly night air as the door clicks shut behind me. This is the nicest any man has been when I have changed my mind about having sex with them, the worst being… I block the memory. Even after a lot of therapy, I can't bear to think about it.

I take out my mobile and start dialling my local taxi firm. As I type in 01332, the phone chirps a warning message; I have 30 seconds of battery life. This proves to be a lie as two seconds later, the screen goes dead.

"Oh, for Christ's sake."

I look backwards towards Pete's house before stumbling away into the night. It's a long walk home; I knew I should have worn my trainers.

15

PETE'S STORY - BAMBI'S MUM

As I vomit the contents of my stomach across the top of my brand new Reebok trainers, two things occur to me. First, it's unfair I am so unfit, my belly doesn't stick out, I haven't developed moobs, and I'm still young, well, youngish. But as Penny sprints away from me like a gazelle, disappearing out of sight, I collapse and spew my guts up. I realise I'm skinny unfit, but maybe not so much the skinny part as for the last few months, it's taken more effort to button my Levi jeans.

The view of Penny's pert bum sprinting away makes me want to be a better or at least fitter person. Kale is so far unmentioned, but Penny cancelled our drinking date because of her busy schedule and asked if I wanted to go running. I stupidly said yes. I haven't run since I was twelve. I borrowed Dave's new tracksuit he bought because the stunner outside the gym had offered him the best sexual experience of his life, and by that, I mean an unbreakable 18-month membership. The 128-page contract can be cancelled within the first week but only during the thirty-minute period between 3.30 p.m. and 4.00 p.m. on a Tuesday, during a full eclipse or in the event of a comet passing into Earth's atmosphere - in person at their office in the Outer Hebrides. I think they also made Dave sign it in blood; I keep telling him to *always read the small print.*

Second, it hurt that Maze left and said we shouldn't talk again. We were getting on so well. The sight of her in high heels had cancelled out my short person bias, and then I met her parents. Mine dying so young had made me emotionally stunted in some respects. Maze's were such fun, even in November. They gave me the Christmas spirit I have always been lacking.

Agonising pain shoots through my head as I try to remember the exact details of her leaving. I vaguely recall she said we shouldn't see each other again. I rub my forehead; my memory is messed up. The fact I keep losing time is also scary. I spit to clear my throat; it feels raw and unpleasant, much like my very soul.

Hurry up. You can do it; run now. I force myself to stand straight and take a deep breath. I need to catch up to Penny or at least end our run a respectable distance behind. She is waiting for me at the other end of the park, jogging on the spot in a tight, all revealing, virtually spray-on tracksuit showing off her finely muscled thighs, taut six-pack, and beautifully firm breasts. My God, how does she find time for a life? It soon becomes apparent with work and the gym twice a day she doesn't, hence me running very badly after her and trying to pretend we are even the slightest bit suitable. The trouble is, though I understand we aren't; I am currently unemployed, broke, and depressed. I find myself attracted to the girl with the strange neck tattoo who is totally unsuitable for me, and she just brutally dumped me. All I have left is the vague idea this hot pixie-haired Olympian is my last chance at happiness.

I pull up beside Penny and pretend to be in full health as I jog energetically up and down. I have around ten seconds before I collapse. "That was great, a real cardiac workout."

She runs her hands through her short blond hair and smiles. "I think you mean cardio workout. You look tired. Do you fancy coming back to mine for a coffee and a chat?"

My heart is beating so fast I can hardly hear, let alone speak. I'm struggling just to breathe but nod yes, and hope she doesn't realise how knackered I am. Her place at least is nearby, an ultra-modern city centre flat inside a sleek glass-fronted building. Her front door leads into an all-white mini-malist hallway leading to a large open plan living space—the complete opposite of my outdated house. Which is so trapped in the eighties, I expect Toyah Wilcox to wander through at any moment.

My first thought is, where are all the stains and the kettle (she has a boiling water dispenser tap instead—now this is the future). Penny pulls off her trainers at the front door and sticks the kettle on, well, walks over and turns a tap. I'm still getting used to the future bit. I pick up the only picture frame marring the empty surfaces.

"Where was this taken?" The picture shows a much younger Penny on skis in a snow-covered scene.

"That's near my family home in Sweden. My parents moved us there for work when I was five, and I spent my teenage years growing up in the snow. We moved back to the UK when I turned eighteen. I still holiday over there when I can; it's a beautiful country. Have you ever been?"

"I have, but only for work. I never got out to see the sights."

"That's a shame."

Penny unexpectedly peels off her top to reveal her sports bra and ridiculous toned physique. "I'm just going to take a quick shower." She sensually bites her bottom lip, giving me a lingering glance, then turns and heads towards the bathroom. My British reserve is upset again, and I wonder if this is an invitation to join her. If I follow and it isn't, then I will be branded a pervert. This could be worse than when I offered my seat on the bus to a pregnant woman, only to find out she was merely overweight.

Seconds later, Penny partly re-appears. First, her leg and arm snake out seductively from behind the doorframe—her long toned leg draped around like it's a stripper pole. Then out peeps her head and the top of her naked shoulders. I marvel at how little I see and how much I imagine. My eyes take in the snake tattoo that wraps around her thigh and goes upwards.

"Want to join me?"

My caveman brain keeps telling me she's nude and probably very bendy. Well, it's hard to concentrate on anything else.

"Rain check," I say. "We should get to know each other first." *Why the hell did I just say that?*

Now I can tell by Penny's puzzled expression she has never been turned down for sex, whereas being a man, I'm quite used to it.

"Well, if you're sure." She pouts then stands in the open doorway, confident in her nakedness. Her perfectly smooth skin glistens with beads of sweat. My gaze drops lower, the snake tattoo starts mid-thigh and climbs upward, the cobra face staring at me from the most unexpected intimate position. While some people look better with their clothes on, she isn't one of these, and I gulp at the sight. Her smile tells me she thinks I should change my mind. Perhaps it's the fact I'm well and truly shattered by my run, but I stay resolute, and

Penny leaves disappointed. I hold my head in my hands as she disappears. *What did I just do?*

Five minutes later, she joins me on the sofa, now dressed in a white towelling dressing gown, beautifully camouflaged against the matching leather.

"Where are all the stains from spilt alcohol?" I ask, as this seems to be a miracle level event on the scale of Jesus turning water into wine or Michael Jackson never having his mostly plastic face ripped off and chewed by Bubbles the chimp. I regularly get my carpet professionally cleaned every three months due to the amount of Shiraz I spill, and the mouse entrails dropped by my cat in some deluded attempt at winning my affections. Mr Tiddles totally fails at catching spiders, which terrify me. I point him directly at them, but he just yawns and goes for a nap. A massive one took up residence in my bathroom, and I had to find an excuse to invite Dave around so he could dispose of it.

"I only drink when I go out or on special occasions, so it's not a problem."

Penny's response troubles me on so many levels as I am currently using alcohol as a crutch to get through life.

"So, how are we going to get to know each other better?" She stretches one leg out beside me, revealing a tantalising amount of bare flesh, mere inches from my hand.

"Why don't you tell me about work?" This is the mildest question I can think of, and women usually love to talk about their day. Penny appears pre-occupied.

"Look, sorry, I thought we were going to have sex; I can't concentrate till I come. As we are both adults, would you mind If I sorted myself out?"

I blush, my natural response. "Sure," I say, somewhat flustered. Even at thirty-plus, I am not adult enough for this question.

Penny now lays back, pulls open her dressing gown and starts to pleasure herself. I thought she would go to the bedroom, but no, she is happily masturbating in front of me. I've been brought up to believe this act to be shameful and turns you blind; also, nice girls don't. Penny obviously grew up under a completely different set of rules as she moans in happy bliss. Do I watch or turn away politely? This is the next question on my mind when she suddenly seizes my hand, positioning it on her upper thigh. Now I'm ill at ease. I can either leave the room or join in.

Surely leaving is the worst option and the one I can't come back from, so I slide my hand down and kiss her knee. She moans and grasps my hair in a tight grip, pushing my head downwards. Is this what being a woman is like? I said no, but somehow, I'm being coerced or manipulated into giving Penny oral sex. Several minutes later, she screams the house down, climaxing annoyingly loudly. Maybe for my benefit, or perhaps she's playing who's got the best sex life with her neighbours. Now she tells me about her day; dressing gown left casually open.

My eyes glaze over in under a minute as she talks about work, and I really wanted to be interested in her life. Being a personal assistant sounds as bad as any of my previous jobs. From selling shoes at sixteen to bar work at eighteen, Tom Cruise in Cocktail I wasn't and just avoided getting fired for the most broken glasses in one week.

After five more minutes, the urge to smash my coffee cup and stick the jagged remains in my eye becomes an increasingly popular idea.

"Penny," I interrupt.

"Yes."

"I…" I do the only thing possible to shut her up, and moments later, my face is once again between her lithe thighs. Soon, she is again yelling out to inform the neighbours her sex life has transcended to a whole higher level than theirs.

Her hand strokes my head as we lie there afterwards. "You're amazing at that."

I glance up at the cobra tattoo an inch from my face. It's fantastic work, but this probably isn't the time to ask about the artist.

"Penny, I just realised I'm late for a business meeting. I completely forgot." I back this up by staring at my wristwatch in fake dismay. "I'm going to have to run. This was great." I get up and straighten my clothes. "I'll call you later." I make the generic phone me gesture with my hand against my chin and ear, and I rush out of the flat. As soon as the door shuts behind me, I wipe my mouth and pull out my mobile - speed dialling my only friend who can't possibly understand.

"Dave, I need to talk. Fancy meeting me for a beer?"

"It's the middle of the day."

"When has that ever stopped you?"

"Well, never, but I'm at work. You know what a vital service I provide."

Not another one. "You sell life insurance to old people."

"Yes, but I'm good at it, and the old gits just love me."

"There is a hot young barmaid you haven't seen before."

There is a pause on the other end of the line. "When and where?"

Twenty minutes later, and we are in the Red Dragon pub, chatting. The first thing we hear as we order a pint is the television spewing out yet more theories on our local serial killer.

"What do you think he does with the bodies?" I ask Dave as we take a seat at an empty table.

"That's easy. He keeps them in his living room and plays Twister with them."

I sit thinking about this; the scene is quite horrific when you play it over in your head.

"Dave, you are one sick puppy. What made you think of that?"

He shrugs. "Or... have you seen the movie American Pie?"

"No, just no." I shut Dave down as I have an inkling where his mind is going. Taking a sip of lager, I pause to reflect. "It has to be a single man, doesn't it?"

"Well, it could be a woman, equal opportunities and all that. But she would have to be pretty strong. All the figures suggest serial killers are white males between the age of thirty and fifty."

"What figures?"

"Grissom said it on an episode of CSI, so it has to be true."

I look around the bar at my fellow patrons. "That means nearly everybody in here could be the killer, including us."

Dave nods. "Well, apart from me and you. I think we know we aren't running around murdering people."

"Yes, apart from us." I bite my lower lip and drink some more. The conversation now turns to Penny.

"She did a Harvey Weinstein on you," Dave says. "You felt you had to for your career. She deffo took advantage of you, mate. I do have one question."

"Yes."

"What the hell is wrong with you? Penny's got an incredible body, and you said no?"

"I've had a weird week, and I wasn't in the mood. Now you mention it; she did Weinstein me. I did say no, I think. This is weird."

I can tell Dave is having trouble with the fact I didn't automatically want to sleep with a gorgeous woman. I don't tell him I have a strange attraction to Maze; I know he wouldn't understand. He is a straight shag and dump them when they become too needy kind of bloke. Some of his girlfriends have been wonderful and kind people, and I even told him he would be hard pushed to do better. Obviously, he has never heeded my advice, whereas I sometimes listen to his, right or wrong.

Shaun interrupts us with two beers. "Do you want to know the time?" He makes a dramatic show of reading his Omega, "3.15," he says with glee and wanders off.

"That bloke is weird, and there is a smell in the air." Dave sniffs. "Yes, the odour of poor people." I don't mention the watch, and as the beers seem to be free, I can't complain. The new barmaid doesn't start for another hour, so I have Dave's attention till then. The pub has a particular urine-filled cat litter tray smell, and in daylight, the place looks worse than ever. My fingers nudge hardened chewing gum as I try to level our rocking table.

"So, what am I supposed to do now?" I ask, taking a sip from my pint of Stella.

"Well, you have several problems. You have no money and no way of earning a real income until you get your money back in a few months. Second, you need to get out and meet slutty women."

"An intelligent and interesting female," I counter.

Dave ignores me and continues. "Now, in my experience, younger ladies are better because they haven't been screwed over by life yet, and as it happens, they won't have heard half my chat up lines either. Get a job in a fancy restaurant; you will have an admittedly piss poor income but access to all the waitresses. You could always slip your number to single women out for a meal with their parents, desperate to have a baby thirty-year-olds or even the odd woman bored by her boyfriend—this one will have to be done carefully to avoid being punched. Well, what do you think?"

I mull this over. This isn't the worst idea Dave has ever come up with. A low wage combined with my credit cards means I can make it through the next few months. Then I'm back. I did bar work in my early years and can be surly and drop food on the floor. Do they still have the five-second rule?

"You know what? Why the hell not? My life could do with some mixing up."

Dave nods, pleased. "See, I'm always right." He isn't, but it would be churlish of me to mention it. "Now, I have a treat for us." He pauses to let my interest rise. "We are going speed dating."

My face remains blank. "As in, you get five minutes to talk to a woman, then do it all over again?" I thought this practice out of date, but I'd never tried it and Derby is always ten to fifteen years behind London or every other major city in the UK, so why not?

"You get four minutes, but it's more than enough time to get to see them close up. Suss out if they're needy, vulnerable or a bunny boiler. You can find out everything essential in a few opening lines. Now here I was thinking you would say no. You are finally opening your mind to life's possibilities."

I blink, puzzled, as Dave's voice slows with every word spoken like he's a clockwork toy running out of power. As I place my pint down, I find it magically transforms into a Southern Comfort. The very molecules of the glass seem to change before my eyes as I set it down on a copper-plated tabletop in an entirely different pub. My outfit has also changed to a white shirt and jacket, and Dave has morphed into an extremely rough-looking woman, one shade of orange darker than Donald Trump. For a second, in the dim light, I thought it was him.

"...I always swallow." I don't recall any of our conversation up to this point but perk up at this insight. Luckily I'm saved by a buzzer, and I follow suit as the men all move to the next table. I make out Dave a few tables away, he winks. I try to remember when he said the speed date was and work how many days of memory I'm now missing. The most worrying aspect is that I'm not more concerned as I take up my next position. A quick check of the list I'm carrying shows I already had three dates, all marked unsuitable. I tick the same for my last one, fairly sure Dave with be doing the opposite after their chat.

"Hi, Pete."

I glance up, not expecting to recognise the person opposite. After all, I'm wearing a small name-tag.

"Hi, Maze." I hope the next four minutes aren't going to be uncomfortable. Her hair is the grey shade so popular with young women right now. When she hits thirty, it will be another matter, and she will go to any means to destroy any trace of it. The colour suits her. I don't check to see if her trainers match, but I suspect they might.

"I didn't think I'd see you on something like this."

She smiles. "Yes, I didn't think there would be anybody I knew here."

"I like your new hair colour; it suits you. So did your parents get off on their vacation?" I make small talk; she is easy to chat to, and it's not even awkward.

"Met anybody interesting?" she asks.

"Well," I relay what my last date said.

"Dirty cow. I was hoping for a few more people, but I suppose it's quiet because it's so close to Christmas."

"By the way, my best mate Dave is here. He's a serial dirtbag; I'd avoid him if I were you." I motion towards his location with a subtle nod of the head, " At a guess, I bet he's wearing a fake name-tag."

"Thanks for the info. So far, nobody special either. I got on quite well with the big bloke over there."

I turn to see a hulk of a man, taller than Jace and thicker muscled with it. "But?" I ask, feeling slightly inferior.

"Well, he won't fit in my clothes, and he seems okay. It's just..."

"He may have a shrunken steroid dick," I finish for her, and we wriggle our pinkie fingers in tandem; she laughs, and so do I.

The buzzer goes, and I give Maze a wistful smile as I move on to the next table.

Taking my seat, I glance up at my next companion. She's dressed in an electric blue silk ball gown, low cut with a tightly cinched waist—long ringlets of curly brown hair flowing downwards all topped off by a diamanté tiara to finish the look. Sort of Elsa meets Scarlett O'Hara. She stands there, tapping her foot and glancing at the barstool in front of her. I check out her name-tag nestled over her ample bosom; it reads – *Are u my Prince Charming?* She pouts and taps her foot some more. Then it clicks.

"Here, let me get that for you." I stand up, pulling her stool out and ushering her into the seat.

"Why, thank you, kind sir. You may call me Aurora," she utters in a perfect American southern belle accent, slow, drawn-out and seductive. Close up; she is quite beautiful with delicate features, a small button nose and pouty red lips. This is all ruined after she sits and starts firing off questions in her real voice, which is much more a manic high pitched helium accentuated squeal that grates like fingernails on chalkboard.

"Sooo, what is your favourite Disney movie?"

I think for a second. "Toy Story."

Her face falls in disappointment. "That's Pixar, not Disney."

"Err, The Incredibles."

A shake of the head follows. "That's Pixar too."

"Monsters vs…" I stop as I see her pinched expression and narrowing eyes. Racking my brains; I finally come up with an answer, "Beauty and the Beast."

I saw this movie because Dave really fancies Emma Watson. He even bribed me to accompany him to the cinema and ruined it for all the parents at the 3 o'clock matinee that day, convinced we were paedophiles out to snatch their children.

It didn't help him shouting, *'I would'* at Emma's first appearance and then later rustling his popcorn whenever she was on screen. We don't discuss Harry Potter films as I am afraid to ask which movie first piqued Dave's interest.

Aurora's face lights up, and a huge grin appears. She reaches over and touches my hand. "That's my favourite film too. The animation and the songs are just so wonderful."

"Okay, next question. Magic mirror or magic candle?"

"Candle." I take a 50/50, and I guess it is the correct answer as she leans closer and lightly rubs her foot against mine.

"I wasn't sure about you at first." She pauses and pulls out a compact from her purse. Touching up her lip gloss, she continues, "You look like a Disney baddie, handsome but with an egomaniacal charm, and I am searching for my true prince, my soul mate and hero. Your answers tell me so much about you."

"Last question, and this is a difficult one, so take your

time. Which Disney character would you least like to be?"
She sits back and stares inquisitively at me.

I try not to look at her impressively boosted cleavage
that's on generous display as I am trying to downplay my
baddie persona. Such a strange question, and I mistakenly go
for the first thing to leap into my brain.

"Bambi's mum."

Silence followed by a sharp slap across my cheek. "That's
sick, you horrible, horrible man."

I am saved from any further abuse by the buzzer as I jump
up and move on to my next encounter, who has just witnessed
me being assaulted and assumes it's all my fault. As I go to
sit down, she shakes her head and points me to the next table.
Taking the hint, I move along, a real shame as she is quite
attractive.

A bright red knitted wool jumper adorned with a cat's
face greets me. The woman wearing it is what I would
describe as homely. She has on a pair of fifties looking thick
horn-rimmed glasses, giving her a librarian vibe. The name-
tag reads Miranda.

"Are you a cat or a dog person?" she asks, animatedly
bouncing up and down.

I get the idea she's been snorting catnip like a demented
coke head. "I'm a cat person; I have a beautiful little Sphynx
called Mr Tiddles."

"Ahh, that's wonderful. I just love all cats, but Meezers
are my favourite. I'd have a houseful if I could." She brushes
a tuft of fluff off her jumper at this point.

"British short hair?" I ask.

"My God. How did you know?" Her amazed expression
tells me she thinks I'm psychic.

I point to her top. "You have one on the front of your
jumper."

"Oh, yes, silly me. That's Harry; I knitted him myself. I'm so glad you like cats. I can't imagine going out with a dog person; they're awful people. Perhaps you would like to meet all my fur babies?" She stares at me hopefully.

"And how many fur babies do you have?"

"Oh, not many, twenty-six at last count."

I love cats, but that number is plain mad. One is hard work—making sure Mr Tiddles wears his knitted top when the temperature falls is quite the hassle.

The layer of cat hair covering her plain black skirt gives it an unusual sparkling sheen. I see Miranda has hand-drawn a cat motif on either side of her name-tag, complete with curly whiskers.

"Would you like some treats for your pussy; I always carry extra." She plonks her oversize handbag on the table between us, and she spends the next minute searching through its many compartments. She offers them to me as the buzzer sounds. I reach over and grab a handful, just to be polite. "Thanks, that's so kind of you."

"Well, maybe one day we can meet up, and you can meet my babies? They would all like to meet you, especially Mr Prawn Balls."

I take the high ground, refuse to let myself make any jokes, and move on to my next date. Her name-tag reads Sarah, and I can't quite make out her ethnicity because of all the fake tan plastered over her face and body, white, perhaps mixed race, possibly Indian. I'm dazzled by her perfect pure white teeth, but the thought of makeup ruined sheets puts me off. Her dress appears to be a size too small, and her cleavage is threatening to pop out, which does get my attention.

"Do you like children?" she asks abruptly, her accent giving nothing away.

"Um, I haven't really thought about it."

"I have. I want eight."

'*Have you thought about the state your vagina will be in after all those kids? And are you going to carry on working, or would you like me to pay for the upkeep? Because I'm going to have to get a job slinging crack cocaine. A 20k a year office job isn't going to cut it,*' is what I briefly think about saying, but when I do speak, it's, "That's nice, one every year?"

"Don't be silly, who has the time, anyway it would ruin my figure, (her hands run down the front of her extra tight dress) I'm going to do a Brad and Jolie and adopt some beautiful African babies."

I don't mention that it probably split Brad and Jolie up, and working-class people don't tend to have this option in life. I choose to say something complementary instead, "That's a beautiful dress you're wearing."

A smile spreads across her face, made more dazzling by those perfect teeth. "Thanks, I knew I would find at least one gentleman amongst all these dicks. That tall guy just stared at me for a whole four minutes and barely said a word—what a weirdo. And the short guy insulted me, he said... Well, I'm not going into that, and him," her head turns towards my mate Dave, "he said we should blow this joint and go to a hotel like I'm a cheap slut. You're the first decent guy I've come across, and I spent so much time picking the perfect outfit. Wait, I'll give you a twirl."

Sarah stands and shows off her outfit, a skin-tight off the shoulder bright blue calf-length dress with matching glittery skyscraper high heels. Her boobs are only just secured in place with the help of a tonne of tit tape but may explode outwards at any second, which is quite appealing to all the men in the room. She turns around to show me the zip detail that runs the entire length down the back to a lengthy split at the bottom revealing her shapely legs. It is an alluring dress.

"Does my bum look too small in this?" she asks me while trying to bend her neck into an unnatural position to see for herself. Now I have never understood the sudden rush of the female population to get a fat bum. It comes naturally with age, so why would you hunt one down.

"No, you look stunning."

"I know this is forward, but how about we get a drink somewhere else? I've had enough of this speed dating lark. I thought I met a lot of numpties online, but this place." She pauses, a hopeful sparkle in her eyes. She is probably quite attractive underneath all that makeup, and I know it will make Maze jealous to see us leave together. A quick scan of the room tells me the nights a bust, anyway.

"Yeah, let's go get a drink." I stand and offer her my arm, playing the gentleman she thinks I am. As we leave the pub, I hear a wolf whistle in the background and smile, knowing it's Dave without even looking back.

"Animals," mutters Sarah as I steer us across the road to some newly opened cocktail bar which still reeks from a fresh coat of paint. We make it to an empty table decorated with coconuts and plastic flowers. Picking up the menu, I nearly faint at the prices. I still remember the days when you could get a pint and a bag of nuts for under three pounds.

"I want a Slow Comfortable Screw," Sarah says suggestively.

It takes a moment before I realise she's flirting with me. I'm so out of practice; this must be the reason that people watch Love Island. I suddenly regret purposely never watching a single moment. An embarrassed looking waitress now appears at our table, dressed in a hula skirt and a bikini top made from two coconuts, her plus size figure not suiting the outfit.

"Can we get a Slow Comfortable Screw and a Margarita, please?"

She presses the screen on her iPad like device. "That will be eighteen pounds, please."

She gives me a dirty look as I hand over a twenty-pound note. "We take contactless payments now," she says, like I'm some sort of Luddite. Now I have only just got the hang of WhatsApp, so the thought of sticking my card details into my phone leaves me in dread, plus I'm always dropping it down the toilet. I had to buy a waterproof mobile as I did it so often. Even though my current phone has more power than the original Apollo Space programme, I just send a few text messages and watch cute cat videos. I delete everything Dave sends me as it is invariably porn or some poor bastard having his head cut off. He is weird like that. Being a man also means I will upgrade as soon as the first reliable foldable phone gets launched. Once you work out how not to look a tool while unfurling it in public, your cute cat video will be a few pixels better. Who cares that it costs more than the first car I ever bought? Of course, it will need to be completely waterproof.

"Sorry, I only have cash."

The waitress turns in a huff and goes to the bar for change. At nine pounds a drink, I guess service with a smile is a bridge too far.

"So, what do you do for a living?" I ask Sarah.

"Beautician." The answer explains a lot. "But I want to launch my own makeup range one day. I have my own YouTube channel, showing just makeup techniques for now, but I'm going to add other things. I only have three hundred followers, but it's just getting going. My mum thinks I should be happy working in Boots, but I know there is more for me out there." She stops and smiles like she's said too much.

"I think you should go as far as you can in life. I have the number of an excellent accountant if you need one in the future."

"Thanks, that's so kind of you." She places her hand on top of mine. "Everybody else I know is so negative. Why can't people just say positive things?" Our drinks arrive and are dumped unceremoniously in front of us.

Sarah waits until the waitress is out of earshot. "Miserable bitch, she's way too fat for that outfit. I'm surprised she can fit her arse through the tables."

After a brief pause, "Can I have a taste of your Margarita?" I hand it over; she takes a sip, leaving a smudged lipstick mark around the rim, "Umm, salty."

I'm at a loss for words; I really must start watching Love Island

16

MAZE'S STORY - VOW OF CELIBACY

"Yes, I know you liked him, but we split up last week. No, I don't want to talk about it."

Talking to my mum, who is relaxing on the beach in Mexico somewhere, getting served a cocktail while burning her pale English skin like a sausage on the barbecue is no fun from the cold confines of the UK.

"No, I can't ring him up. We are officially over. Tonight, I'm going to meet new people at a speed dating event. Mr Right might be seated opposite, and hopefully, he won't already have a wife and three kids."

She doesn't sound convinced on the other end of the line.

"Got to go, have a great time. I'll ring you tomorrow and tell you how it went." I turn the phone off and get back to the difficult job of getting ready.

Examining my tired features in the mirror, I realise I need to pull off a miracle level event in the next thirty minutes. My hair resembles a bird's nest, and I'm developing deep puffy bags under my eyes. I squeeze the biggest between my fingers. Am I getting old or just need way more sleep? Either way, I decide to plaster myself in makeup and ten minutes later end up looking like I've been dead for a month at least. Now too much blusher leaves me looking like a freaky horror doll straight out of a movie. It's not the look I was going for, though it will appeal to certain men, probably not the type I want to meet. I start over and eventually achieve something satisfactory. After applying endless hair mousse, my tangled mess becomes just about acceptable. Now what to wear? I trust India's judgement, but unfortunately for me, she left an hour ago on her own date.

My clothing is strewn all over the floor; why I don't hang them all up nicely is a mystery to solve another day. My first choice of a jacket with shoulder pads marks me out as an extra from Miami Vice. My second outfit accentuates my belly even when I breathe in. I now regret the doughnut I ate at dinner. If I could find my scales, I'd weigh myself and start sulking. I'm going to starve myself every second day till my top fits again. After trying everything I own on at least twice, I leave the house wearing my favourite go-to outfit of a mini-skirt and T-shirt, paired with a cute faux fur jacket I picked up at New Look the other week. My trainers even match my new hair colour. That's better; cute and youthful again. My confidence rises as I manage to grab the first taxi outside. Tonight is the night I'm going to find *the one*. I groan inwardly as I pull up outside the speed dating venue, and see a few dweebs smoking outside.

The pub is your average boozer that used to be trendy but now relies on gimmicks like escape room events to get people in, but at least the drinks are cheaper. I sign in and pay my fee; the organisers explain I will get four minutes to chat to every man, and then a buzzer goes, and we move on. I get a little name-tag to wear, simple. I buy a beer and sip it out of the bottle; this way, nobody gets to roofie my drink.

Oh no, walking through the door is Pete. How is it

possible that we keep bumping into each other like this? I shift behind a couple of girls so he doesn't see me, which is stupid because if, like most of us here, he's going to tonight's event, then we will end up sitting opposite each other at some point. I decide to leave, but I just paid my fee for this evening, plus I have nothing better to do, so I come back out of hiding. I'm annoyed as Pete fails to notice my presence while getting a drink at the bar. He even laughs. How dare he be in a good mood.

I try to focus on the upcoming event and conduct a judgemental examination of the potential men, all shown off by their tiny name-tags. It's thin pickings. Calming my nerves by knocking back my drink in one go and quickly grabbing another bottle, the buzzer goes, and I take up my first position. Sitting opposite me is Steven, who, at first glance, appears okay. He's presentably dressed in a dark blue suit with a red and white striped tie. I go to say hello, and he interrupts me, which gets on my nerves straight away.

"You're shorter than the girls I usually go for; you should wear heels."

I sit there shocked for a second as Steven is barely five and a half feet tall and a ginger too. He carries on.

"You would be more attractive if you wear more makeup, and that hideous doodle on your neck could do with covering up."

I take a deep slug of my beer, trying not to punch the ginger creep straight in his ugly mush.

"I work in a law firm; when I get a promotion, I will be move to the London office. It's just so provincial here."

"Don't let me stop you." He's oblivious to my sarcasm. The four minutes drag on painfully, with Steven forgetting to ask me a single question and boring me about his extraordinary career. The buzzer sounds, and I'm off like a greyhound to the bar, leaving him with a shocked expression; he can't believe I'm not begging for his number. What a tool.

After grabbing an emergency beer, I return. My next date is eagerly waiting for me; he stands as I approach and rushes around the table to pull out my barstool.

"I think I can manage my own chair, mate." He looks so disappointed I relent, but he mistimes his attempt to push my stool forward until after I've sat down and struggles away to no avail, huffing in exertion before giving up. I move it myself, and he retreats to his own chair, embarrassed.

"Welcome." He stands and tries to doff his hat, which he forgets is sitting on the table. He goes red and tries again, tipping it and bowing. "What is thine name, beautiful lady?"

"Hi, I am the venerable lady Maze." I play along. His outfit of top hat and steampunk-inspired thick-rimmed glasses suggests a harmless virgin, while his ankle-length coat drags along the floor by a good five inches, obviously made for a six-foot frame.

"I am Sir Gawain, my lady."

"Do a lot of roleplaying, do you?"

"I love LARPing; I am a twelfth level Chaotic Good Wizard and Knight of the Round Table." He rises and bows again. "Which character class are you, Evil Witch?" he asks, pointing at my neck tattoo.

I take a sip of my beer. Gawain has a coke which I resist throwing in his face. Brushing aside his comment, I carry on, "Do you have any other hobbies apart from?" I point to his outfit.

"Well, when I'm not being a wizard, I love watching Disney films. I have the entire collection on Blu-Ray."

"I bet you do." I smile; this is hopeless.

"I just love Beauty and the Beast; it's such a beautiful love story. I hope to meet the lady of my dreams someday."

He has a kind face, and his chubby cheeks go a shade of beet-root red as he stares over at me. "What's your favourite Disney movie?"

I don't want to upset him by saying I don't watch cartoons, only anime and manga, so I try to think of one. What's that one they show clips of every Christmas with that friendly old man with the grey beard singing to cartoon birds? Now, how does it go, zip a dee do something or other?

"Song of the South," I say, remembering the title.

Gawain blanches and stares at the table. "I'm just going to the toilet." He scurries off, leaving me there. Wait, what just happened? I realise he's not coming back.

I stand. "Hey, you're the one that's dumped, nerd boy." I sit quickly back down as people stare at me.

The buzzer sounds two minutes later, and a taller man around mid-twenties appears. He has brownish curly hair and thick-rimmed glasses, which are a must with the hipster crowd; sadly, he seems more of a stamp collector. He has a small plastic bag next to his drink which looks like orange juice. I hope he's not teetotal, and there's at least a double vodka in there. I'll give him the benefit of the doubt for now.

"Hi, my name is Maze, a pleasure to meet you, John."

He holds his hand out somewhat awkwardly, and we shake for at least five seconds too long, and it becomes weird.

I can't resist any longer; being a nosy bitch. "So, what's in the bag?"

"My mum made me sandwiches in case I got hungry. They are egg and cress." He opens one up; the smell is horrendous. "Would you like a bite?" He holds it right under my nose, and I pull as far back as possible without seeming rude.

"No thanks, I ate earlier." He takes a mouthful and puts it back away.

"Are you close to your mum?"

"Oh yes, she's sitting over there. She came to make sure I don't meet any nasty women."

I glance over to where he indicates and notice a little grey-haired woman in her late fifties looking back, knitting away effortlessly. Her unblinking eyes give me a frosty once over as she shakes her head slowly like I'm unclean.

"Sorry, I can't talk to you anymore. Mum doesn't like you."

I'm dumbfounded and sit there with my anger stewing away till the buzzer goes several minutes later. Surely all the men can't be this bad or can they? From previous experience it's entirely possible. I wait patiently, my beer empty. I wish I'd bought several at once. My next date is hugely impressive, at least six and a half feet tall and all muscle. Not as good looking as a young Dolph Lungren, but at this point, I will take anything. His name-tag reads Charles, and he speaks first.

"Hello Maze, a pleasure to meet you." His voice is surprisingly soft.

"You haven't got your mum with you?" I relay the details of my last encounter.

"No, she's quite dead. For a while now."

Well, at least he's not a mummy's boy. "Do a lot a working out, do you?" I'm not sure why I asked, as it's obvious.

"I like to stay in shape." He flexes his bulging arm. I immediately turn back into a schoolgirl and giggle as I press his huge bicep, impressive. I wonder if he can still get it up? - the number of steroids he probably took to get in this shape. I do approximately zero exercise apart from the odd occasion of running for the bus when I've got up late, so this could be a future problem.

"I work out lots, too." I lie, hoping he doesn't question me about my exercise regime.

Charles asks a few questions about my life, which is a first so far tonight, and we chat for a while before the buzzer sounds. We have nothing in common, but I do want to see him naked, so I mark him down as a match.

The next date is awful, and now the moment I have been dreading, Pete sits down opposite. In the week following my departure from his house, I have decided he isn't a serial killer; my instincts can't be that far off. But Pete is carrying a lot of emotional baggage, so I stick to my original decision. Though now looking over, I wonder what he's going to say. His tone is charming and friendly, just the opposite of what I was hoping for. Being a prick would have made him a lot easier to deal with. We chat easily for four minutes, and then he leaves me sitting there. *Stay strong,* I tell myself; you made the correct choice. My heart tells me differently.

Two more distinctly average men follow in the next eight minutes. They are either too short or… just not Pete. I clear my mind and prepare to give my next date a fair chance. Unfortunately, he just happens to be the most boring man I ever met. He keeps telling me about fishing, which I have less than zero interest in. My mind wanders as he drones on, and I keep staring over to where Pete is flirting outrageously with some overly made up slut who's practically popping out of her dress. Well, I suppose some men like that kind of thing, actually it seems like Pete does too.

"I use a copper tube fly; I swear by it." My date is still droning on, but my eyes keep sliding over to the table on my right. Pete is getting on with his date far too well. The sound of their laughter annoys me a lot more than it should. I suddenly place my hand on my companion's arm, his name already forgotten.

"That's so funny." I laugh like I heard the most hilarious joke in the world and all so Pete can hear me at the next table.

"Fishing is a very serious business." My date, offended by my levity, removes his hand.

I doubt he's ever been laid in his life, and he never will with this attitude. Now I can't quite believe it, but Pete is getting up, my hopes he has had enough of his date are smashed against the rocks as he holds out his arm, and yes, they leave together before the end of the night. My eyes shoot daggers at the back of the tart as she totters out of the pub on ridiculously high heels. I hope she trips over and lands on her face.

"Stop. Fishing is boring; if you want to get laid, talk about something else and perhaps show some interest and ask some questions," I say to my date moments before the buzzer goes. As he starts to cry, I decide that's it. Enough of tonight's utter fiasco.

Impulsively, I get up and go over to Charles, who towers above me like the Iron Giant and ask him if he wants to go somewhere else for a drink. If he refuses, I will join a convent. He smiles and nods. Relief washes over me, I'm too young to be a nun, and I'm quite sure vibrators are against the vow of celibacy, even the quiet ones that don't resemble a huge cock.

"So, where do you want to get a drink?" I ask.

"I know a place, this way."

We head off outside and walk down the street. The last time I remember somebody towering over me like this was when I was seven and dad took me to the pictures. This cherished memory reverberates around my head as I fail to notice we are heading down increasingly deserted side streets. Charles encases my hand in his giant, firm grip. *Please don't have a tiny shrivelled steroid ravaged penis* is the thought that keeps going around in my head like a bad song on repeat.

"I can't wait for you to meet my mother," Charles casually says as we stroll along.

That's a bit soon, I think, and then I remember what he said about her.

"I thought you said your mum was dead."

I get a weird feeling running down the back of my spine and try to remove my hand from his grasp; it's held tight. I look around. We are entirely alone on an empty street. Oh shit, my creep radar goes off big time. His hands fasten around my waist. Lifting me off the floor with his powerful arms, he plants a surprisingly tender kiss on my lips, which is a pleasant change from having a tongue stuffed in my mouth and swished about like you're searching for treasure.

"My flat is just around the corner. Why don't we go for a drink there?" I turn off my creep radar as he gently lowers me back down to the floor. It's broke anyway—I can't tell a regular guy from a nutter anymore.

"Okay, let's go." I put all concerns out of my mind; I really need to get laid. Seeing Pete has made me horny.

His flat has a standard height entrance, and he bends to get through the front door and again at the living room. I don't have any of these problems.

"Drink?" he asks, but I have other things in mind as I push him backwards on the settee and drop my coat to the floor. Stripping off my T-shirt off, I wait for his excited reaction to my sheer bra, then climb on top of him. It's like climbing a mountain. I run my hands all over his rippling muscles and grind myself against him wantonly. I don't feel a lot down below, and the thought he might have a shrunken steroid dick resurfaces. It's very progressive that he's letting me take charge, but that's not the mood I'm in tonight.

Pressing his hand to my breast, I whisper in his ear, "I want you to prove what a man you are and give it to me, hard."

That's it; I can't be any more direct. Charles picks me up in his powerful arms and carries me through to the bedroom. Dropping me down, he strips his shirt off. His steroid-enhanced physique is magnificent. I hurriedly undress, unclipping my bra and sliding my panties off. Biting my lip in excitement as he removes his trousers, I blink in surprise. Damn, I've gone to bed with Action Man. Disappointment fills me as he peels off his underwear. The flat area where his junk should be could be moulded plastic just like the toy. I'm left with something that resembles a stunted earthworm. I just can't get a break. Still, maybe it's a grower, and I'm here now in desperate need of sex.

"Condom," I remind him, and he scrabbles about in the bedside drawer and gets one out. He fiddles with it, and next, he's on top of me, kissing me and then, with absolutely no foreplay, starts pounding me against the headboard. He moans and seems to be enjoying himself. Me, I can't feel anything down below, apart from his taut abs pressing against me.

Don't ask if it's in yet? Don't ask if it's in yet? I tell myself numerous times, but as he pounds me with increased intensity, I finally snap, "Is it in yet?"

He looks surprised. "Yes, I'm about to come. I can't hold back any longer," he groans. His weird mashed up purple near come face reminds me of Hulk Hogan having a heart attack. I'm worried he might die, leaving me stuck here to die of malnutrition and found by the neighbours in six months' time - just a tiny skeleton. He carries on pounding away, and I stare heavenward in the hope that God gives me a much-needed orgasm. The only things I do see are the cobwebs on the ceiling, and the lampshade could do with a good clean. There is also a shelf on the wall next to the bed. Bored, I try to make out what's on there—nothing but a weirdly shaped vase. It's got writing on the side in a fancy engraved font that's hard to read.

Edna Stevens
Best Mum in the World
Always in My Memory

I squint to make out what it says and then realise it's an urn with Charles's dead mum's ashes inside, and with every shove against the headboard, the oddly shaped jar is gradually moving towards thin air. An extra firm thrust leaving it balancing precariously on the edge.

"Charles, Charles, CHARLES!" The last one is a near scream, but he stupidly thinks I'm coming and beams at me with a pleased expression on his distorted purple face.

"I'm coming too," he shouts and, with one last thrust manages to dislodge the urn. My hand shoots out to catch it but clips the side, sending it on another trajectory, where it smashes onto Charles's head. A cloud of his dead mum's ashes explodes outwards, filling the room in a blinding cloud of debris. He stumbles upright, dazed, and confused by the smack to the head and now by the dense powder stinging his eyes.

"Mummy," he says, standing up on the bed and hitting his head on the lampshade. Taking a step back, he falls off and smashes the wardrobe with his huge frame. He lies in the wreckage, unmoving. I'd be more concerned, but I've got a mouthful of dead mum I'm trying to spit out. Plus, I'm completely covered. She's even in my vagina; there's no way I'm going to be able to persuade Charles to go down on me now. He groans from where he collapsed. At least he's not dead—try explaining that to the police.

"Mummy, I'm so sorry." He's crying now, and I decide it's time I leave. Grabbing my clothes, I make a hurried and embarrassed exit.

17

PETE'S STORY - I'M NOT AN ANIMAL

I knew the makeup would be a nightmare to shift. Spraying an extra dose of Vanish on my sheets and stuffing them back in the washing machine for a second go, I turn the temperature dial to maximum and pray they don't dissolve. Sarah left an hour earlier. She was barely recognisable when I bumped into her leaving the bathroom. Without the thick layer of greasepaint, she's a pale imitation of the young woman from the previous evening, much less enticing even though wearing the same figure enhancing dress. The lack of makeup also seemed to dent her self-confidence, and from the over the top woman of last night, she now appeared shy and embarrassed. This could also have something to do with her insistence that I *do her up the bum,* always a delicate subject to broach the following morning.

I tried to bypass the awkwardness by making her a cup of strong coffee and providing biscuits, the good ones, McVitie's Dark Chocolate. I'm not an animal; Lidl home brand just won't do. We swapped phone numbers, and I told her to call if she needed any business advice, and after seeing her safely into a taxi, I took a couple of painkillers, vowing never to drink again. This vow is made on a semi-regular basis and usually lasts until seven o'clock the same evening when I snap and open a bottle of wine so my damn headache will go away.

My phone keeps beeping, showing an unusually high number of missed calls. No doubt, Dave wants to check how last night went. My sister is another, doing her duty and keeping tabs on me. Penny's number causes me to stop and think. Avoiding her is silly, but I'm unsure what to say. Should I confront her with the fact she has the most boring job in existence? She is intelligent and attractive but is probably jogging twenty miles through a forest, not exactly the thing I'm up for. Other numbers I don't recognise and typically wouldn't answer.

William from Microsoft has an unerring interest in fixing my PC and has singled me out of seven billion people to help. I couldn't get somebody out to fix it even if I offered double the going rate, so it's blatantly a con. Plus, William possesses a thick Nigerian accent and has no idea what is happening in EastEnders, so his claim to be in central London isn't particularly believable. When I'm bored, I chat to him anyway. He tells me about his six kids and how I really should let him fix my laptop; he calls every week now. Such a nice bloke.

I wander back into the living room and make the mistake of switching on daytime television. Where does Jeremy Kyle find them, the most depressing selection of under-educated, unemployable misfits in existence? Today Shannon, who already has three children by two different fathers, thinks her current boyfriend cheated with her own mum. A pregnancy test is arranged live on the show as she may also be knocked up again. This episode might be one of the better ones, so I sit down to enjoy the degradation when a loud knocking from the front door interrupts. It's the police; they have that knock, the one that says power has gone to my head. The famous quote, *'Power tends to corrupt, and absolute power corrupts absolutely'*, is especially apt when it comes to the Derbyshire force. A blue uniform is all it takes, and off they go, speeding ticket pad in hand.

I reluctantly open the door to find two police officers outside, one male and one female. The woman speaks, and I can't help myself as my snap judgement kicks in:

---

1. Height – *five feet nothing tall - too short for me and way too small to be tackling and arresting bank robbers etc. – fail. (I suppose being short is perfect for doling out speeding tickets as you don't have to bend down to talk through the car window)*

2. Age - *I take her to be between 27-35 – pass.*

3. Appearance – *Asian with dark straight black hair tied back in a ponytail. Slim, wearing a minimum of makeup. Uniform not flattering – pass.*

4. Body Art & Accessories - *No sign of a wedding or engagement ring – pass.*

Taser, CS Gas, radio, handcuffs, and truncheon – all fail - apart from the handcuffs, which might be fun. Being a police-woman means she can drink me under the table, which isn't necessarily a bad thing.

Universal Attractiveness Rating System - 7 out of 10, but she gets a 4 point reduction as she may be here to arrest me.

*My eyes take in all this information, sends it to my brain and
a split second later, I have an answer:*
Possible life partner = ~~PASS~~ / FAIL
*Just like that, the policewoman is written out of my future -
unless she does actually arrest me.*

"Peter Walker?" she asks.

For some reason, I get the urge to lie, so much I make up a fake name: Clive Standen. I work out how to get out of the country by renting a boat and sailing over to France and living under my assumed name while eking out a living as a peasant farmer while playing boules and drinking Pernod with the locals. The only trouble is my entire French vocabulary ends at saying, "Une bouteille de limonade, s'il vous plait," that and my name. Not exactly the required language skills for a perfect thirty-year hideout. Law enforcement at the door always makes me uncomfortable, guilty conscience maybe?

"Yes."

"I think you know why we're here, sir?"

I really didn't. "Are you lost, need directions?" Sarcasm comes easily.

She doesn't appreciate my attempt at humour and withdraws her notebook like it's a club and precedes to beat me with it, figuratively, not literally.

"We have received reports of a car belonging to you causing a nuisance. Speeding, playing loud music, honking the horn late at night and revving the engine in a racist manner."

"Sorry, did you say revving my engine in a racist

manner?" A white-hot pain suddenly grips me as I think about the night with the horn.

"Yes, there are families from ethnic backgrounds living in that street, and you are intimidating them with your revving engine. This is a serious accusation."

Shit, this is serious. The police are all over any, even imagined claims of racism with even more fervour than handing out speeding tickets. The trouble is, I have no idea what the hell I'm up to when in one of my fugue states. Cautious now, I remain silent as she continues.

"Do you know the amount of paperwork it would cause if we were to arrest you for racist engine revving?"

I don't but hopefully, a shed load as she brought it up. I shake my head.

"A lot, and we know why you're there. If you have a problem with your car, then take the previous owner to the small claims court, don't sit outside his house, causing a nuisance. Any more of this, and we will have no choice but to arrest you. Do you understand?"

Not really, not a clue to what's going on, but it looks like I will get a pass, so I drop the sarcasm. "Sorry officer, won't do it again."

"Good. Make sure we don't have to return as I won't be as pleasant next time."

I close the door carefully; thankful I'm not spending a night in the cells. If only I knew what was wrong with me. To be honest, I've just stopped thinking about it. The hospital scan was clear; perhaps I am going mad. I stew on this thought as I go back into the kitchen and pour myself a large glass of wine. The sun is over the yardarm somewhere. My lack of knowledge of what a yardarm is doesn't influence the Merlot—it tastes magnificent. The pain in my temple gradually recedes when I get another knock at the door.

"What the hell now?" Stomping through the house, animosity building, ready to tell anybody but the postman to go and have intercourse with themselves, I fling the door open and am surprised to find Maze standing there. I should be annoyed, but I'm secretly pleased. Though she appears distressed, shaking, and red-eyed, covered in…

"Jesus, have you been on a cocaine bender?" I ask as she's completely coated in fine white powder.

She shakes her head in the negative, but I don't believe her. I wet the end of my finger and capture some of the powdery substance, bringing it back to my tongue.

"Don't!" she yells. Too late, an unpleasant flavour fills my mouth. It isn't coke, not that I'm an expert, but I tried it at a party in my youth.

"What the hell is this?"

"It's somebody's mum."

"Sorry, can you repeat that?"

"It's the ashes of somebody's dead mother."

It takes a moment to process this information before I take a slug of wine out of my glass and spit it out past Maze's head in a fine mist.

"Can I?" She takes the offered glass and follows suit. I do hope Kev from neighbourhood watch isn't spying. He's going to spread the rumour that I drink unbelievably rubbish wine, and at ten-thirty in the morning too. Maze drains the rest of the glass in a single gulp.

"How?" I ask.

"Look, can I take a shower? This was the nearest place I could get to; I lost my house key and India isn't back till later. I need to get this off me." She brushes some powder off her shoulder but merely creates a swirling cloud around her head.

Now my phone rings, not the usual tones I set for my friends, the theme from the X-files plays, which is strange as

I once tried to watch an episode and turned it off after a plastic alien appeared. I glance down at the screen. It reads: Head Shrink. As I've never seen this entry before; I'm more than a little intrigued.

"Maze, why don't you run upstairs and take a shower," I say, looking down at her shaking figure. "Upstairs to the left. There are towels are in the drawer."

She runs past me and disappears. I am dying to hear her story, but first, I press answer and cradle the phone to my ear. I've never been one to hold it in front of my chin like a penis extension. It's just so—The Apprentice.

"Hello"

"Peter, glad to catch you," a friendly, well-spoken female voice says. "It's Doctor Summer." I have no idea who that is, but she appears to know me.

"Hi, Doctor Summer," I reply cautiously.

"Just a reminder, you have an appointment at eleven. I only phoned because you missed the last one."

"And how many appointments have we had so far?"

"This will be number six."

My phone contact reads - Head Shrink - so I put 2+2 together and work out I have been seeing a psychiatrist for half a year. I wonder briefly if this voice is lying to me but deep down, I recognise the soothing tone. There is a small chance I may be bat shit crazy.

"Balls," I mutter to myself.

"Sorry?"

"Oh, nothing, Doc, I'll be there." I pause as I realise I don't know where her office is. I have a deep-rooted fear of being sectioned under the mental health act ever since watching 'One Flew Over the Cuckoo's Nest'. Nobody is going to fry my brain; I am quite fond of it the way it is. What should I do?

"Could you give me your postcode again? I've got a new sat-nav in the car." Did that sound natural? Doctor Summer reels it off in a neutral tone and says goodbye. I think I got away with it. Now I have a dilemma. On the one hand, Maze is upstairs showering, and I want to know why I got to taste someone's dead mum, and on the other, I need to know why I'm in therapy. I decide the appointment comes first. Grabbing my jacket and keys, I sprint upstairs to the bathroom. Behind the closed door, my outdated nineties shower chugs away painfully, forcing out the last of my pitiful water pressure.

I knock. "Maze, I'm going out for an hour, but look, why don't you hang around, and we can chat when I get back?"

I wait for a second. "Lock up if you decide to go; there is a spare key by the front door," I shout when no answer is forthcoming.

I rush out to the car and then spend five minutes trying to input the postcode into my car's sat nav. Far from being a simple task, someone has designed it to be a Mensa IQ test, which I fail. It's only after punching the thing twice in frustration that it goes through, and we are off. I get up to ten miles an hour before I hit gridlocked traffic at the first junction and crawl the rest of the way there. Derby City Council's planning department have decided it's a great idea to block both entrances to the Wyvern Retail Park from the A52, which forces all traffic through the City Centre while also having major road works in four different spots. Chaos ensues. I have the idea in my head that most of the Council have Alzheimer's, and instead of coherent planning, they are merely re-enacting the plot to RoboCop they happened to see on the TV last night.

"You have arrived at your destination," the stilted computer voice informs me as I pull into the car park of a large Victorian building. I decide that downloading a Danny Dyer voice over for the sat-nav is now a priority as being referred to as 'Ya' muppet' will make my daily commute so much more bearable. I get the last space of only eight, which front the building. By some miracle, I'm only a few minutes late, and the receptionist directs me down a narrow corridor and into a mini waiting room, none of which are familiar so far. I take a seat on a low-slung black leather chair, all quite tasteful. There is a single door into what I assume is Doctor Summer's office. A small red light off to the right indicates she is in session or having a crafty cigarette break.

Already bored as I've forgotten my phone, I lean over and peruse the magazine collection left out on a small oval coffee table. My suspicious mind wonders if a hidden camera in the ceiling above records your choice and files it away for later use. All the periodicals are at least eighteen months out of date because who can resist reading a copy of PC User with Windows 8 on the front cover? I almost pick up a Cosmopolitan, but Miley Cyrus's annoying tongue stuck out expression puts me off. It's so over-exposed I'm surprised it doesn't have its own Instagram feed. Surely with all those Hannah Montana millions in the bank, she could just retire. Unless Billy Ray spent the lot on stick on ponytails? I grab a Car Mechanics weekly and start thumbing through the pages. I read the article *'How to change the diff on a Ford Mustang'* intently, even though my mechanical skill level on the 0-10 scale is somewhere around minus one million. I have trouble opening the petrol filler cap, but the very act of reading this article makes me feel a whole level of manly man higher. I'm now sure I can fix a broken-down Mustang with only an elastic band and paperclip if required.

A buzzer sounds, and the light next to the door changes from red to green. I stand, ready to walk over when the door opens, and Doctor Summer appears. I now understand why I set the X-files ring tone as she resembles Gillian Anderson from a distance. Closer up, I see she's older by a few years, but still, the resemblance is uncanny. My snap judgement thing doesn't kick in as the Doctor has reached the age women become invisible to me, over fifty. She beckons me through, and I enter her plush office. A thick cream carpet gives it a cosy appearance. She has her work desk set out in the corner and placed to the left is a red leather Chesterfield chair. I'm excited to see a couch on which to lie back on and spill your innermost feelings, just like in all the American movies I've ever watched.

Behind the desk is a framed certificate with her name, followed by a long list of letters indicating all her qualifications. Now I realise I've been here before as the same thought strikes me again, and I wonder if she made them all up. I make the same vow to check to see they are real that I do every time I visit and then completely forget about as soon as I leave.

"Hello, Peter." Her soothing voice fills the air. At £50 per twenty minutes session, it better be worth it; I've just seen her price list on the wall. Typically, you can get this service on the NHS, but the earliest available appointment is in the year 2379. At least I'm talking to a woman; I'd expect a male Doctor to tell me to *man up*.

"You missed our last session, but it's good to have you back. Shall we continue where we left off?" She looks happy to see me; I bet she's imagining me as a crisp £50 note and thinking of a new house extension with a swimming pool annexe.

"Have a seat." She indicates the Chesterfield, but I settle for the couch and lie down, relaxed. Doctor Summer flashes me a patient smile; I guess I always refuse the chair and choose the couch as I feel this is how the American's do it, and they sure do need their therapy.

"Perhaps you would like to have a seat opposite?" she suggests again.

"No, I'm good here." It is so much easier to talk about your emotions if you aren't looking directly at someone.

"So, shall we carry on where we left off?"

I would if I remembered a single minute, now I have a dilemma, I can't say I'm losing time and having blackouts, or she will ship me off to the funny farm.

"I met a woman." As I'm paying a fortune, she can give me dating advice. "I met a woman; I like a lot. We keep bumping into each other more than is normal."

"Are you suggesting she is behind these unusual number of meetings?" She scribbles something in her pad, commenting on my levels of paranoid delusion.

"No, I mean, I think its fate or a weird connection. We seem to run into each other like we are somehow linked. Is this even possible?"

"Do you think this is a possibility, Peter?"

"I'm not sure, maybe. She's not quite like anybody I met before. I thought we were over, but then out of the blue, she showed up this morning, covered in somebody's dead mum. I even took a taste."

Deathly silence meets this announcement, followed by a nervous shuffling; I turn to catch her hand snaking towards an emergency button she has hidden under her desk. I hastily explain that Maze turned up covered in ashes and not dismembered body parts.

"I haven't got the full story yet, but I'm sure there is a simple explanation."

"And did you deem the decision to taste the powder to be a good one?"

"I thought it was coke." I'm not making this sound any better.

"Do you take many illegal substances, Peter?"

"No, it's not what you think. She was all shaky and wide-eyed, head to toe in white powder, I thought she was having a bad time, so I checked to make sure. I haven't taken anything illegal since my late teens." I glance over at the Doctor who's scribbling away in a small notebook; she has a deep frown line above her nose. I guess this isn't the best time to mention my excessive drinking.

"It's good you're meeting new people, healthy, part of your ongoing recovery, though perhaps this woman may be unsuitable. You have had a lot of stress, Peter. Take it slowly."

I nod but then realise she can't see me, so I say, "Sure."

"Shall we go back to the subject of your wife?"

Red hot pain slices through my brain at this sentence, and I grip the couch so hard my fingers go numb.

"Okay." Just saying this one word is the equivalent of running the marathon barefoot over broken glass.

"Now, we have tried this in the past, but I would like to try again. I would like you to repeat back after me the next sentence I say. If this is too difficult, we can try writing it down. I believe this far into treatment, you are ready."

"Okay," I say tentatively, how hard could it be?

"My," she pauses.

"My," I repeat.

"Wife."

A white-hot pains sears through my eye socket, and my vision blurs fades to a pinprick of light. My heart rate shoots up, and I hear the thud of it beating wildly in my chest, "W…" I stumble and try again, "Wi…"

"That's terrific, Peter; you're nearly there." Doctor Summer encourages me.

"Wife," I manage to spit it out—my jaw aches as if I just had a tooth extraction minus anaesthetic.

"Is," she pauses.

Before I say anymore the door to the office explodes inward with some force. And we are interrupted by Wonder Woman who appears to be having a bad day, perhaps having been expelled from the burning man festival for having on a too revealing costume. I don't mean the actual Wonder Woman, that would be weird plus she's not a real person, sorry comic book nerds. The impressive figure strides confidently across the room. She has some of Gal Gadot's features and from my horizontal position appears to tower over six feet tall. Her outfit of black fur boots and tight black leather hot pants accentuate her long muscular legs, the rest of the ensemble consists of a minuscule top of black leather bands, that against all logic keeps her impressive cleavage in place. Whereas Penny is lean and finely muscled from a mainly cardio workout, it is apparent this woman lifts a lot of heavy weights. I have no doubt she would destroy me in an arm wrestle. She notices me staring and with a quick turn of the head appraises and dismisses me all in a split second.

"Lila, I'm currently in session. You will have to wait," Doctor Summer protests.

"I can't wait." Lila turns to me. "You don't mind, do you, Little Man?"

Now, I'm glad of the interruption but don't much like being called 'Little Man'. My gaze automatically drops to my groin area to see if I have suddenly shrunken. Lila carries on.

"Nobody believes I'm a time traveller, and it's getting on my nerves."

I perk up at hearing this. This is going to be one hell of a story. She now sits on the side of the couch, and I scoot over, giving her more room.

"Lila, you need to make an appointment. You can't just burst in whenever you want."

I interrupt, "It's fine; we can carry on next time."

"Well, if you're sure."

I nod and direct my next question to Lila, "How do you travel in time? Do you have a magic sword that can break the space-time dimensional barriers?" I'm intrigued by her outfit, which suggests a sword of power or at least a magical whip. Perhaps I watched too many He-Man cartoons when I was little.

"You're special, aren't you?"

I don't think she means this in a positive way as she turns and gives me a judgemental once over. I shrug, and Doctor Summer chips in, "Look, therapy is private, so I'm going to have to ask you to leave now, Peter."

"Oh, alright." I get up to leave, and Lila takes pity on me, shoving her arm out and showing me her wrist. Sitting there is what appears to be an oversized digital watch.

"I simply punch in the date and press the red button, and it takes me there."

"Cool." While this is no way near as good as a magic sword—I don't let my disappointment show.

"I like the outfit by the way."

"In your dreams, Little Man." This retort brings a smile to my face as I wander back outside to my car and join the slow crawl of traffic home.

———

Thirty minutes later, and I'm back. I open my front door in the grip of trepidation and search for signs of life.

"Maze," I shout.

A crunching sound announces her location, and she appears from the kitchen chewing on a piece of toast. I'm momentarily speechless because she is wrapped in the smallest towel possible, which hugs every contour of her still damp body.

"Hi, there." She stops chewing, and we exchange glances.

"I think you may be wearing one of the tea towels by mistake."

I blush as I make out the nipple piercing I never knew existed but still can't pull my eyes from this tiny piece of cloth that's barely protecting her modesty, mere inches away. She smiles, and I must be dreaming because her hand goes to the tucked in corner and pulls it loose. I follow the towels descent to where it lies by her feet, leaving her glistening naked body before me.

Shit, it's going to happen. That's all my mind keeps telling me as I stand frozen to the spot. Maze's initial confident smile wavers as I stand doing nothing, *do something* I tell myself; the shock wears off. This is happening. I return the smile and step forward. As we are about to embrace, the sole of my foot slips on the puddle of water Maze has dripped all over the wooden flooring. Next, I'm flying backwards, arms flailing for a grip; my right hand connects with Maze's face as I topple back and smash down onto the hard flooring. My universe goes dark.

18

PETE'S STORY - JAPANESE CAR WEEK

S pending time in hospital is one of life's most miserable experiences, but being stuck here at Christmas is intolerable. First off, I imagine all the Doctors are holidaying in Hawaii, playing golf, sipping a Pina Colada, and getting a tan while I lie here bored, staring at the ceiling. Second, staffing is the bare minimum, so instead of a genuine turkey dinner, you get served some inedible rubber monstrosity that has no resemblance to real meat. I spit most of mine into a napkin and throw it secretly into the waste bin. I don't complain as it's all free.

The National Health Service is brilliant, even if rampant corruption is slurping away all its funds. Every pack of painkillers you can buy for twenty pence is costing the nation £13.80, but who am I to fight injustice, especially as I'm so banged up again. I should get a rewards card for staying so often, and I'd be dead already if I were in America, as my insurance would have run out.

This ward is similar to all the others I've previously stayed in, the only difference being the number above the entrance, and the coffee tastes better in this one. By better, I mean one step up from engine oil drinkable. There are four beds, with my roommates being two decrepit old men who keep mentioning the war and an annoying builder called Ray, who finds everything hilarious. My painful attempt to get out of bed and reach the bathroom has him in fits of hysterics as I ease myself gently to the floor and stagger over, every muscle in my body aching. It feels like I spent the last year of my life in Guantanamo Bay being tortured by bored U.S. soldiers, for which Barack Obama somehow got the Nobel Peace Prize. I bet Donald Trump now offers a golf club membership to anybody giving up useful information.

"I bet these two old codgers could race you," Ray bellows in laughter as I again take an eternity to reach the bathroom. I slam the door and stand unsteadily before the toilet, one hand on the metal support and the other messing with my pyjama bottoms. Because of my weakened state I give up and slump down to urinate in the seated position, grateful for a breather. I sigh as nothing comes out, then strain several times, disappointed by the pitiful amount of liquid released; it really wasn't worth the effort required to get here. I finish and rely on the two metal bars on either side to pull myself upright and, after a quick wash of my hands, return to Ray's tiresome banter.

"Mate, I thought you died in there. I nearly got the nurse to organise a search party."

I resist the urge to punch him and sigh miserably as I slide back into bed. My spirits rise as I check the wall clock, the one permanently lit to prevent you from getting any meaningful sleep. It's visiting time any second. The simple pleasure of another persons' company is a beautiful thing. Maze enters the room, punctual as ever.

"That's quite a shiner you got there, love. Has Pete been beating you again?" Ray explodes in laughter. It's the fourth time he's made a variation of the same tired joke. Maze's expression tells me she has had enough.

"Hi." She marches over and picks up his chart from the bottom of the bed. After a careful examination, she stares straight at him in an acting master class. "Ray, I am so sorry," she says and puts it back. After, she sits opposite me on the bed and winks. I struggle to keep a straight face as a range of emotions play over Ray's face, and when he can't contain himself any longer, he gets up and runs off frantically looking for a Doctor to tell him what's wrong.

"Now that wasn't very nice. Remind me never to get on your bad side." I laugh and immediately wish I hadn't as pain racks my body.

"The guy is a dick. What does he find so hilarious all the time?"

"No idea. Your eye is looking better, though." She has disguised the bruise with a layer of makeup, but the deep black colouring still shows through slightly. "Your parents do believe I didn't hit you on purpose, don't they?"

"Of course. Dad would have murdered you otherwise."

"A comforting thought."

"Hey, they like you. They're mad at me for nearly killing you. So, when are you getting out?"

"A few more days, they are insisting on another MRI, but the machine's been down for repairs, and the backlog is huge."

Another visitor arrives. The impressive figure of Jace enters the room.

He grins. "How's the hero feeling today?" he says and presents me with what looks like a mini florist shop of pink and red flowers.

The last time I saw a bunch this big, I had forgotten an anniversary, and my credit card was buying me out of sleeping in the spare room. I smile, remembering another occasion when I accidentally let my wife know the real feelings I harboured towards her favourite outfit. The memory of her indignant pained expression when I said it and then my own fallen features when I realised the hell about to be unleashed makes me laugh out loud.

Maze stares over inquisitively. "What are you smiling about?"

"I was..." A sharp pain erupts in my left temple and thuds through my head with all the panache of a learner driver trying to reverse park, causing me to close my eyes. "It was… a memory, no it's gone." I shake my head. "No, can't remember a thing. Strange, it was so vivid and now nothing."

Jace places his bouquet on the bedside cabinet, where it overhangs the edges. "There you go, hero. A bit of colour to brighten this dreary place."

"I'm hardly a hero. I fell over and hit my head, again. That makes me a bit of a joke."

"No, it doesn't, honey." He grabs a thin plastic visitor chair and sits by my side. It creaks and flexes under his substantial frame but doesn't break.

"Thanks for coming guys, but you didn't have to visit on Christmas day. Go spend some time with your family." I know Maze's parents are in Mexico, but I think her sister is with her husband nearby.

Everybody is being so pleasant; I can't wait to visit my local branch of NatWest and ask for a statement so the staff can treat me like a pariah. Jace stays for the next twenty minutes making small talk.

"Now, are you two going to go out on a date? I can't stand seeing this much pent-up tension in a room."

"As soon as Pete gets released," Maze replies.

"I'm glad to hear it." He seems genuinely pleased.

"Something safe, the cinema?" I suggest.

"Movies," she corrects me incorrectly, "you make it sound like we're going to see Ben-Hur in CinemaScope." I happen to like Ben-Hur, the Charlton Heston original, not the abysmal remake, but now is not the time to mention it.

"How did you get so dragged up in your million-pound mansion with Olympic sized swimming pool add-on?" I say just to annoy her. "Get home-schooled?"

She doesn't answer, which is unlike her, and then I get it. "You went to private school, didn't you? I bet it was all dreadfully jolly hockey sticks?" An angry thunderstorm builds on her face; I sit back, smirking. "Did you meet any of the Royals?"

"Dick." She hits my legs through the bedsheet.

I give a false wince in pain, then sit back with an even bigger grin on my face.

"Now you two behave, play nice, or I'll bang your heads together."

We both laugh, and Maze takes my hand. "Will do, Jace."

"Okay, take care, you pair." Visit over, he leaves us to it.

"So, what do you want to see?" I ask Maze.

"Oh, the new Avengers film in 3D."

I groan inwardly. Not another sci-fi piece of crap that's all action and no story, which she loves so much.

"Sure, let's do that." I force a weak smile. This must be love. We are alone again, well apart from the two uncon-scious patients who may or may not be deceased.

"So?" Maze says, standing in front of me, her hand tenderly touching the side of my face.

"I—" We get rudely interrupted as my best mate Dave bursts into the ward.

"Got you some por—" He abruptly sticks a magazine

behind his back as he sees I'm not alone. "Er, a Top Gear magazine."

"Do they normally feature a nude oriental woman on the front?" Maze raises her eyebrows questioningly and stands there, hand on hip.

"It's Japanese car week. There's an article on the new Supra."

"Well, I guess I will leave you to it, don't injure your wrist, staring at all those vehicles." Maze laughs and leaves us to it. I wait until she's out of the room.

"Dave, mate."

"Sorry, I didn't realise you had company." He throws the magazine over; I wince in pain as I lean over to grab it and quickly hide it as a nurse arrives to take my blood pressure for what must be the hundredth time today.

Dave perks up as the young woman straps the blood pressure cuff around my arm. "You know you shouldn't wear makeup; it's messing with perfection."

I can't quite believe he said that.

She giggles. "You're a cheeky one, aren't you?"

I now realise he's pulled again. A couple more outrageous lines later, and the nurse passes him her phone number. As she disappears back into the ward, I stare at him.

"What? I can't be affable while visiting my ill friend?" He pretends I have hurt his feelings.

"Are you chatting up nurses on every visit?"

"Of course not." He nods the opposite.

"Dave, I'm ill."

"Yes, but life is short. I don't understand why you're not getting some sympathy shags; you are practically living here."

I'm envious of Dave's simple view of life. Why can't I be

more like him? My mobile phone chooses this point to meow from the side of the bed.

"Want me to get that for you?"

"No, it's my sister."

"She's worried about you. Talk to her."

I'm being childish, but I don't care; Dave gives me his hangdog expression.

"Okay, next time she phones," I reluctantly agree.

"Good, now when are you getting out?"

"Another few days."

"Have you seen the movie Unbreakable?"

I nod. Who hasn't?

"Maybe that's you, hear me out. You survived a terrible fire as a kid, several accidents and knocks to the head. You are unbreakable; maybe you should become a vigilante and fight crime."

"Seriously, you want me to don a cape and a pair of tights and tackle criminals. Have you been drinking today?"

"Yes, started at nine. Christmas is brilliant, isn't it? The only day you can start early and not get judged." He stares down at where my legs are positioned under the sheet. "Nobody wants to see you in tights, mate. But give it a thought."

"Dave, I've got a secret."

"Are you a cross-dresser? Sorry about the crack about your legs. I'm sure you look great in heels."

"No, don't be stupid."

"Thank God for that. You had me worried then. Mate, you would make one hideous looking bird."

I decide not to take offence, even though I'm sure I would make a semi-attractive female. "No, there is something that I've been keeping to myself. I've been seeing a psychiatrist." I pause, expecting laughter or some retort about manning up.

Dave looks pensive. "I've known for a while, with every-thing…" he can't think of the right thing to say and leaves it there. There is an awkward silence between us, so I try to lighten the tone.

I met somebody there, a woman, Lila. She thinks she can travel in time. She might be perfect for you."

"What does she look like?"

"Unusual, tall with long muscular legs, impressive arm muscles too and well stacked up top. Long black flowing hair. Pretty in a certain way but tough-looking, I wouldn't have messed with her, and oh, she wasn't wearing very much at all."

"Exactly, how much?" Dave is intrigued.

"Well, leather hot pants and furry boots and a bondage-style top comprised of only a couple of thin leather straps. I guess she must get cold out." I wonder if I imagined the whole thing.

"Was she hot? Say Xena Warrior Princess fit, or does she look like someone on the Russian woman's shot-put team who may have previously pissed standing up?"

"You watched Xena?" I thought I knew everything about Dave.

"Well, sort of. I was waiting for some hot lesbian action. Not that I ever got any. False advertising. Now answer the question."

"She was all woman." I try to remember what Xena looked like but can't remember having never seen it. "She's like an Olympic athlete, tall and powerful who likes to weight train and could snap you in half if she wanted." I realise my description is rubbish, and try again, "She was hot, just the right side of muscle versus I have now taken so many steroids that l now resemble the incredible hulk with a beard." I leave it at that.

"And why didn't you give her my number?"

"Seriously, Dave, you're interested? What about the bit where she believes she's a time traveller? That might not be her only issue."

"Well, we all have our flaws, and I've got a brick wall in my garden that I've been planning to demolish. It sounds like Lila could give me a hand."

I'm unsure how Dave's mind works sometimes.

"Why don't you go out with her?" he suggests.

"Maze. I think she might mind."

"You know it doesn't count if they don't find out? Now repeat after me - do you believe in love at first sight, or should I walk by again?"

"What, you want me to give her a cheesy chat-up line?"

"Definitely, that line is an extra sharp cupid's arrow—use it at your own risk."

We are interrupted again, this time by an older nurse who tuts at me when she spots Dave's porn magazine peeping out from under the covers where I hid it earlier.

"It's got an article on the new Toyota Supra."

She shakes her head, disappointed.

19

PETE'S STORY - UTILITY BELT

I rub my eyes long and hard. "Could you repeat that?" I swear a school-kid is waving his fountain pen at me. Through the gloom and my current bout of vertigo, it's difficult to tell.

"I ain't fucking kidding mate, gimme your money, or I'll stick you good."

Why I'm standing in a dark alley at night is a mystery. Then it comes to me; I am wearing my all-black outfit with matching leather gloves, another blackout. The schoolboy seems to have morphed into Daniel Radcliffe wearing a pair of round glasses. I step back as he now waves a wand dangerously close to my face.

"Harry, get that out of my face before I stick it up your Expellianus." My head is throbbing, and I feel drunk, but not in the good way. I don't have time for this crap.

"You think I'm kidding, bruv." He steps forward, his wand magically slicing open my stomach.

We stand staring at each other for a second before I realise Daniel is no longer wearing glasses and is now sporting a swallow neck tattoo, and his wand is actually an evil-looking knife. I touch the wound with my hand, blood staining the fingertips of my glove. My rather fetching black roll-neck top is ruined, and I have no idea where I buy them from. My annoyance turns to fear as the increasing pain breaks through my fugue state.

"Gimme your wallet, bruv, last chance." He stands to his full height of five feet nothing and waves the blade about menacingly. Dirty tracksuit bottoms and an ill-fitting Adidas top swamp his emaciated figure.

Patting my pockets, I discover I haven't brought it out, not even my mobile phone to pacify him with. Now I'm in trouble. I hold my hands up in a surrender gesture. "Sorry, kid, but I have nothing on me. I wasn't expecting to get mugged."

He edges closer; knife held out.

"Perhaps I can send you a cheque? Give me your name and address, and I'll post it out first thing, promise." His scowling expression informs me he's not overly enamoured by my offer. "Hey, take my watch; it's all I have." I unclip it and dangle it in front of his face.

"What the hell am I gonna do with a bleeding Seiko? That wouldn't even buy me a bag of chips? You're dead, mate."

Would you like to know what your last thoughts are, just before you die? Luckily, I don't have time for any as out of the darkness strides a superhero. One I have met before.

My mugger turns and waves his blade. "What do you want cu—"

His sentence is cut short as a fist mashes his nose. I wince at the cracking sound and blink as blood flies everywhere. He staggers back, knife temporally forgotten as he makes an ill-judged attempt to pull it back from its now squashed position against his cheek. "You bit—"

A knee to the stomach expels all air and maybe a rib bone

or two from his lungs. Now doubled over, a powerful leg clad in furry boot stamps down on his kneecap; a sideways blow. A high pitch squeal accompanies the unnatural angle of the appendage as my mugger falls to the floor crying, snot, phlegm, and tears covering his mangled features.

"Take that," I mutter under my breath. My saviour in the same outfit as before is the woman I'd met briefly at my therapist's.

"Hi, Lila, nice to see you again."

She shakes her head. "I can't leave you alone for five minutes, can I, Little Man?" She kneels and takes the lock knife from the mugger's twitching fingers. Wiping it clean on his soiled top, she folds it closed and slides it down the inside of her left boot.

"Hey, he's a little man. I'm six foot tall. It's just… he had a big knife." Now I remember he cut me. "Jesus, he stabbed me. I think I'm dying." My body's adrenaline has numbed the pain, which is fast returning.

"Don't be such a baby. I bet it's a paper cut."

"I'm done for, you need to get me to a hospital."

"Let me take a look." She walks over and pushes me back against the alleyway wall. Kneeling, she examines the wound.

"You know I would normally get bought a drink first."

My quip is met with silence, then excruciating pain as Lila probes the cut. "It's nothing; I can fix this."

I glance down, worried. "Maybe take me to the hospital."

She pulls my roll-neck half-up, exposing my stomach. "Hold this."

I place my hand over the bloodied garment and strain to see what's happening.

Lila gets a tube of something out of her hot pants. Has she got a utility belt on there like Batman?

I feel the warmth of some sort of liquid applied to the

wound. "Now, place your fingers here." Lila guides my free hand down. "Count down from five slowly."

"Why?"

"Just do it."

I frown. "Five, four, three, two, one."

Lila stands up. "All good, Little Man."

"The name's Pete." My voice echoes loudly down the alleyway. "Pete," I repeat in a whisper, afraid somebody is listening.

Lila smirks. "You're fine, Little Man."

"Was that antiseptic cream?"

"Superglue."

I pause. "Sorry, can you repeat that because I think I heard you say superglue?"

"Yes, you heard correctly, superglue."

"Lila, I'm not an eighty-four piece Airfix model." I panic and bend my neck to examine my makeshift emergency adhesive surgery.

"What? It's sorted, all fixed."

"Jesus, get me to the hospital; I may need an operation."

Lila slaps me lightly across the cheek. "Calm down, you're fine, and you know we can't go, not with the police searching for us."

I thought I heard a distant police helicopter in the background, the rhythmic thud of rotor blades spinning in the darkness, quite a familiar background noise in this city.

"Lila, what did you do?"

"What did I do?" She pokes me in the chest with her finger. "What did I do? Mr I get a lot more interesting when changed into my all-black outfit with matching gloves. Mr lets get a car and tear up and down a side street, pulling doughnuts, terrifying the neighbours before crashing into somebody's front garden and killing their entire gnome collection. Then sticking a rag into the fuel tank, lighting it with your cigarette, and watching it explode. What did I do?"

I knew there was a weird taste in my mouth; I don't smoke. I cover my eyes with my hand, hoping this is all a dream. "I crashed my Porsche and set it on fire. Jesus, the police will be at my house waiting to arrest me."

"Of course, you didn't."

"No." I stare at her through the gaps in my fingers. "No?" I say again.

"No, we stole a car. I thought that's why you're wearing gloves, no DNA evidence."

"Stole a car," I repeat. "Wait, I have no idea how to steal a car."

Lila shrugs. "I have some skills."

"I can tell." I glance at the poor bastard groaning on the floor. Unsure what to do next, I decide to level with my accomplice. After all, she thinks she can travel in time. Who's she to judge? "Lila, um, this might sound strange, but I have been losing track of time recently. I don't remember this." I indicate my outfit. "I remember nothing about today if this still is today."

"That explains a lot," she steps close and stares directly into my eyes, "you really don't have a clue, do you?"

"That's what I just said." I pull my top down, prying my fingers loose from the glue.

"Let's get a drink, and I'll fill you in on our adventure. You're paying."

The phrase adventure fills me with dread. "I don't have any money on me."

She holds up my credit card; there must be some sort of utility belt on those hot pants.

Ten minutes later, we are in a private booth in one of the town's quieter pubs. I'm paranoid everybody sees my bloodied top, but in reality, people are admiring Lila's figure in her skimpy barely there bondage-inspired outfit. Few of the regulars will have seen someone like Lila in here before. The usual clientele typically sports a beer belly and full Gandalf beard. I understand it's in the CAMRA requirements for full membership. I take a swallow of my Grolsch lager and sit back to enjoy the ice-cold liquid's effects. My vision swims, and I close my eyes, relaxed at last.

"So, go for it. What exactly did we do today?" I sit back, trying to get comfortable.

Lila has three drinks before her, and she pushes them around, deciding which one to down first. The double gin and tonic, bottle of Desperados or a pint of real scrumpy cider, resplendent with floating bits of God knows what? This being a real ale pub, I received a lecture when purchasing the drinks and a '*why not try a pint of Old Slapper*' instead of my mass-produced beverage. You'd have thought I'd shagged the barman's mum by the look I get when I insisted on my Grolsch. Why sell it if they don't want you to purchase one? She goes with the gin and takes a sip. "Well, I bumped into you at Doctor Summer's place, I was coming out of a session, and there you were. Looking all sad and pathetic."

"Yes, don't sugarcoat any of it for me."

"Anyway, you asked if I had broken the fifth dimension with my sword of power recently?" Lila reprimands me with a firm raise of her perfectly sculptured eyebrows.

I decide not to smirk, especially as she can snap me in half with minimum exertion.

"Sorry, that was a dick thing to say."

"Yes, it was, but you looked all sad and pathetic, so I

didn't hit you. Instead, I offered to take you on an adventure, and we went into the future."

She now has my full attention.

"I set my time travel device," she holds out her arm displaying the oversize digital watch type bracelet, "not sword of power, then we jumped five, then ten and finally forty years into the future."

"What marvels did we experience?" My interest is piqued.

"Absolutely none. Nothing at all. It is exactly the same backwards shit hole city. Why do you even live here? I'm only here because I'm hiding," her voice lowers, now barely a whisper, "from the Time Bureau, what's your excuse?"

"The Time Bureau?" I know I shouldn't feed Lila's delusion, but I'm intrigued.

She drains the bottle of Desperados in an impressively short time. "The time police, they oversee the rooting out of illegal time travellers. Now I know little about them apart from they dress all in black, and recently," she leans forward conspiratorially, "they might have come up with a way to track me."

I move closer, my voice low, "What like those two at the bar?"

"Which two?"

I point at the pair of dark-suited characters who just walked in. "Them." I turn back, and Lila is gone. Vanished completely. I scan the entire bar. Where the hell did she go so fast? And she still has my credit card. I take her pint of scrumpy as a consolation prize and take a long gulp, not bad. The two figures walk over, both men, both identically attired in black suits, black shirt plus tie and of course black shoes. I don't dwell on thoughts of underwear. The lead male, who appears to be around forty, stops right in front of our table.

They don't have any drinks, which is odd; only what looks like some sort of iPad with an antenna attached. It hums as he passes it over Lila's vacant seat. They both look questioningly at me.

"You should try a pint of Old Slapper; I hear it's excellent."

20

MAZE'S STORY - FOUR-POSTER BED

As I stumble along, trailing behind lost like an abandoned trophy wife at a posh golf club, desperately in search of the only set of ladies' toilets, I take the opportunity to check out Pete's rear. He has a fine pair of calf muscles on show, plus his tight shorts hug every curve with each long stride. I resist the urge to ask again if he's feeling okay. After his recent hospital visit, he finds my concerned questions increasingly annoying and now refuses to discuss the topic at all.

The sun's heat beats down on us relentlessly, almost as if somebody up there is looking out for me. Personally, I put it all down to global warming. Getting such a scorching day in winter is unheard of, and I hear the constant murmur of complaints from all around.

"It's too hot," moan a nearby middle-aged couple as I take a misstep and nearly end up in the man's arms.

"Sorry." I again regret the decision to wear my high heels. How was I supposed to know that our second official date would be a day out in York? Home of the worst street surfaces in existence.

"It is a bloody shambles," I mumble under my breath as I navigate the narrow cobbled street, all the while ducking left and right out of the way of a hoard of smiling photo mad Japanese tourists. Try living here is all I can think. That would wipe the grin off your face. I am feeling claustrophobic in the crowd and weirded out by all the happiness. Maybe the Japanese are all high on a secret happy pill; I wish the NHS could get some in quick sharp.

"Photo, please." I get a mobile phone thrust in my hands for perhaps the eighth time today by an excited pair of teenagers who seem to have recently discovered girl power by the state of their clothes, though I do quite like the pink tutu which I'm sure I could work into a cute outfit. I snap a couple of shots and hand the phone back. I also love the fact that I'm no longer the shortest person in the room or street. My heels propel me skywards, and I get a Godlike feeling of power just being able to see over the top of people's heads.

"You Hugh Grant, Four Weddings and Funeral?" My new, excitable friends jump up and down and touch Pete's arm as he makes an appearance, fearing he lost me in the crowd. He doesn't quite know what to make of this and stands there dumbfounded for a second.

"Thank you." He says, and the girls snap a few photos of him and run off giggling.

"Hi, Hugh," I say with a smirk firmly in place.

"You know what that makes you?"

I shake my head. "What?"

"An extremely short Andie MacDowell."

I'm pleased for a second until I realise she must be about eighty by now.

"Hey, do all white people look the same to them, the racist little shitbags? And what's with the manic cheerfulness? You'd think having your country nuked would put you in a bad mood."

"I'd be happy if they levelled Derby," Pete replies, "Mind you, all that would be left along with the radioactive cockroaches would be glow in the dark mamba addicts and some corrupt politicians." He laughs. "It's a good job I'm not running for Prime Minister. That would be my first order."

I take Pete by the arm, only half to steady myself. "I think you would make a great leader of our nation."

"Really? Have you been on the vodka already? What about the B word?"

I secretly check my breath, worried he can smell the few drinks I had to settle my nerves earlier on. Nothing, he must be joking. "What B word?"

He gives me a look and raises his eyebrows.

"Oh, Brexit." It has as much chance of happening as repeating Candyman five times in a row and expecting a visit from Mr stumpy hook bee face.

I say it under my breath just to tempt fate, "Brexit, Brexit, Brexit, Brexit, Brexit." There, said it, now I hope Candyman hasn't misheard and tries to stick his stump where it shouldn't go, at least without a lot of lube, or even worse, that Australian millionaire dickhead who likes to walk his girlfriends on dog leads makes an appearance.

Pete stares down at my heels. "So, are you ready for the three-mile walk around the wall?"

"You're kidding? I'm lucky I haven't tripped and broken my leg. No way am I hiking up and down a crumbling wall."

"It's supposed to have exceptional views."

I change the subject in the only way possible. "Hey over there," I point, "a shop that only sells things with cats on them. You want to go in, don't you?"

"No." He shakes his head, but I can see the excitement grow in his eyes.

"Come on." I drag him inside, to be accosted by the most immense amount of feline related tat I have ever seen. Pete offers to buy me a hat with a cat motif, but even I can't find a suitable outfit for that. As I'm dragged around three floors, I soon regret the decision to come inside. After about an hour, we finally leave with Pete having bought a cushion with a Sphynx cat emblazoned on it.

"It's a present for Mr Tiddles," he insists.

I'm not overly fond of Pete's cat because he seems to have taken a dislike to me and hides completely whenever I appear. I have yet to set eyes on the elusive little bugger.

"Shall we get something to eat?" I really mean drink. I am absolutely gagging for a beer as it's nearly 1 p.m. "Somewhere near, I can't walk in these shoes."

"Maze, I thought you would wear your trainers. You practically live in them, anyway."

"Well, I didn't know you would surprise me with a day trip to York. I wanted to be all sultry and feminine for you."

"That's great, but you won't to be very ladylike, face down on the floor with people trampling all over you. Come on." He grabs my hand and drags me into a small boutique shop, and I am instantly in heaven—faced with row upon row of Converse trainers in every colour imaginable. Christmas has come early. After careful consideration, I pick a pair of high tops (white with pink laces and matching roses on the side). I'm thinking of that tutu outfit again. Pete blanches as the bill comes to £69.99 at the till. I give him a kiss on the cheek as he hands his credit card over.

"You know you can buy these for a fiver in Primark?"

"No, you can't. These are quality." I slip off my heels,

putting them carefully in the box and then fasten up my new trainers; they fit like a glove. That's better. I can walk again.

Happy now, I demand we find somewhere to eat, and we end up in the Valhalla bar. It has a strange mix of customers, rammed full of huge beer-bellied biker types in leather and denim, and tourists from all around the world. We get two pints of pilsner and a bag of crisps to share and sit down at the only available seat opposite an ancient couple. The old man has a two-foot-long camera on a strap around his neck. Hearing their accent, I say, "Are you two Ame—" only to be interrupted by Pete. "So, where are you guys from?"

"Montreal," the old man says. So, I was right; they are American.

"Are you wholesome youngsters from the Great Britain?"

"Well, technically, we are from England," Pete says.

"We just love this place; we are off to the Edinburgh next and then the city of Wales. We are going to that place they filmed the Prisoner in."

"Portmeirion, it's beautiful there. Plenty to photograph."

I wonder if he intends to take me there, as I've never been. I make a mental note to wear more appropriate footwear. We stay in the pub for another pint, and I feel happily intoxicated as soon as we leave and hit the fresh air.

"So, when do we have to drive back?" I ask, not wanting our date to end.

"Well, I sort of booked us a hotel for the night, if you want that is?"

A wave of excitement shoots through me. "And does this hotel have matching twin beds?"

Pete blushes, "Um, it has a huge four-poster bed."

I stand right up close and stare upwards at him. "And what are we going to be doing in this enormous bed?" I smile as he goes an even deeper shade of red.

"Oh, that." I take his hot and sticky hand. "Perhaps we should go and test the mattress out, you know, just to make sure it's the right firmness."

It turns out to be perfect, so comfy that we end up staying an extra two days while hardly leaving the room at all.

21

PETE'S STORY - BROKEN MIRROR

Three months is the golden zone for any relationship when your other half is the most beautiful and perfect human being in the universe. They can do no wrong, nothing whatsoever. It is difficult to be this flawless, and most normal people can only keep this façade in place for twelve weeks max. I have kept mine in place for barely seven weeks so far. February is here, along with a respite in Britain's freezing weather. Like a melting iceberg, the first cracks have appeared in our perfect relationship. You can tell when we aren't getting on because I use her actual name *'Helen'* in my superior tone, and she refers to me as *'twat face'* in her whiny voice. They say familiarity breeds contempt, and we have been living in each other's pockets ever since I got released from the hospital. It all started with an argument about leaving the toilet seat lid up, strangely directed at Maze and not myself and snowballed into something more.

"Maze, can you put the toilet seat down?"

"Sure." She mostly ignores me while stuffing crisps into her face while watching some rubbish sci-fi show on Netflix.

"Maze," I say again, leaning over and pausing the television.

"Hey, I'm watching that." She stares over, biting her lower lip, annoyed.

"Seriously, why do you waste your time on that piece of crap? Spock has a beard. When was that a thing? It makes no sense."

"Hey, we can't all series link Grantchester. I like sci-fi. You should give it a try."

I go back to my original complaint. "You can't keep leaving the lid up."

"Why the hell not?"

She gets all defensive, so I try a different tack. "The cat might fall in and drown," I speak slowly as if to a little kid.

"Why is he retarded?"

I grind my teeth before continuing, "No, Mr Tiddles is a clever little Sphynx, but if he slips, he might get stuck and drown in there. It's got a soft close lid, so can you just put it down?"

"I hate to break it to you, but your cat has run away." Maze switches her television show back on.

A white-hot pain pulses through my brain, so all-consuming that I can't speak for a second. I grab the remote and switch the TV off.

"My cat hasn't run off; he just has good taste and avoids you."

"Pete, I haven't seen or heard him once in all the time I have known you." A concerned expression crosses her features.

"How about last night when he went mad on his wheel?" I refer to the unbelievably expensive, one-metre giant hamster wheel for cats that cost more than my first car.

Maze shrugs guiltily.

"Please tell me you didn't go on the cat wheel, Helen?" I pointedly use her real name.

"Well, it looked fun. I only had one spin before I fell off."

"It's not a toy, and you probably broke it."

"Are you saying I'm fat?" Voices are raised as we face-off over the remote control like it's the demilitarised zone.

"Well, you have put on a few pounds." I stare at her flat stomach just to annoy her. It works, and World War III ensues, as we have our first significant row. Of course, I eventually apologise and say everything was, is, and will always be my fault.

Later, as we lie in bed, Maze snoring loudly like a wounded animal, my thoughts go to Mr Tiddles. I don't recall him sitting on my knee recently. In fact, the last time I saw him was… I'm not even sure. Maze's aspersion that he ran off months ago keeps hitting me in the face like a rather unpleasant school bully.

Now unable to sleep, I slip out of bed and go hunting for my missing feline. Mr Tiddles is not in his favourite basket or hidden under the settee, nor in a random box I left lying around for him. I check the expensive cat tree he refused even to sit on, much preferring to play with the packaging. My cat is nowhere to be found. I search the final place he might be, high up on the kitchen cupboards where he knows he's not allowed like I have any choice, nothing again. Opening his food cupboard, I notice it is crammed with tins, hundreds of them, all unopened and stacked one upon the other, filling it to the brim. They tumble out and spill over the floor, one rolling past my foot. My heart rate slows, I shiver, a red filter drops over my vision as I stare at the little circular tin hitting the opposite wall. A strange smile erupts onto my face like it received a texted emoji, as I fade ghost-like into myself.

The rumble of the car engine draws me back to reality as I glance down at my leather-clad gloved hands, which grip the steering wheel tightly, and I realise where I'm heading. Excitement and dread fill me in equal measure. *Is this the time?* On the seat next to me is a thing of beauty, the magnum revolver, a bleak instrument of death waiting for me to use her, calling out to me. My breathing slows as I make a right turn and, to my horror, find that the road is closed for construction work. A glowing neon sign on wheels blocks my way. It reads *open at six*. Then it wavers like a heat-induced mirage in the desert and changes to, *Don't do it!* I smash my hands against the wheel ineffectively, biting my tongue in rage, the iron taste of blood filling my mouth.

"Where have you been?"

I pause, realising Maze is asking me a question. I stare at my surroundings, puzzled; I'm back home in the living room. Maybe I was dreaming, but my black outfit suggests otherwise.

"Nowhere," I lie.

"Really, then why are you dressed like that? Are you seeing another woman? I think it's about time we talk about this." She pushes past me and pulls open the bureau drawer. "Pete, why do you have a gun?"

I scan the interior. "What? There is nothing in there; it's empty."

"That's what you're going with."

I nod because it is, apart from a couple of petrol receipts, some loose change, and an old Nokia charger from the previous decade.

"Well, how about now?" Maze stands before me in a purposeful two-handed arm's outstretched pose.

"Have you been taking mime classes? Is that why you have a beret in your wardrobe? You're standing there holding nothing. Can we go to bed now? I just went for a drive; I don't need an argument."

"Seriously, you aren't going to discuss this?" Her still empty hands sag as if she's holding something heavy.

"I'd ask for a refund of your tuition fees if I were you."

She points towards the wall. "Well, how can I do this?"

An explosive blast deafens me as blinding smoke fills the room, stinging my eyes. Maze is shocked, and I stare at the gun that has appeared in her hands as if by magic. I see it now, a monster of a weapon gripped in her trembling fingers. My vision blurs as she splits into two, then three separate people, all standing there in stunned surprise. White-hot pain explodes in my head as my life fractures into pieces like a broken mirror.

22

PETE'S STORY – 5 YEARS AGO – LONDON

D ave paws at his shirt collar. "Is this too small?"

"No, it's fine, and you look very Bond." That's if James were several stones over-weight as Dave's cummerbund is protruding an extra few inches from under his jacket.

"How did you talk me into this?"

"I said you would enjoy the culture."

"No, I remember, you promised me posh totty. Now, where are they? These old bags are all around ninety and dried up. This isn't an interval; it's the menopause." He laughs at his own joke.

Dangling the carrot of upper-class women was my only way of getting Dave to agree to dress up and accompany me to the ballet. We booked a hotel and travelled down to London by train for the weekend. Derby is too backward for anything more than panto, plus the Council are up to their old tricks, and after a small fire at the Assembly Rooms—Derby's premier entertainment venue is permanently closed. While I could repair the place for fifty quid, the five million insurance pay-out has already disappeared.

"An attractive woman." I nudge Dave, and his head swivels around. "Well, what do you think?"

He gives her the once over. Mine and Dave's opinion on women differ. Whereas I see an alluring older woman in her forties, reeking of wealth and privilege, wearing a floor-length figure-hugging dress that is sexy but classy, Dave's answer shows his different view.

"Still a bit menopausal, but I'll give her a go. Let me think of an appropriate chat-up line." He uses his razor-sharp memory to search through his list, no google required for him. Now, if he'd only remember to pay me back that twenty pounds I lent him.

"Got it, now experience the master in action." Pulling himself up to his full height, he marches straight over and delivers his line. It works as she laughs, and they continue chatting. The man is a pulling God; he really should do a TED talk on the subject.

As I take a sip of my overpriced champagne and peruse the foyer, my eyes lock with a beautiful woman only a few metres away, her piercing eyes, one bright blue and the other soft green stare right back at me. She gives me a slight smile before glancing away to continue talking to her friend. My snap judgement kicks straight in with automatic passes. I find out later her heterochromia isn't real as one of her blue coloured contact lenses fell out, and her bust is also enhanced with an extremely effective push-up bra. Even her height is exaggerated with a massively high pair of heels, but by the time I find these things out, it's already way too late as shortly, I will be completely in love with this woman.

Taking a calming breath, I try to remember all the pulling advice Dave has given me over the years, and the first thing is you have twenty seconds after eye contact to make a move. Valuable time is wasted thinking about the reason why. Down to fifteen seconds. What should I say? Easy chat up lines aren't me, or should I try one? Dave claims a ninety percent success rate, shit down to ten seconds, it's now or never.

Taking a swift gulp of champagne, I stroll over as casually as one can in these situations. She senses my approach and smiles as I step up to her and her friend, who's just about invisible to me. I'm going to go with a line I once heard, but my mind suddenly goes blank, and if I don't speak now, I will look like a weirdo. *Say Something.*

"Hi, I'm Pete. I hope you don't mind me introducing myself." Shit, blown it. What the hell was that? Dave will be so disappointed. I'm going to have to scuttle off and hide out of sight for the rest of the night, but no, wait, it's okay.

"Emily," the beautiful woman I'm talking to introduces herself, "and this is my friend Rachel."

She offers me her hand, which for a second I nearly shake but kiss lightly instead. After all, we are dressed up to the nines, drinking champagne at the ballet. I have gone up two class levels merely by being here. Emily seems pleased, and I carry on trying to impress.

Dave's voice echoes in my head with dating advice, '*complement her*'.

'That's the most amazing dress you're wearing,' I almost say, but Dave's voice comes in again, '*don't alienate the friend, bad idea. Always think threesome*'.

"You are both wearing the most amazing dresses."

Dave's voice sounds again in my head, '*After the initial complement, tone it down unless they are utter scrubbers, then go for it with any filth you like.*'

"What do you think of the ballet?" Emily strikes me as a classy lady. We chat casually, as I desperately try to appear calm, and collected even though I have butterflies in my stomach and a lump lodged in my throat.

Dave now appears. I guess it didn't go too well with his forty-year-old, so I introduce him, and he works out the woman who has my interest straight away.

Looking Rachel directly in the eyes, he comes out with another line, "That's a beautiful dress. Can I talk you out of it?" It sounds so natural when he says it, and she laughs. Our limited time together goes painfully quickly as the end of the interval buzzer sounds, and people start returning to their seats.

"Would you like to go for a drink after?" I ask hopefully, fearing my world will end if she says no. She briefly converses with her friend.

"We would love that. Meet you in the lobby after." She kisses me on the cheek, and we watch them walk away.

"You have a stupid look about you."

Immediately, I force the enormous grin off my face. "I don't know what you mean."

"So, what colour hair does Rachel have?"

"Blonde," I guess incorrectly.

Dave shakes his head at me. "You're in love, I can tell."

"Rubbish, she's pretty, that's all. Are you okay with going for a drink after?"

"Sure, Rachel has huge norks. I'm more than happy to take one for the team, but you need to calm down. Next thing, you'll be asking for her hand in marriage."

"Don't be so stupid."

A few months later.

My freshly purchased engagement ring is trying to burn a hole through the thin material of my trouser pocket. I know it's in my imagination, but I swear I can feel the heat radiating off it. Now I understand how Gollum felt in the Hobbit. Brushing a bead of sweat off my forehead, I think, *what's the worst that can happen?* The thought she might say no terrifies me. My thumb brushes against the single one-carat diamond; I hope it's the perfect size. Now I worry it will look too small. What is she thinks it's too big and ostentatious? Would any woman say it's too enormous, probably not? I try to clear my mind by breathing deeply and counting to ten. It helps, but Dave's voice keeps interrupting my thoughts.

"*You're mad. Why ruin a good thing? The only thing marriage does is destroy your sex life and bank account.*"

Cheers, Dave. I knew I could count on you for advice. That had been a few days ago, but here I am about to propose, anyway. Checking my hair to make sure it's perfect, I do a quick stock take, looking truly outstanding. Who wouldn't marry me? Five minutes later, my life is destroyed as Emily fails to say yes. I surprised her and went down on one knee and presented the ring in my open palm.

"Emily, you are the best thing to happen in my life. Will you be my wife?"

I want to cry when she doesn't ecstatically yell out the word 'yes', and a troubled expression appears on her face instead of the joyous one I was hoping for.

"Peter." I realise I'm in trouble as she uses my full name. She pauses, and I get a firm grip of myself, there will be no crying, and I will take it like a man until after she leaves, then drink myself unconscious while watching Dirty Dancing and crying pathetically.

"Peter, I have been trying to find a good time to tell you. I guess I can't leave it any longer. I'm already married."

I stare at her, puzzled; my brain expected a straightforward yes or no, not what she just said. Slowly getting to my feet, my hand clenches the ring tightly, and I now see Emily in a new light.

"Can you repeat that as I think I misheard?"

She nervously stares down at her feet. The ring disappearing into my clenched hand hasn't gone unnoticed.

"I meant to tell you, but we have been having such an amazing time. I just couldn't find the right moment. We are getting divorced. I know I should have mentioned it, but everything was going so well. I didn't want to ruin things... Please tell me I haven't ruined everything?"

"No, but this seems premature." I stare down at the ring in my palm.

She places her hand over mine. "It's so beautiful, and if you are still asking, then the answer is yes, as soon as is legally possible. I would love to be your wife."

"Really?"

"Of course."

"I was worried you would say no."

"Never." We hug, and the world is perfect, though I throw it in her face when we eventually have our first argument. I can be quite petty.

23

PETE'S STORY – ONE YEAR AGO

My nostrils twitch from an unpleasant odour. Opening one eyelid, I find a bright blue alien orb peering right back at me, less than an inch away. Fishy breath assaults my senses as a paw extends and taps the end of my nose to wake me; the claw extended the tiniest amount to suggest impending violence. I grab my Sphynx cat in a bearhug, and he purrs away happily. It's early morning, and Mr greedy wants feeding. Yes, I know I could be anybody, and he will probably eat me if I die and he can't to get his favourite treats, but I love Mr Tiddles just the same. If the nose press fails, then he will march his dirty feet all over the pillows to annoy me into wakefulness.

"You spoil that cat, and I swear you love him more than me," my wife says from the open doorway.

"Now, you know I love you both equally," I say, then whisper in the cat's ear, "Don't listen; I love you the most." I yawn. I'm not really a whole person till I consume several cups of strong coffee. Some mornings, I'm damn near mono-syllabic until 10 a.m.

Emily leans against the bedroom door frame, mostly

dressed but struggling to do her trousers up. I smile as I slide out of bed and wander over. She brings out the best in me. I always think what bullshit it is when I hear people say their partner makes them a better person, but with Emily, it's so true—she makes me my best self. I know I sound a bellend but don't worry; I don't have the urge to grow a hipster beard and wear a beret just yet.

My hand slides over her lightly, protruding stomach. "Perhaps now would be the time for some fat clothes."

"I believe the phrase is maternity, and these will do for a while longer." She finishes fastening the top button with a struggle.

"What if it's twins and you turn the size of a bus?" I lose my smile as that thought suddenly terrifies me. I'm not sure I have the maturity level for one child, let alone two.

Emily grins. "What if it's triplets? We will have to buy a bigger house. You know I think it runs in the family, every second or third generation." She laughs as a look of panic crosses my face, leaving me temporarily unable to speak. My job in I.T. is steady, but with Emily's income no longer coming in, a bigger house is simply out of the question. Plus, we need a new car. My BMW Z3 is tiny, and while I refer to it as vintage, it's merely old. We will need something a lot more practical with five seats, and I'm not sure the finances will stretch to running two vehicles side by side. What about a future college fund? It never stops.

Emily touching the side of my face brings me back to the real world. "Stop worrying about money. We will be fine." She kisses me, and I feel the same thrill as the first time, even after three years of marriage.

"Maybe I could help you undress again?" My hands slide around her waist as I kiss her neck.

She laughs and brushes me away. "Now that's what got us

in this predicament in the first place. Anyway, don't we have to get the cat to the vet soon?"

"I can be super quick."

"Not something to be so proud of." We end up in a passionate clinch until she whispers, "Mr Tiddles is watching us." My jealous feline is peering at us from the end of the bed. I quickly get dressed.

"Okay, are you ready for this? Action stations." I rush out of the room as Emily closes the door quickly to prevent a Houdini style escape. Grabbing the cat carrier from the kitchen, I return, knock once and swiftly enter. Mr Tiddles has seen us, and he makes a magnificent attempt to rush the door but a moment too late as it closes just in time. He now stares indignantly at me and gives his loudest annoyed meow, which is one octave off a baby crying. Now, as I chase the little sod around the bed, I briefly wonder if this is what having children will be like? Can I play fetch with them, or is that inappropriate with toddlers? The thought of nappies is equally unpleasant, but I have a plan to get Emily to do most of the changes just by being useless or unavailable.

"Got you," I shout as I finally catch the elusive Mr Tiddles. He meows loudly in my face as I kiss him on his wet nose and place him carefully in his carrier, making sure the door locks are fully engaged. He is known to prise them open and escape.

Now his vexed meowing starts from inside the cage, and he won't stop till he gets out again. Emily stares at me.

"What? He's my baby." I shrug.

"You are going to be a brilliant father."

I check to see if she's making fun of me; she isn't. But I'm not so sure about the brilliant bit myself. My parents dying so young and my Aunt single-handedly raising me have left me without a role model to copy. Whether that's good or bad is yet to be seen. Dave told me his father was a drunk and a womaniser which funnily enough is what he became, and he seems amazingly happy.

"Let's get this little sod to the vet before he drives us mad." I stop Emily as she goes to pick up the carrier. "And what do you think you're doing, Missus?"

"Oh, for God's sake, I'm not a cripple."

I shake my head slowly. "No heavy lifting."

"So, I can't do the washing?" A smug expression appears on her exquisite face.

"Well, I didn't say that. Just move a few bits of clothing at a time and not a heavy basket."

"You know you can be a bit of a dick, don't you?"

I smile and nod happily. The meowing from inside the carrier increases in volume and starts to penetrate my brain. "Let's get a move on."

We hurry outside to my BMW, where I act the gentleman and open the passenger door. Emily sits down in the sculpted seats, scrunched uncomfortably, and I feel guilty for not buying a sensible vehicle straight away. She covers her eyes in what is now an old joke that the bright red leather interior is too garish to view without sunglasses. Personally, I think it complements the black exterior to perfection and is half the reason I bought the car. James Bond driving one in the movie Goldeneye didn't hurt my choice either.

"Seat belt."

Emily clicks herself in. I hand over the cat carrier, which she ledges on her knees, giving her barely room to breathe, the open-door end facing me because Mr Tiddles will want the reassurance of my close proximity.

I shut the door and get in the driver's side. Sliding the seat back to accommodate my six-foot frame, I turn to my wife. "I will search for a new car this weekend, promise."

"Good. I want a red SUV and petrol, don't forget."

Diesel cars are suddenly bad for your health, worse than chewing blue asbestos, according to our government, who are the same people who forced us into one in the first place with road tax cuts and promises that we were saving the planet.

"Petrol, got it." While Emily is thinking of a small, economical engine, I imagine a V6 with an obscene amount of horsepower.

"I might not be able to get a red one." Emily slumps back in her seat, disappointed. But for the past ten years, silver and grey seem to be the most popular colour on British roads, and our finances only allow for a second-hand motor.

She thinks it over. "Okay, but nothing in that brown colour that resembles poo or white either, as you can never keep it clean."

"Sure." I turn the key and the 2.8-litre engine bursts into life. Pressing the clutch and selecting first gear, I make up my mind.

"I'm going to get an automatic too." The last few years have seen a massive increase in traffic jams. We set off and, within a few streets, hit roadworks. Yes, an automatic is just the thing.

"Do you want to know the sex of the baby?" Emily casually asks while playing with the radio, looking for something classical for our unborn child to listen to.

I know this is a trick question. "No, it should be a surprise."

"What colour are we going to paint the spare room then?" She teases, finding a suitable station at last and turns it up to drown out the cat's pitiful meowing. Mr Tiddles is really feeling sorry for himself now. "I will leave it up to you if you want to know."

I reach over and take her hand in mine. "Look, boy or

girl, I will be happy with either outcome. Our son will become a famous soccer star, and if we have a girl, she will learn to be a world-class ballerina."

"Why can't she be a footballer?"

"Seriously, can you even name a single female player?" This is before I learnt Mia Hamm had her own N64 game. "You can name plenty of male players, though."

Emily huffs, "Yes, but that's only because they're in the news charged with rape."

"Well, we would bring up our son with a morals code like Dexter."

"What, you want our son to follow a serial killer's code?"

"Or daughter," I chip in, then laugh. "Let it be a surprise." I try to slide my hand onto Emily's stomach, but there is no room with the cat carrier there. "And I will buy a big sensible SUV at the weekend." *With a massively powerful engine.* Traffic now clears, and I put my foot down.

"How about names?" This is one of our favourite topics and one we can't agree on. "Rupert, if it's a boy and Delphine if it's a girl, if it's got two-heads we'll call it Bumble and sell it into a circus of freaks."

"Peter, I know you're joking, but don't you think that's a bit sick?" She gives me the *'you have gone too far'* look. I only get called Peter when she thinks I have done something wrong. It's quite a useful pointer as I haven't a clue what goes on in the female mind.

I ignore the stare. "Yes, nobody should be called Rupert, but Delphine is growing on me; let's add it to the collection." Our list of possible children's names is already well over three hundred and getting bigger by the hour.

All our conversations these days seem to be about our forthcoming child. I hope we don't become one of those couples who bore you with every single detail of their kids' life. Andy and Jen used to be close friends, but after they showed us a poo their child had done in his potty—I couldn't face talking to them again. They didn't notice being so obsessed, but when we made excuses not to go to a thirty-plus kids' party, they did, and you would have thought we had arranged for Gary Glitter to be the children's entertainer by their anger. We haven't spoken for a while, but I'm led to believe when you have a child of your own, then all is forgiven as you are invited into the proud parent owners' club.

Another worry of mine is what if we get an ugly baby? While parents tend to think their children are beautiful, we all know this is often not the case. I have been referring to a work colleague's kid as *'Ugly Baby'* for so long now; she is in secondary school. Obviously not to her face. That would be unnecessarily cruel, but the kid did have a huge bonce. I pray we have a pretty child or much better friends than myself.

Traffic slows, free-flowing in the opposite direction but gridlocked my way and our speed drops from thirty to twenty to a full stop. I'm stuck opposite a junction, and I admire a sleek silver Porsche Cayman as it approaches. Maybe I could get a second-hand Cayenne, Porsche's SUV with the 4.5-litre engine? Big and safe. I'll give Emily the NCAP rating and the number of airbags to seal the deal. I will search the local car dealers this weekend.

The approaching sports car isn't slowing down as it nears the stop sign. I can now make out the man behind the wheel, arguing into his mobile phone, held close to his mouth. Stress lines criss-cross his forehead, and I smile at the way his comb-over is trying to save his hairstyle. Too late, he glances up, and our gaze meets as he desperately attempts to brake. Time slows as his wheels scream, worn brake pads on metal.

His car's front-end skids over the stop line and smashes into our side door with a loud crunching of bent metal and plastic. Breaking glass sprays the interior as the momentum pushes us over the centre line into the road opposite. The engine dies, and I'm left with the sound of the cat madly screaming and thrashing manically around his cage.

"Em, are you alright?" I stare around wildly, broken glass everywhere. Emily is bleeding from a cut to her cheek and one above the left eye. She seems dazed, her eyes glazed in shock.

She blinks. "I think I'm alright. Pete, Pete!" The last word is a half scream as I glance back around to see the speeding articulated lorry, which hits us like a toy, flipping us backwards into the air. My head strikes the steering wheel hard, and I black out momentarily as we spin several times before slamming down onto the fabric roof, which bends and rips. One of the windscreen uprights snaps with an agonised metallic shriek.

Blood oozes from my mouth, the iron taste bitter against my tongue. I squeeze my eyes shut against the sticky, blinding flow. A cold, sharp pain radiates out from where the seatbelt saved me and probably broke my ribs too. I think I'm upside down, but concentration is near impossible as waves of excruciating pain pulse through my body, leaving me in unrelenting agony. My head is tilted to the side and squashed against the ground where the roof should be. Little of the vehicle remaining intact, my left arm seems to be the only thing I can still move without nearly blacking out.

"Emily," I say in what might only be a whisper. Silence greets me, utter silence, no sound at all, not human or animal, I'm all alone. The harsh odour of petrol fills the car, fumes stinging my eyes as my only working hand makes a futile attempt to undo my stuck seatbelt. I fall into a semi-conscious daze as blood rushes to my head.

The smell of my own seared flesh awakens me in a different place and time. Flames leap across the ceiling like a wild animal, sparks igniting my Ninja Turtles print duvet I wrapped myself in for protection. I am a child again, and my worst, most terrifying nightmare is happening all over. I batter the flames that burn through my T-shirt and scar my flesh, crying out for my parents to come and save me, but they are already unconscious from smoke inhalation and soon to die. My younger self huddles in the corner, confident they will rescue me. Fear keeping me stuck there as the entire house erupts in a tinderbox of burning memories.

Death is calling out to me through the raging flames, claiming me for herself. The screams of my younger sister save me. Kate is the most important thing in my life, and the need to help overcomes my fear. Somehow I crawl over to her room, where I find her hiding under the bed. Grabbing her hand, we escape the raging inferno.

I always remember this bit in a fairy tale way, me pulling Kate from under the bed and us simply skipping down the stairs and out the door into the fresh air, almost Disney like. Now I recall the real details, both of us crying and choking, the slow crawl to the stairs, me staring over through the open doorway to see my parent's bodies in their burning room. Holding my hand over Kate's eyes so she can't see the horror, my arm getting so severely burned, I needed multiple skin grafts as I shielded my sister through the living hell our house has now become.

Wake Up. Wake Up. Wake up.

The agony of my broken body drags me back into the real world. Disorientated, I struggle against my seatbelt. All I see is a red tinge as I try to swivel my head towards the crushed section of the car. Nausea, pain, and hopelessness fill me. The muffled sound of people outside reaches me, seemingly from far away.

"Helps on the way. We called an ambulance." A man's voice, I think.

My hand reaches out to the unmoving body in the next seat. "Em, don't leave me, please don't leave me." I pass out again.

Wake Up. Wake Up. Wake Up.

24

PETE'S STORY – REALITY CHECK

Opening my eyes, I again see Maze standing there in a thinning cloud of smoke. The three versions of her fuse back into one, and I reach over and take the Magnum revolver out of her trembling grip—guilt flooding through me as our hands touch briefly. I never meant to cause her any pain. The ringing in my ears recedes as I survey the damage Maze has wrought; she quite effectively murdered my clock as it drops off the wall to die on the floor.

Large chunks of my fractured memory have returned, not all of it, just the horrible soul-destroying pieces I tried so hard to suppress. My entire life ended that day with Emily's death, crushed when the windscreen failed to hold the car's weight. And all my fault. If only I'd bought a big safe SUV bristling with airbags that would have survived the crash intact. Tears sting my eyes as I resist the overpowering urge to stick the gun in my mouth and pull the trigger.

The court case replays in my mind. The driver of the lorry was foreign and had a fake licence. He fled the country before the police could catch him, though he probably would have gotten a slap on the wrists. That's precisely what Porsche owner Eric Griffiths got. He received a five hundred pound fine along with a three-month driving ban for taking my wife's life—an utter travesty. He was back on the road before I could even walk again.

At first, the constant pain kept my mind blank. The day would start with a simple breakfast and afterwards exercising my damaged limbs. Followed by staring out the window until lunch. Each afternoon I did my daily walk, travelling a few steps extra each time. As I healed, the physical aches lessened, but my mental torment grew. My large circle of friends shrank rapidly to near zero. After one brief visit, I no longer heard from them. I mean, what do you say to somebody who has lost everything? The couples we knew were the first to go, then Emily's single friends and finally mine too, embarrassment, selfishness or just not wanting to see a sad broken reminder of the past, who knows? Dave was my only constant visitor, and I fear I was too much even for his optimistic spirit. My employer was good to me. Paying full sick pay, so I had no money worries, but afterwards, I quit my I.T. job—all those sympathetic and well-intentioned comments were more than I could endure.

Months later, I received the all-clear, and that was it—abandoned to my new life of nothingness. That's when fate stepped in. Instead of staring vacantly out of the window one day, I chose to waste time by looking up cars on AutoTrader. Before the accident, I'd spent many happy hours daydreaming of vehicles I could never afford. Jaguar F Types, Nissan GT-Rs, even the footballers' favourite, the Bentley Continental, which being the size of a barge, is entirely impractical; it would never fit in the Aldi car park on shopping day. Today I searched the Porsche section. Entering *lowest priced first*, the vehicle that soon pops up and now registered as a Cat S accident damage repair was the exact car that destroyed my existence. I never believed in a divine destiny until that moment, and by the end of the day, the car belonged to me. Luck or fate? It didn't matter—a plan formed in my head, one of vengeance.

The look on Eric's face was priceless when I first drove past in the car he used to kill my family. Recognition, horror, followed by pure fear. He knew it wasn't over. That I would never let it end. Detouring randomly by his house whenever I went out, sometimes twice a day, caused me to receive several visits from the police who warned me against stalking, but they couldn't stop me as I had made no threats, plus the car was road legal, taxed, and insured.

I now recall the police visit when Maze had been in the house. Again, they advised me to take a different route to work. They didn't realise I had moved things on to a home invasion by then.

I lift the revolver, clicking open the cylinder and checking the number of bullets left. Down to two, but that's all I need, one for Eric and the final one for me.

Maze is staring right at me; she senses I'm not quite the same person she first met, and how could I be? I only got through the pain by drinking myself unconscious most nights, stuck on the never-ending wheel of self-pity and despair. Blocking out a massive part of my life was the only way I could carry on. Now all I can think of is killing another human being.

"Sorry about your clock," she apologises as our ears finally stop ringing.

"My wife is dead; she was expecting our first child." I stand there numb with grief, unsure what response to expect, but I get a flashback from my sister's renewal ceremony, the severe pain in my head and a sentence Maze said to me, at the time I didn't hear, now it becomes clear, and the scene plays back in my head.

"Yes, you pair are the talking point of the night. I over-heard one couple asking if the kids were safe with you. I mean. I did overhear something else, and I wanted to say I'm so deeply sorry about your wife. I heard she died in a car crash. That must have been awful for you."

Maze's voice fills the room, here and now this time. "Are you alright? I didn't know your wife was pregnant. Come here." She hugs me tight. But nothing will ever be okay again, and all I feel right now is searing pain from this embrace, that, and a profound, unbearable loss. Pushing Maze gently away, I take the Magnum and leave.

"I'm sorry. I have to go. Take care of yourself."

She shouts after me, "Have to go where?"

———

This is it. As I drive over to Eric's, I notice every house on the journey. Imagining happy families inside laughing and enjoying themselves. I'm calm now, even programming the sat-nav on my mobile to bypass the roadworks with a wide countryside detour. I still can't figure out the in-built one, and if I start hitting it, then I won't stop. My left hand grips the gun tightly as the scenery turns green and leafy.

"Don't do this."

I swerve the car, almost clipping the curb at the sound of Emily's voice coming from the passenger seat. I turn to see her sitting there exactly as I remember.

"You're not here, Em. You're in my head." I try to ignore

her as she wants to stop me. The hand she places over mine feels real, the same warm skin. I swear I can even detect the scar in the palm of her hand, done when she was monkeying around with a knife as a teenager.

"He killed you and got off scot-free. Nothing, no punishment, no consequences, and he gets to live, playing happy families, is that fair?"

Her hand takes mine, loosening my grip on the revolver. It drops into the passenger footwell. She tenderly kisses each finger. "Please don't do this. All I want is for you to be happy; you're too pretty for prison life," I smile sadly before the anger sets back in. Emily always possessed the magic ability to cheer me up.

"How do I carry on without you?" Full-blown tears streak down my face, blurring my vision. Outside, it goes dark, and the rain hits the windscreen in heavy droplets, a downpour to match my own inner turmoil. Then lightning streaks across the sky in jagged bolts of power. I switch the headlights on to full beam, but they hardly illuminate the road ahead. Now the thunder strikes, an ominous sound, and a portent to my future.

"Do anything but this." Emily dissolves into thin air, leaving me alone. My hand passes through the space she just occupied, seeking her out.

"Anything but this," I repeat as I smash my forehead against the steering wheel, once, then twice, a third time leaves blood on the rim. Wow, that truly hurt. I sense Emily's reassuring hand on my knee.

"Okay, I know what to do now."

I'm not going to kill Eric even though he deserves punishment. It wouldn't make a difference, and perhaps I never had it in me to take another's life. My right foot presses the accelerator pedal down to the floor, the surge in power pushing me back in the seat. I watch transfixed as the red speedo needle rises through 50, passes 75 and goes even higher. As it nears 85, I pull the wheel to the right, and the car leaves the road with a roar. Silence follows as I close my eyes and think of Emily, barely noticing the Porsche Cayman's violent impact as it hits the swollen river that runs alongside. The thunder and lightning reach a crescendo as I sink under the raging water, the cold brown liquid flooding the footwell, rising to my ankles, knees, then chest. My last breath held tight as I go under the water, a natural reflex of the body wanting to hang onto life. Shutting my eyes, I welcome the coming darkness.

———

I'm floating now. Far away is a wavering light, beckoning me forward. My arm stretches out towards it as an unseen force pulls me violently away. I wake with a start, coughing up lungs full of rancid water. An unpleasant damp sensation hitting my face. Millions upon millions of snowflakes are falling, and I see them all so clearly as I gaze around confused. The sky is almost black as cold gnaws away at my extremities, and I shiver. I'm lying on my back, staring upwards. *What the hell just happened?* I vaguely remember powerful arms dragging me here and pumping my chest. My hand goes over and rubs the sore area. A gentle kiss, I remember that and a voice.

"Stop trying to die, Little Man."

I sit up painfully, my bruised body protesting, throat sore. Walking away and about to disappear in the distance is Lila. The Amazonian looking woman from my psychiatrist's office, still in the weather inappropriate outfit of leather hot pants and matching top.

"Wait," I croak, voice failing. I lose sight of her as she

crests a small hill. Desperate to talk, I drag myself to my feet and stumble after, slipping several times in the mud, but as I finally make the top, she has vanished. Exhausted, I slump to the floor. Maybe I imagined her. The weather changes suddenly, turning to rain, and in moments it washes all the snow away. All I can do is laugh, stuck in the middle of nowhere, soaked to the skin, my car lost under the water like it never existed and absolutely nobody in sight. Laughter turns to tears, and I can feel again—the pain, the cold, the damp. I am alive.

———

Staggering down dark, deserted countryside lanes, two cars pass by, but nobody stops to give a bedraggled figure a lift. I don't blame them; I've seen *The Hitcher* too. After an hour, the darkness is interrupted by the sickly yellow beam of a vehicle's headlights. Shaking from the cold, I stick my thumb out and hope they don't drive past. Covering my eyes against the glare, I wait to see if it stops. Too tall and boxy to be a car. The rough engine sound and squeal of brakes suggest a worn-out Ford Transit van. It pulls up beside me. The once shiny chrome wheels are pitted and dull. The paintwork a rusty patchwork of colours, possibly bronze at one point. It has an odd shape that rings bells at the back of my mind. As the driver winds down his mirrored window, I realise why I can't place it. He is seated on the wrong side. The van is an American relic of the seventies or early eighties, judging by its state. It's not quite Scooby-Doo or A-Team, somewhere in between.

"Need a lift?"

The deep gruff voice disturbs me as the driver turns and

grins madly, and I see teeth the colour of molasses. Dark Aviator style sunglasses improbably covering his eyes.

"I'm all wet, and I wouldn't want to ruin your seats." I make excuses as my subconscious is screaming wrong'un at full volume.

"Plenty of room beside harmless old me," he drawls, patting the passenger seat.

I'm cold, exhausted, and at least another hour from home. I almost relent and accept the offer of a lift. Still, something here concerns me, the wide variety of objects hanging down from the roof lining, dashboard, and window—like one of those desperately sad sports bars that mount football shirts everywhere to make up for watering down the overpriced beer. I can't imagine the diamanté tiara is a present from his daughter, or else he would keep it sparkling clean instead of covered in a blackish residue. Hanging next to it is a gold Saint Christopher pendant and a silver Star of David in an unusual show of solidarity. My eyes travel back to the tiara as a haunting sense of déjà vu unnerves me. I almost remember it from somewhere. But then I see something that instantly makes up my mind, furry dice around the rear-view mirror, and not ironically placed either. That's a firm no.

"Look, I'm fine. I'll walk. It's all good."

"If you're sure. Guess I'll see you around." The manic grin stays firmly in place as he winds the window back up and drives off. Did I just hear a thudding noise against the back doors as it speeds away?

The only signs of life on the entire street are the lights blazing from my front windows. I pause at the front door, guessing Maze is waiting up for me. What I don't expect is a row of chairs and a small crowd of people. Dave and Jace are present, as well as my sister Kate. Even Maze's flatmate India is here, healing crystal in hand.

"Please have a seat," Maze says in a commanding voice as I wander through the door.

I stand there dripping on the carpet. "What's this?" I ask, glancing at the one empty chair facing them.

"It's an intervention."

"But I'm not American," I say, puzzled.

"You don't have to be for this. Now, this is a safe place. We have come together," Maze indicates my friends with a hand gesture, "because we are all very worried about you. Wait, is that lipstick on your face?" Her voice changes out of that caring tone into something harsher.

"Safe place, honey," Jace intercedes on my behalf.

"Funny story that," I say, then give up and slump down on the empty chair. The walk back has worn me out. "Tell you when I get my breath."

Maze angrily paces up and down, but Jace makes her take a seat.

She starts again. "You haven't been acting right, and I couldn't keep it to myself. I told them about the gun you have. Where is it, Pete?"

"I threw it in the river," I can see her staring at my wet clothing, that a two-hour walk has failed to dry out, "with the car and myself," I add.

"What? God, are you alright?"

We now stare at each other awkwardly until I eventually speak, "This woman pulled me out of the river and saved my life, gave me CPR, and told me to, 'Stop trying to die, Little Man," then kissed me on the cheek and disappeared. Maze looks dubious, and I know Dave is dying to ask how she knows I'm a little man. Because he's on best behaviour, he restrains himself.

"Were you trying to die?" Maze finally asks, and now all my friends stare at me intently.

"Maybe, possibly. Yes." That last word is tough for me to utter and takes what seems an eternity to say aloud.

Maze can't help herself and rushes over and throws her arms around me. "We can get you help, counselling, we all love you, things will get better."

A small, almost childlike cry emanating from a mysterious cardboard box at my sister's feet grabs my attention.

"What's in the box?" I ask as the lid pops open and a wrinkled nose appears, followed by a familiar pair of eyes that stare at me mischievously, one blue, one green.

"It's your horrible cat, and I'm sick of looking after it. He keeps leaving oily marks on my furniture," she wrinkles her nose in disgust, "and it's got a funny smell."

"Mr Tiddles." I hold my arms out, and he races forward. I hug him tight. "Don't listen to that nasty woman," I whisper while holding back a surge of emotions. "I thought you were dead."

"Yes, don't thank your long-suffering sister who had to put up with the little rat when you were in the hospital and then while you run around having a breakdown."

"Kate," Maze says sternly.

"You're not a rat," I whisper to Mr Tiddles, holding him up in the air and kissing his head.

"He peed on my favourite velvet chaise longue." My sister sighs.

"Did you do it on purpose?" I ask, holding him closer. A firm meow and an extended claw signal a definite yes. "Good boy, such a nasty woman. I bet she bought that cheap cat food you don't like. You're home now, and I'm not letting you out of my sight again."

A warm purr follows, and I start to cry. My emotions finally escaping their prison of grief. Maze puts her arms around me, and suddenly I'm in the middle of a rugby scrum of love as everyone piles around. Even my sister joins in after a while.

25

PETE'S STORY - ONE MONTH LATER

The smooth texture of the white marble is cold to the touch but oddly reassuring as my fingers move over the thin veins of gold to trace the indent of my wife's name, as I sit struggling with my emotions.

"Such a beautiful headstone, Em. Sorry I haven't visited recently. I have been having a few problems, and had to take a break from reality for a while, but I'm back now."

A sudden gust of wind shakes the tree above my head and dislodges several fragrant pink blossoms that float gently to the ground.

"Is that you, Em?" I smile, no longer sure what I believe. "Maze is here, and she brought flowers. She's going to wait in the car and come over in a bit, said she'll give us some time together. Hey, did you know the new Vauxhall Insignia doesn't have a slot for compact discs, and they claim that's the future? And the thing is enormous. Why make a car that's too large for a parking space? Yes, I figure it's for fat businessmen trying to make up for having a micropenis too. I needed a rental, and it's in that bright red colour you always loved; I've been naughty and reported mine stolen. Yes, I know. Look, I'm going back to being a law-abiding citizen soon, but you don't get a pay-out for deliberately driving your car into a river, and I can use the money."

The wind increases as if in a warning, and I pull my jacket tight against the chill. "I haven't seen Lila. If it weren't for this scar on my stomach and the fact she's still charging my credit card to eat out, I'd swear she was all in my imagination. I'm not sure if she pulled me from my sinking car or not. Perhaps that was my subconscious saving me. I mean, how would she know where I was going to crash? Did she happen to be out for a stroll in the midnight rain? But just in case, I'm going to give her until the end of the month before I cancel my credit card, sound fair? Hopefully, she might buy a coat too. I worry she's going to get cold running round in that skimpy outfit. Hey, I tried not to notice, but I'm only human."

Making sure nobody is in sight, I remove a small metal hip-flask from my inside pocket and take a substantial gulp. The smooth taste of Southern Comfort fills my mouth and warms my insides.

"It's the good stuff, 100 proof." I pour a small amount on the grave. "Nice? No, I'm not getting a drinking problem. It's just… I… I miss you." I fight back a tear threatening to form in my eye. No blubbing today.

I sit quietly for a while, listening to the wind howling through the leaves and the few solitary birds brave enough to stick around.

"I nearly forgot. I have some fantastic news. That dick that killed you has moved. He's upped sticks and gone. It might be something to do with his gnome collection being deliberately smashed or the exploding car in his front yard, but as I told the police for a solid five hours—*nothing to do with me.*"

I take another sip from my flask. "Shall we talk about the

elephant in the room? No, I don't mean Maze is putting on weight. I wanted to make sure you are okay with things? What, you think she might be too young for me. Well, possibly. I mean, nobody knows for sure if a relationship is going to work. It could end badly for both of us. Are you alright with me taking the risk? Maybe there is that Twilight level of everlasting love beneath the surface. Okay, bad example, now that Kristen Stewart is a full-time lesbian. I bet that was a big shock for Team Edward." I pause. "She isn't you, Em, but…"

The sound of light footsteps on the gravel path announces Maze's arrival.

"You alright?"

I nod and smile.

She respectfully places a small bunch of Chrysanthemums on the grave. "Go on, give us a drink out of your hidden flask."

"What flask?" I deny. How the hell did she know?

"This one." She reaches over and pulls it from my inside pocket. Expertly spinning the screw top off, she downs the rest of the contents in one.

"Wow, impressive," I say. "Don't leave any for me."

"Hey, you're driving." She hands it back. "Do you need some more time?"

"No, I'm good now."

We stroll leisurely back down the uneven path, close but separate. The wind howls in ever increasing-intensity, sky darkening by the second. A full-blown storm is approaching fast. Our fingers touch and Maze entwines her hand with mine.

The first droplets of rain hit the ground as we reach the parked car. Maze comes to a halt by the passenger door. "I think it's time we get Mr Tiddles a friend."

"Are you suggesting we buy a cat together? Because that's a lot of commitment."

She grins. "I sort of already have. We just need to pick her up, like now."

I stand there, unbelieving. "You're serious?"

"Deadly, Mr Tiddles must have had a horrible time with your sister, and I thought... well, it will be our own little family unit."

"Let's go then." I pull open the door and slide behind the steering wheel, excitedly clicking my seatbelt in place and starting the engine. "So, where to?"

"Not far, Kent."

I do a double-take. "Sorry, I thought you said not far."

"Don't you just drive down the motorway?"

"Not really, Kent is basically as far as you can go before falling into the sea before France, and you have to drive around London in the most horrendous traffic possible. If there are roadworks or a single accident along the way, it can easily be a ten-hour round trip."

"Oops, still." She pulls out her mobile and shows me a picture of an adorable fluffy silver kitten with huge paws and a long bushy tail. It's a Maine Coon. I was told that's a good make."

I grin. "I think you mean breed, and we are going to need a bigger cat tree; they can grow up to four feet long."

She frowns, concerned. "You don't think she might eat Mr Tiddles, do you?"

I unclip my seat belt and lean across the cavernous interior to kiss Maze. "I am sure they will be a perfect fit, just like us."

She grins back at me. "Great, because I said we'd be there in two hours. Sorry."

"Well, I guess I better get a move on." I slide the gear lever into drive.

Maze immediately kicks off her trainers and places her feet on the dash. Ignoring my disapproving stare, she leans over, flicks on the radio and precedes to sing along tunelessly to some insufferable chart hit. I glance over, smile, and shake my head before finally joining in with my own tone-deaf rendition.

The End.

AFTERWORD

Many thanks for reading my first novel - Bound To End Badly. If you enjoyed it then PLEASE leave a review. Why? Because without your kind words my book becomes invisible. As a new author I also read and appreciate every single comment.

American Readers - I apologise for spelling words with an S instead of a Z, but we did have the language first. (Though after 20 years of The Simpsons, even I think doughnut is spelled donut.)

I wanted to write a book for many years, so having your business shut down and being forced to stay at home during the current pandemic, proved an unexpected opportunity of endless time. What I didn't realise was the amount of work that actually goes into the finished product. I now have a fresh appreciation of all the novels I have ever read—good, average, and rubbish.

My book is set in my home city of Derby. Is the place as bad as I make out, and should you visit? Well, I hear there is a gem of a video games shop called Retro World where one might get their copy of a certain book signed, but apart from that… everything with any intrinsic architectural value has been torn down over the years and replaced with a poor quality square, concrete or glass box. Our beautiful art deco bus station was just one of many to be destroyed. The new one is so well designed that if more than two buses try to park at once, then the whole of Derby City Centre becomes gridlocked. Brilliant.

Mamba is, unfortunately, the drug of choice here, and the sight of shambling zombie-like figures is an all too common sight. Though I have never actually been attacked on a night out in Derby (only in Burton upon Trent – where I woke in the hospital with a fractured cheekbone and a head the size of the Elephant Man).

The Red Dragon pub in the book is fictitious but loosely based on three different pubs from my misspent youth in Derby. Two from Spondon – The Anglers Arms & The Yarn Spinner – where I started underage drinking at 17 and the third from Chaddesden – The Spinning Wheel (who remembers the keyboard player?) – All are sadly no longer with us, having being re-developed into housing, a retirement home and a supermarket.

As I write this, the British Prime Minister has leaked the date of our release from quarantine to the Daily Mail online – 21st June 2021 – I am already looking forward to an ice-cold pint and seeing my friends and family again.

Take Care – Rob Tiochta - Feb. 2021

(PS My unusual surname is originally from the Ukraine. I
have heard every pronunciation possible over the years but
choc-ta is the way to say it.)

ACKNOWLEDGMENTS

I would like to thank my wife, Jane, for putting up with me – especially during these long months of closely confined quarantine, and for all the endless help she gave.

A big thanks to all my beta readers, especially Claire & Karen for all the advice they gave.

A big thank you to Sarah Kempton for the amazing audio performance and hopefully see you for the sequel.

Printed in Great Britain
by Amazon

78755515R00161